A Beautiful Satan III

By

RJ Champ

DC Bookdiva Publications
#245 4401-A Connecticut Ave NW
Washington, DC 20008
www.dcbookdiva.com

Publisher's Note: This is a work of fiction. Names, characters, places, and incidents are a product of the author's imagination. Locales and public names are sometimes used for atmospheric purposes. Any resemblance to actual people, living or dead, or to businesses, companies, events, institutions, or locales is completely coincidental.

Ordering Information:
Quantity sales. Special discounts are available on quantity purchases by corporations, associations, and others. For details, contact the "Special Sales Department" at the address above.

ISBN: 978-0-9907854-2-2

Prelude

12:24 a.m.

"Shhh!" Natasha hushed herself when she heard the front door open.

"Dashia!" Shane stepped inside the apartment and closed the door behind. "Big Poppa is in the house! Come out here and show me some love, girl!" he said, sporting a wide, expectant grin. His grin faded slightly when a cloak of silence greeted him.

He proceeded to the sofa, slipped off his blazer, and placed it across the sofa's arm. His eyes casually roamed the exquisite interior, taking stock of the expensive Arabian décor dominating the apartment and the half-empty bottle of red wine on the mini bar.

"Pretty nice place your girlfriend has here," he muttered, facing the gold-framed wall mirror. "What she do for a living?" he inquired, loosening his black silk tie. "She better be a company CEO, a bank president, or owner of a Fortune 500 company. If not, then I know she's knee-deep in illegal activities," he remarked nonchalantly as he did an about-face and headed for the bedroom.

Shane paused in the doorway. His eyes took a minute to get acclimated to the dark room.

"Dashia... Girl, you know I don't like it when you drink yourself into a stupor like that. I'm in the mood to fuck. I don't want a ragdoll I gotta be tossing around the damn bed," he expressed to her, moving to the right side of the bed. He flopped down on the edge of the mattress and started unfastening his shirt. Shane huffed, "Gotdamnit, I thought I made myself clear. Didn't we both agree on this?" He got aggravated by her lack of response.

"Oh, I get it." He clenched his jaw, snatched off his shirt, and fell back on the bed. He paused before sliding up on her backside. "You're testing me, right?" he said tight-lipped in her ear. When she didn't respond this time, he really got pissed.

"Dashia! What in the hell is your - " He yanked her by the shoulder and Dashia's head rolled over - limp - dead!

Shane's eyes leaped from his skull, totally horrified by the mangled and lipless face staring at him with stone dead eyes.

"What the fuck!" he cursed as he catapulted off the bed in one mighty lurch. He stumbled backward, startled and disturbed, his heart pounding in his chest as he tried to catch his breath. Shane couldn't tear his eyes away from the ghastly sight, even though his instincts were sounding off warning bells loud and clear in his head.

Five feet behind him, the shadow in the corner came to life. Natasha's black form moved like a phantom camouflaged in darkness as she closed in on the unsuspecting Shane.

A small black billy club rose in the air for a second before swooping down in a powerful arc. It crashed hard into the base of Shane's skull - not once, not twice, but three vicious blows! She cracked him in the head and sent him crashing to the floor, completely unconscious.

"You dirty dick muthafucka!" Natasha hissed scathingly as she whipped out her switchblade. She stood over him like some sort of dark, threatening she-devil, casting her death gaze upon Shane as he lay perfectly still.

A wicked diamond-smile burst off Natasha's face in 3-D as she savored the moment before the kill. A second later, she keeled down beside his head and pressed the sharp edge firmly against his thick Adam's apple. Natasha inhaled deeply and a rush of pure evilness aroused her core.

"You piece of shit for a man!" she snarled in a deadly tone. "Reap what you sow, Shane, cuz bitches like you don't deserve life..." She pressed on the blade. Her adrenaline pumped hard in her veins and her breathing grew deep. A sadistic grin spread on her face as she applied more pressure to his Adam's apple. Natasha groaned excitedly when the blade pierced Shane's skin.

"Bitch!"

Natasha jumped, startled.

"What in the hell are you doing? Have you lost your muthafuckin' mind? Get your filthy hands off of him! And get the hell away from Shane. Now!"

Natasha's head snapped back and a look of complete shock was flash-frozen on her face, Oh my God!" Natasha stammered, completely astounded, shaken, and confused. "Angel?" she uttered, breathless, her tone cautious but alarmed. "No, that's impossible. What are you doing?"

"Fuck that!" Angel snapped. "Let's go!"

Natasha's anger-filled disposition changed to a look of utter disorientation. Angel's spirit was strong tonight; she could feel it surging and ebbing, like waves on a beach.

Natasha whipped her head around. "Shane, you're one lucky black bitch!" she conceded reluctantly. "If it was up to me, I'd cut off your dick and stuff it down your slimy-ass throat!" She paused and cast an evil look down on Shane's unconscious frame. It was easy to see Natasha was fighting with herself. Absolute hate surged heavily in her body language. She was but a millisecond away from sticking Shane in the ass with her blade.

"I said let's go!" The voice that was Angel barked aggressively.

"Lucky bitch!" Natasha spat. She gave Shane a hard kick to the groin before storming out.

Chapter One

The elevator ride up to the 12th floor was so gentle and smooth that Nadia and Mecca were unaware the mechanical platform was moving at all. When the elevator stopped on the 12th floor and a subtle ding sounded, both Nadia and Mecca were impressed by the elevator's quiet arrival. The women watch as the gold metal doors parted — so soft — without a hitch or sound. If you weren't paying attention, you could easily miss your intended floor.

As soon as Nadia and Mecca stepped off of the elevator, the stunning detective pair attracted a number of unwanted stares.

"What's this department composed of, Nadia?" Mecca inquired, flashing a hostile sneer when they blew by the gawking crowd of suited men lingering in the hallway. "Humph...looks to me like a bunch of horny-ass heathens who lack the proper etiquette or wherewithal to deal with strong, intelligent woman like you and me. Ain't that right, girlfriend?"

Nadia twisted her head and snorted, "Amen to that, Mecca!" She flipped the men off before they both ducked inside apartment 1244.

Once inside, the women's eyes were instantly drawn to the commotion surrounding the sofa. Chief Holt sat there holding a cold pack to the back of his head and beside him, a young paramedic with bright, curly orange hair and a pale face virtually overwhelmed with freckles fumbled with the contents of a First Aid Kit. Mecca glanced at the paramedic's name tag – Ted Andrew.

"What's the deal, Nadia? What was the chief doing here?" Mecca voiced suspiciously.

A dry smirk cracked the corner of Nadia's mouth. "Humph. What you think he was doing here? It doesn't take a rocket scientist to figure that out," she remarked snidely.

Mecca cringed at the thought and quickly brushed Nadia's remark aside. "Nadia, look at the little white boy paramedic," she whispered. "Doesn't he remind you of the caricature on the cover of Mad magazine?" She gave Nadia a playful shot to the ribs with her elbow.

Nadia stumbled slightly and covered her mouth. "Go 'head Mecca," she chuckled under her breath. "You know that ain't right."

"Excuse me, Detectives, but the Chief is none of your concern. I have men already assigned to his matter," Tony Woo expressed seriously. His short, pudgy frame stood firm in the bedroom doorway, his short arms folded over his chest. "Come. Your assistance is needed in here with me...and it would behoove you to get in here ASAP. Close the door on your way in," the Forensic Chief finished as he disappeared from the doorway.

Mecca stopped, stared, hung her hand on her hip, and rolled her head all in one motion. "What? I know that li'l fuck ain't talking to me like that?" she said, clearly appalled by his tone and demeanor.
Without missing a beat, Nadia took Mecca by the arm. "C'mon, Mecca, we have a job to do," she spoke calmly. "This isn't the time or the place; you know that. So let's get in there and analyze this bullshit and handle our business."

Thirty seconds later, both women were standing at the foot of the bed, their eyes glued to the tormented sight of Dashia's bloodied and mangled face. Nadia and Mecca looked absolutely disturbed by the warped nature by which their colleague was slain.

"The psychotic bastard cut off her lips!" Mecca hissed, feeling a sense of outrage pierce her insides. "But why?" she groaned, her facial expression taking on a painful and profound look.

Nadia was completely taken aback by what she saw. It took her some time to gather herself after seeing her friend in such a horrible state. She willed herself to stand there and absorb the travesty before her. A moment later she inhaled and exhaled – slow, deep controlled breaths. Nadia could feel the pain, the regret, and the anger colliding in her core. The voice of reason spoke to her. This isn't the first time I've had to endure losing a close friend, and I know this won't be the last. So get a grip on yourself, Nadia! She pressed her right hand firmly against her breastbone. Nadia struggled to hold back the tears threatening to burst free as she gazed upon the hideous corpse with a strangee look in her eye. Nadia took three shallow breaths and vowed passionately, "That sonofabitch is gonna pay for this, with God Almighty as my witness!" Nadia stopped short, turned to Mecca, and swallowed hard before adding, "I promise you, Mecca, we're gonna get this sick - "

Tony Woo cut in. "Hold that thought," he advised with his meaty index finger waving in the air. "It's good to see the emotional bonding and the both of you feeding off the grief of a fallen comrade." He stopped short and looked from Mecca to Nadia. "But I'd advise the both of you to save your emotional display for later on at a more appropriate juncture. Right now..." Tony lingered and stepped around to the left side of the bed. "Our deceased colleague deserves our devoted, undivided, aggressive and concise attention." He took a deep breath and allowed his eye to rove over the enclosed terrain, finally coming to rest on Dashia's corpse.

"Time of death was between midnight and 1 a.m. this morning," Tony said, straightforward and to the point. "Dispatch received an anonymous call from this address at exactly 1:15 a.m. Yes, you heard me right: our perp phoned from right here inside the residence immediately following the murder." Tony Woo took a deep breath and exhaled. "It's written all over your face. Yes, Chief Holt can count himself one lucky man. Evidently, he was not on our perp's radar for reasons unbeknown to us," he finished saying as he turned on his heels.

Tony clasped his hands behind his back and went on. "As you can see..." This time when he spoke, the tone of his voice took on a weird, hypnotic authority. "Our perp, he's neat, meticulous. Hopefully we can find something worthwhile out of all this savagery. Look at this." Tony indicated the bloody gash in the throat. "Carotid artery severed, at least five inches deep, and he's a lefty. Check out the wound pattern and blood splatter."

Mecca watched and listened intently. Her right index finger pressed under her bottom lip. "Excuse me, sir," she spoke up. "But how long has the perp been doing this, exactly?" Mecca felt stuffy all of a sudden. She unbuttoned her baby blue blazer, shrugged it off, and slung it over her shoulder.

Without hesitation, Tony answered, "Long enough to perfect a signature M.O., and his violence is escalating expeditiously. He's changed the stage. He usually murders primarily indoors so he can manipulate the crime scene. If this is our man, and I have no doubt it is...this would be his first indoor slaying since the murders started up again. Keep in mind, our man is extremely adept at staging his murder scenes. No prints, no hairs, no fibers...this sicko is like a ghost."

"Why would he make such a drastic change?" asked Nadia.

"He's losing control. Can't you tell?" Mecca said, moving to the right side of the bed.

Mecca's reply made Tony Woo light up inside. He bit back the smile that was threatening to show on his face, adding evenly, "Detective Tomay, that is precisely correct about his escalation in violence." Tony paused briefly and removed his gold-wired frames off his expressionless face. He looked both women directly in the eye. "It pains me to say, but the more this predator maims, the worse he becomes."

While examining the corpse, Nadia pulled back the covers. What she witnessed made her gasp. "Oh shit!" Nadia winced. "Her rectum...there's so much blood, and the anal opening is so large. Looks like he carved it out!"

Everyone in the room was so involved with the critical death assessment that no one noticed when the chief pushed open the door and stood quietly taking mental notes.

Before he spoke, the chief made his presence known. He cleared his throat, extra loud. "Ahem!" Once he had the room's undivided attention, he walked in, straightened his tie, and spoke in a low-slung monotone.

"The way Sergeant Webb died...death was a blessing." Shane hesitated and shook his head in disgust. "We owe this woman," he said flatly. "Before this, I wanted to hang this sick fuck up by his nut sack and make him suffer." He sighed. "Now he's made it personal, and I want to skin his sick ass alive!"

It was quite apparent to everyone in the room. You could see it in his face and body expression. The chief's mind was focused, sharp like a razor.

"Detective Dozier...Detective Tomay." The cadence in Shane's voice created an aura that was deep, cryptic, and moody. "It's time to shake up this city like it's never been shaken before. I'd like it done before the Feds move in and take over this investigation. You see how they're hovering outside like vultures. I'm keeping them at bay, but that won't last for very long. A little birdie told me that a special unit has been analyzing our cases." His tone turned grim. "I need to see results, because I'll be damned if I allow those bastards the chance to steal this case out from under me. Do you understand what I'm getting at?" The chief took two steps forward. His deep-set eyes grabbed hold of Nadia first, then Mecca. He continued in a low, rumbling drawl. "Detectives, I'm giving you the green light. The streets are yours. Get out there and kick some ass, ladies. That's a direct order!"

Watching silently from the sideline, Tony Woo didn't utter a word although he knew the chief was crossing the line. Tony also realized the severity of the situation staring them all in the face. The move Chief Holt initiated was the appropriate action, he rationalized. It was time for the gloves to come off. Miranda Rights? Toss them out the window. The killer they were pursuing wasn't your run-of-the-mill version. He was a cut above the rest. This killer was abstract and beyond the norm. The means in which he tortured and killed his victims was sick, demented, and merciless, beyond comprehension. In order to apprehend this form of killer, it would take tactics and techniques that went beyond the normal boundaries of law enforcement. Everyone on board had to be prepared to suffer the consequences and repercussions that would undoubtedly follow these actions.

Chapter Two

"Law 17: Keep Others in Suspended Terror: Cultivate an Air of Unpredictability"

"Humans are creatures of habit with an insatiable need to see familiarity in other people's actions. Your predictability gives them a sense of control. Turn the tables: Be deliberately unpredictable. Behavior that seems to have no consistency or purpose will keep them off-balance, and they will wear themselves out trying to explain your moves. Taken to an extreme, this strategy can intimidate and terrorize."

48 Laws of Power

12:03 a.m. – Columbia Heights

It was business as usual outside of the Go-Hard-Gangstas drug den. The block was jumping with drug activity, GHG vultures trolling the length of Columbia Road in search of fresh meat to unload their poison. They were so preoccupied with plying their illicit trade that a number of crew members were totally oblivious to the imminent threat lurking within their territorial borders.

A glazed black Eddie Bauer Expedition cruised westbound on Columbia Road. The SUV slowed abruptly and melted into the shadowy blind spot of a large eucalyptus tree and then, without drawing so much as a glance, the sleek black vehicle pulled to the curb and killed the headlights.

Loso was perched at the wheel. A look of unbridled cynicism seethed in his expression as he silently peered through the windshield, his sights focused on their adversary: the GHG's loitering and lounging along the block. Inside, Loso was smiling like a Cheshire cat, thinking to himself, The bammas on the front line slippin' as usual. We could lay this whole fucking block down before these bammas knew what hit 'em!

With that thought in mind, Loso looked over at the big gorilla-looking dude with the long ponytail riding shotgun beside him — Tommy Gunz. You could tell by the crazy-ass look in his eyes that Tommy Gunz was itching to kill something.

"Tommy Gunz, you good, Cuz?" Loso inquired with a sneer.

A sinister smirk twitched in the corner of Tommy Gunz's mouth as he watched the goings-on outside and simultaneously kept a close eye focused on Loso. On impulse, Tommy Gunz right hand moved to his waist. "Yeah, I keep it trill, Slim," Tommy Gunz remarked, dry and gritty, his fingers clutching the fully-loaded Desert Eagle tucked by his scrotum. "Lemme handle this money for y'all cats. I owe this bamma big-time! Santana did me dirty, and I got nothing but hate in my heart for his bitch ass!"

A distressed, muffled moan sounded from the rear of the vehicle. In unison, Loso and Tommy Gunz glanced over their shoulders.

Nightmare flashed his crooked, jagged, yellow-stained teeth in a creepy grin. His wide bulky frame twisted awkwardly as the big brute leaned over the back seat and glared down at the bound and gagged Santana, who was stuffed in the rear cargo area like a load of garbage waiting to be tossed out. Nightmare snatched out his burner. "Shut the fuck up, sucka!" He whacked Santana in the face with the butt of his gun and gave a wicked grin when he noticed tears pooling in the man's eyes. "Ha! Ha! Now I've seen everything!" His cock-eye jumped. "Midnight, check out this shit, dawg! This bamma is crying!" He giggled like a drunken chimpanzee.

With a sudden jerk of his head, Midnight shifted his gaze from the view outside and focused his yellow-tainted stare on the rear compartment. "Fuck that bamma! His time's up. Tomorrow morning, his bitch ass gonna be on the front page of the Washington Post. Day after that? Huh, we'll be cutting his name out of the obituaries and adding his bamma ass to our body count." Murder snorted, as a noticeable sense of finality rose in his voice.

Loso interrupted. "Y'all bammas ready to do this?" he barked, staring through the front windshield. Loso's nature swelled – cold and contemptuous and invigorated, ready to wreak havoc.

Small clusters of young gang members were scattered along both sides of Columbia Road, hanging out on porches, perched on concrete stoops and fences, or loitering just beyond the boundaries of some unlucky homeowner's gated property.

Loso steered the shadowy hunk of rolling metal along the asphalt, and immediately its presence sent a ripple of caution and curiosity surging through the block. Every man stood poised but hesitant, their eye trained on the black SUV, glaring with open hostility brewing in their facial expressions. Their gangsta senses tingled — danger!

Loso and Tommy Gunz noticed a number of young'uns, some flashing the butts of the guns tucked in their waistbands, some more aggressive than others as their fingers hinged on the triggers, giving the staunchest warning looks their cold killer stares could muster.

"A'ight, Tommy Gunz." Loso cut his eye to the right and spoke up. "You up, OG. Go handle your business."

The Eddie Bauer Expedition cruised to a stop directly adjacent to the GHG stash house. The sight of the vehicle instantly brought Knuckles to his feet. He stepped to the front of the porch and wavered for half a second as he scrutinized the Expedition from the top step. He whipped out his pet – a .44 Bulldog. "What the fuck y'all waiting on?" Knuckles admonished his comrades. "Vehicle check, fools! Who dat is? See what those bammas want!" The tinted passenger window glided open.

"What up, young soldier!" Loso shouted from the driver's side. "I got a package for your man, Lucius. He around?"

Popeye cocked his dusty red head slightly to the right. He took two long strides and his long thin frame stood on the edge of the curb. He drew his .40 caliber Smith & Wesson from his waist. "Who you be, Slim?" Popeye grunted, giving himself a fearless mug like he was sucking on a bad lemon. "What the fuck you want with my man Lucius, huh?" His upper torso weaved left and right as he gripped his pistol with an exaggerated show of force and animosity.

Loso fought back the urge to unleash his .45 Semi on the young bamma fronting for his comrades. He bit his tongue and said, "C'mon, soldier, I just told you I got a package for your man. You want me to drop these stacks off with you?" Loso lifted his hand, where thick rubber-band stacks of 100's were clutched casually. "Or should I come back another time? You make the call, soldier."

A flicker of greed and wild curiosity flashed on and then Popeye's face and disappeared. He quickly glanced over his shoulder. His two comrades, Ears and Shorty, were lounging on an old beaten-down fence. The looks on their faces said they both were itching for action. Popeye shifted position and cut his eye toward the porch, where Knuckles stood watching like a hawk.

"Wipe that dumb-ass look off your face, Popeye!" Knuckles scolded him with icy bitterness. "Tell me what those bammas want!"

Popeye's head snapped back, disturbed. He shook his head and blinked in disbelief. "What?" he uttered under his breath. Then he did something he would forever regret. "I got this, Slim!" Popeye scoffed defiantly. His disposition was stout as he turned and eyed the man behind the wheel, tightened his grip on his pistol, and pushed off the curb.

"So how many stacks you working with, Slim?" Popeye peered inside and leaned his free hand on the roof above the passenger door, his pistol dangling carelessly at his side. He glanced over the seat and turned his nose up at the two goons sitting quietly in the rear.

A dark, creepy smile crept up on Loso's grill. He looked Popeye in the face. "I got ten thousand right here," he said coolly as he motioned toward the back. "Plus we bagged that soft bamma-ass nigga Santana for your man Lucius. Tell your boys to grab the bamma out the back door. We got his ass gift wrapped real nice for y'all."

"Oh shit! Hell yeah, that'll work!" Popeye smacked his thin, chapped lips excitedly. "Ears! Shorty!" he called out over his shoulder. "Go 'round the back of the truck and get that package for Lucius!"

Up on the porch, Knuckles was growing more agitated by the second. His left foot tapped incessantly on the porch like it had a mind of its own, while his right hand trembled with angst. He kept rubbing the barrel of his pistol against his right thigh, massaging himself in order to stay calm. "What the fuck is Popeye doing?" Knuckles grumbled when he noticed him order Ears and Shorty to the back of the Expedition.

Loso pressed a button on the dash and the rear cargo door automatically swung open.

Tommy Gunz greeted Ears and Shorty with a crooked grin. The brim of a navy Georgetown cap covered the upper half of his face as he crouched in the rear cargo area.

"Here ya go...this bamma is all yours." Tommy Gunz had stuffed Santana into a large black burlap sack.

Ears and Shorty stared at the black sack. From where they stood, they could easily see the outline of a body inside.

Ears's droopy eyes jumped wide. "Who's in the bag, Cuz?" he asked, rubbing his forehead.
"Is the bamma dead?" Shorty stammered awkwardly.

With a wicked-sounding cackle, Tommy Gunz responded, "Nah, homes, he ain't dead. That wouldn't be any fun. The joy is in the kill, feel me? Just make his ass suffer when you do his bitch ass." Tommy Gunz reared back and gave a strong shove. The sack dropped to the asphalt like a heavy load of potatoes.

"A'ight, Lo!" Tommy Gunz turned and gave Loso an affirmative nod. "It's time to boogie!"

"Ay, playa, you got a bag to put that loot in?" Popeye asked, while fidgeting with his pistol. He stuffed the .40 caliber in the back of his waistband, anxious to get his hands on the money.

"Yeah, here you go...suck on this!" Loso responded, his tone flowing with open contempt now.

"What?" Popeye frowned. Did I hear him right? He looked up and caught the flash of a .45 exploding between his eyes.

The shot rang out like thunder and for a moment it seemed as though time stood still. Nobody moved; nobody breathed. In that brief time span, silence gripped the block.

Slow and carefree, the stream of pedestrian traffic went from a modest 2-mph gait straight to bedlam! The sound of a thousand choppers going off at once sent the entire block into a chaotic frenzy.

Before Ears or Shorty knew what hit them, the forces of gravity knocked them clear off their feet. Tommy Gunz howled a triumphant roar as he unloaded his .50 caliber Desert Eagle on the surprised pair, both men flash-frozen in place as they watched their life flash before their very eyes.

Midnight and Nightmare sprang through the rear windows. AK-47's spit death across the urban landscape and ripped the air like thunder clapping off in the night.

"Aw shit!" Knuckles groaned, dropped to one knee, and bucked off shot after shot after shot, emptying his clip at the fleeing Expedition. Knuckles was so caught up in the moment that his trigger finger looked to be operating on its own accord, pumping away at an empty gun chamber that had gone empty five seconds ago. Knuckles rose to his feet, his heart thumping wildly in his chest, watching his squad open fire from both sides of the block, as the black SUV took evasive maneuvers and high-tailed it out of there.

Knuckles's shoulders sagged and his heart sank when he noticed his man Popeye lying dead in the street, his top-piece pushed back. "Damn, Popeye," he uttered, disgruntled. "You dumb fuck!"

"Hey, Knuckles!" the voice of a comrade yelled out and snapped Knuckles out of his funk. "What's in this black bag? A body?"

A trio of GHG comrades circled the black sack lying in the street. Tommy Gunz peered from the rear cargo area. "Loso, hit the button! Hit it now!" Tommy Gunz barked impatiently.

When Knuckles noticed his comrades kneeling over the sack, warning bells went off in his head. He screamed at the top of his lungs, "No! Get the fuck - "

Kaboom! A deafening thunder rattled the entire block. Shockwaves reverberated with a blast radius that shattered every window within fifty yards of the detonation.

Knuckles was rocked from the powerful explosion. He stumbled backward, trembling with an awful ringing in his ears that galvanized his gut. It took him a moment before his blurred vision refocused. When he finally came around and was able to gather his wits about himself, he cringed at the human devastation lying mangled in the street. The gruesome scene rocked him like a hard body blow to the midsection.

Knuckles paused when he felt something wet on his arms, his neck, and his face. He looked closely at the dark wet splotches littering his arms. Suddenly, his stomach twisted and curled into a knot when he realized what the dark splotches were on his skin. Tiny shards of blood-soaked skin, bones, and guts jumped out at him, and the feeling of nausea overwhelmed him and won. A ten piece chicken wings and mumbo sauce dinner spewed out of his mouth and splattered all over the porch.

This cruel, calculated attack had the desired effect Bad Ass intended. Bad Ass's emergence on the DC gang scene had created a radical equilibrium shift, a vicious rip in the gang hierarchy. A line had been drawn in the sand, and that line was in pure gangsta blood.

###

The following day, word spread through the streets of DC like the plague. Blood had been spilled on the doorsteps of two of the city's most notorious drug gangs – the A-Team and Go-Hard-Gangstas.

Today's headline splashed on the front page of the Washington Post spoke volumes:

More Than A Dozen Gang Members Crucified in an Orgy of Violence!

Two Separate Bombings in NW & SE

Leaves Scores of Gang Affiliates Dead or Wounded in the Street

Columbia Road, NW – A young man presumed to be in his early twenties lies dead in the street, his blood-stained white tee pulled up to give paramedics access to a number of gaping chest wounds. His arms are splayed, eyes wide open on a surprised face. A number of gang affiliates lie bloodied and mangled. It's a virtual war zone.

East Capitol, SE – A powerful explosion rips through a 3-story row-house. Five bodies discovered burned inside.

Washingtonians, what's happening to our Nation's Capital? I'll tell you: it's the gang wars and the drug wars that are tearing at the fabric that binds and holds our free society together. What are we to do? Better yet, what are you going to do? It's time, people, that we make a stand. You have to stand for something. If not, you will undoubtedly fall for anything.

Special Editorial,
Gloria Gomez

Chapter Three

The bright warm sun was adrift in the cloudless sky over our Nation's Capital on this beautiful Monday morning. On the streets below, a cacophony of automobile horns blasted the air, their operators venting their frustration. Along Rockville Pike, the early crush of a.m. traffic clogged the main artery as vehicles crawled, jostled, and bogarted their way toward their intended destinations.

Navigating her way amongst the metal fray, Angel pushed her snow-white Mercedes down the crowded stretch of road. The surface of her automobile glistened in the sunlight as though the paint was latent with crystal gems. The German sedan slowed down and made a right turn into the main entrance of the world-renowned medical facility called N.I.H. – the National Institute of Health.

It didn't take Angel long once she breached the first security checkpoint. She drove halfway around the campus grounds before the facility's main building came into view. The main building was a looming architectural structure that soared fifteen stories above the lush green landscape and was situated at the epicenter of N.I.H.

A sense of calm came over Angel the moment she laid eyes on the towering sandstone building, as if the looming structure engulfed her being with comfort. The faster she closed the distance between the building and herself, the better she felt. A moment later, Angel's Mercedes made a left turn into the underground parking garage.

Angel took the elevator up to the 11th floor and quickly disappeared inside the comfort of her spacious office. She locked the door and moved across the light gray Berber carpet. The bronze nameplate perched on the front ledge of her teak wood office desk caught her eye. Angel hovered over the nameplate for a minute before deciding to pluck it off the desk. Angel placed her prized black crocodile Gonzalez handbag on the desk and read the inscription on the face of the nameplate out loud to herself.

Ms. Angel Rising – Supervisor, Oncology Dept. Nursing Manager. It never failed to amaze her how good she felt every time she recited her much-deserved title. She coined the practice "Angel's version of self-gratifying psychotherapy". The thought made Angel beam all over. She brushed away a light coating of dust from the front of her nameplate before replacing her coveted bronze prize.

Angel reached toward her desk for the slim black Bose remote resting atop the cover of a book titled Act Like A Woman, Think Like A Man by the comedian-turned-author Steve Harvey. She aimed the remote toward the window and the portable Bose sound system situated on the top shelf of a teak wood bookshelf that straddled the wall just beneath the window ledge.

A second later, tranquility flowed from the Bose speakers in the form of Floetry's soft melody "Getting Late". Angel listened as the soothing harmony coursed through the room and massaged her soul. She could actually feel the tension and tightness starting to subside in her neck and shoulders. Floetry's vibe seemed to conjure up feelings of calmness and relaxation in Angel.   She began to hum along with the music as she floated around her desk and sank down into her cushiony black butter-leather contemporary chair, kicked off her black Christian Louboutin stilettos, and relaxed her head on the pillowy headrest.

After a full year's leave of absence, Angel was surprised how the familiar office setting helped alleviate the stress she felt consuming her. Her private office sanctuary provided her with a comforting stress-free environment, something she had missed and didn't realize until today.

Angel found the soothing ambiance incredibly refreshing. She turned her chair, facing the magnificent aerial view of Rockville Pike and the Bethesda Naval Hospital grounds situated on the opposite side of the Pike. The picturesque view coupled with the soft music and quiet office setting was the quintessential stress reliever. Angel sat at home the entire year without lifting a finger.

Wow...who would've thought a work environment could offer so much comfort? She silently confided.

Gradually, as the discomfort left her body, Angel felt her eyelids grow heavier and heavier until she could hold them open no longer and she gave into sleep.

Suddenly, Angel felt herself drowning in a thick cloud of black smoke.
She moved beyond the smoky borders and stumbled upon a bed covered in gold silk linen. Her eyes zoomed in on the woman lying beneath the sheets.

Angel blinked. A moment later, she realized she was on the bed beside the sleeping woman, looking around in a daze.

"Where in the hell am I?" she huffed, looking vexed. "How did I get here?"

Out of nowhere, an eerie, cryptic laugh echoed around the room. The wicked sound gripped Angel's heart and caused her to freeze in place. The fine hairs on the back of her neck stood straight up like stiff blades of grass.

Angel peered directly across the room. Her gaze focused on an oval-shaped mirror hanging on the wall. Suddenly, out of the clear blue, a disturbing image appeared in the mirror.

The whites in Angel's eyes expanded large like silver dollars. "Who in the hell?" Her voice trailed off, her gaze fixated on the woman's face floating in the mirror. She possessed the coldest blue eyes she'd ever witnessed, and the woman's hair... It was a beautiful honey blonde, she conceded silently. Then it dawned on her.

Abruptly, without thinking, Angel jerked her hand up over her mouth. "She resembles the woman the police found buried in my backyard. Natasha Lopez? Oh my Lord!" Angel gasped, astounded. "She sort of looks like me!" she muttered in a low, surprised voice.

"Angel...what are you waiting for?" Natasha snickered, a sinister smirk tucked in the corner of her mouth. "Don't you want to see the gift I left for you? Go 'head, take a look. One less hoe to worry about; one less hoe for Shane to fuck! Ha! Ha! Ha!"

With caution swimming in her face, Angel turned to the left. She cast a startled eye upon the person sleeping beside her. Fear billowed in her eyes as she reluctantly extended her hand and carefully pulled back the covers.

A full head of curly brown locks hung over a woman's face like a thick veil. Gazing upon the prone figure on the bed, Angel wanted out of there. She wanted so badly to turn and run, but she couldn't. Something was holding her there as if she were a puppet on a string, some sort of unforeseen hand guiding her.

Angel watched her hand move toward the curtain of hair covering the woman's face. She tried to fight and stop herself, but for the life of her, she couldn't. Angel was totally stumped. She watched her fingers brush along the mystery woman's soft brown strands, and then they stopped abruptly and hovered over the woman's face.

"Go ahead, Angel," the cryptic voice urged.

Angel huffed, frustrated. "No! I don't want to," she protested.

"Don't you get it?" Natasha countered. "You're not in control anymore. I am!" she stated vehemently.

Angel stared, dumbfounded, and watched her fingers take a handful of hair and push it aside. Angel's heart stopped. "My Lord!" she gasped in horror when she laid eyes on the hideous sight staring up at her. "She's dead!" Angel breathed, catching her breath.

The corpse lying before her was horrible and grotesque, propped up against the pillow like some ghastly, ill-conceived prank. A bony, emaciated face gazed across the room. The flesh on the lower half was gone, totally ripped away, exposing a creepy-looking clenched jaw filled with long, blood-stained teeth.

The grisly find was so overwhelming and unexpected. It galvanized Angel to her core. Every inch of her body was utterly petrified.

"So what do you think, huh, Angel?" The evil face in the mirror sneered demonically and laughed. "Just another dead hoe. Don't worry, Angel. None of these bitches deserve life, and I'm gonna make 'em all suffer 'til death. Ha! Ha! Ha!"

Angel's head lurched violently and her eyes shot toward the ceiling. She could feel her soul rise up from the pit of her stomach and surge sharply in her throat. Angel's mouth popped wide open; a deafening wail pierced the air. But all the screaming in the world couldn't stop the devilish laugh that continued to ring out in her head.

The secretary banged on the door and shouted. "Mrs. Rising! What's wrong? Are you okay? Do you need for me to call security?"

All of a sudden, a weird sensation of falling through the air overcame Angel. A moment before impact, her eyelids shot open and the sprawling panoramic view beyond the window was a welcoming sight.

"Oh my God!" Angel groaned when she felt a sharp pain grip both her thighs. Her eyes instantly fell to the spot, and she cringed when she realized the pain she felt was because of her own doing. Angel's nails dug deep and hard, like talons biting into her thighs. "I'm losing my mind!" Angel stammered in disbelief. Another hard bang sounded on the door, startling her. "Bitch! What the fuck do you want?" she hissed, totally annoyed. That was totally out of character, she thought after the fact.

Angel stood for a minute and took a deep breath to calm her nerves. The mellow tune "Butterflies" by Floetry wafted through the office and its gentle vibe soothed her spirit. The gentle melody prompted her to exhale deeply and movingly.

Thirty seconds later, the office door swung wide.

"Good morning, Diana. It's nice to see you too, but right now is not the time," Angel expressed less than cordially as she slipped a bright white smock over the jade-colored Yves Saint Laurent pants suit she wore. Angel plucked her stethoscope off the wall hook beside the door, draped it around her neck, and stepped outside of the office. She pulled the door shut behind her and locked it.

"Later, Diana," Angel said dismissively. "I have a ton of work that needs my attention." Unfazed by the secretary's perturbed face, Angel moved to Diana's desk, pulled a pink clipboard from a wall-mounted hook above the desk, and started thumbing through the pages.

A thought suddenly occurred to Angel and she hesitated. "Okay, there is one thing you can do for me, Diana," she said over her shoulder while she skimmed the contents on the clipboard. "You can page Nurse Cunningham. Advise her that I'm on post today and that I will be paying the chemo unit a visit very shortly. That'll be all for now,." Angel directed. She walked off down the carpeted corridor without so much as a glance Diana's way.

The Jewish secretary didn't respond verbally. Her petite frame did all the talking. Diana turned up her extra-long snout, rolled her big brown fish eyes and her elongated cranium. She perched her bony hands on her narrow hips and made her impossibly thin lips impossibly thinner when she gave a smug sneer to Angel's back and proceeded to her desk.

Diana plopped down in her chair, snatched the phone off the base, and punched in a number. "Yeah. Tammy?" she snorted with an obvious attitude. "Is Nurse Cunningham on hand? No, that won't be necessary. I just called to give the unit a heads up. My boss...yeah, that bitch is in the building. Girl, you know I almost slapped her ass just a second ago! She doesn't know how lucky she is..."

It didn't take long for the entire office to notice the change in Diana the moment she started hanging out with the facility hoodrats, Laquisha and Martima. The little Jewish chick was getting feistier and more obnoxious by the day.

Ding! The chrome elevator doors parted noiselessly and the attractive Angel, who resembled a Pocahontas stand-in, emerged on the deserted 13th floor. It required a special security clearance in order to gain access, which Angel did not possess.
Upon exiting the elevator on this unit, you were immediately greeted by a bold red enameled sign emblazoned on the wall:
National Institute of Health – Main Building
Disposal Reserve Unit – Authorized Personnel Only

The bright red letters were painted on a chalk-white backdrop and seemed to hover in a state of suspended animation.

Angel lingered in front of the sign with an anxious gleam dancing in her eye as she adjusted her white smock. She peered along the carpeted corridor. Not a soul in sight. Good, she voiced quietly.

Ten paces ahead on the right in the main vestibule, a dark oak security counter resided. That would be Angel's first stop. Stan, the dorky little security guard, should be posted at the security counter, keeping a sharp eye on the traffic arriving and departing from his checkpoint.

Angel was surprised when she found the post un-manned. Empty counter? Now that's not like Stan, she thought to herself, making special adjustments to the cream silk blouse she wore underneath her pants suit, al-lowing some extra cleavage to spill over the top.

The chubby little guard is a freak, Angel quickly realized. His dorky ass would be thrilled to have the privi-lege of feasting his perverted sights on my skin, and he wouldn't care what I was here for or what I was taking off the unit. He'd be too consumed with trying to get a piece of ass! In Angel's mind, that was totally unfathomable, but she still got a big kick out of seeing his red freckled face drool over her. It was a nice ego boost, if nothing else.

Angel paused in front of the counter. "Okay, Stan, where are you?" she said to herself, fingers tapping "The Little Drummer Boy" atop the dark oak counter. Angel's gaze swept east and west along the empty corridor. Still-ness and silence were all she detected. Suddenly she felt a cold chill crawl up her arms that made her shiver with a rash of goose-bumps bubbling on her skin.

"Oh well," she sighed, rubbing her palms together. "I might as well proceed with my inventory inspection," she spoke aloud just in case someone was listening. Angel pro-duced a small notepad from her smock pocket.

Her gaze fell on a stack of clipboards stacked in the top right drawer. She glanced up and down the empty cor-ridor again before looting the drawer. She pushed aside the clipboards one at a time until she found the one that suited her needs, and then she paused and studied the yellow in-ventory forms clamped to the face of it. A mischievous grin appeared in the corner of her mouth. A moment later she glanced over her shoulder and gave the area a quick once over before she slipped the clipboard under her arm, stood up straight, turned, and strutted off toward the corridor's east end.

In no time, Angel's curvy frame stood in front of a large steel gray door, hand propped on her shapely hip.

On the center of the door frame, bold red letters were painted on the smooth gray surface and seemed to jump off the door. The sign read:

Disposal Vault – Authorized Personnel Only

Angel made one last visual inspection of the corridor before swiping an orange access card through the decoder. She lit up when the red LED light changed from red to green.

The heavy steel door glided open smoothly without making a sound. Inside, the room was cold. As soon as Angel walked in, a low humming sounded in her ears. The humming was the motion detector activating the automatic lighting system. The lights flickered overhead and then blinked on in a successive chorus all across the ceiling.

The room's interior was bland. It mirrored the entire floor of the Disposal Reserve. Chalk white walls, gray-tiled floors and steel-framed shelves dominated the décor. Multi-colored plastic crates filled with file folders were placed on the floor beside each steel-framed shelf, and an assortment of cardboard boxes was stacked accordingly along the shelves. The contents of the boxes covered the medical spectrum of the N.I.H. facility, from discarded medical files to obsolete equipment to outdated and ill-conceived narcotics.

The moment Angel stepped inside of the vault, she made a beeline for the section where the prized pain meds were stored. She rushed around a tall steel structure. A growing sense of anxiety and triumph soared in her expression when she laid eyes on a gray metal bin sitting alone on the bottom shelf. The bin looked out of place just sitting there like that.

Angel didn't waste any time. She instantly knelt in front of the bin and lifted the top. Her eyes lit up when she saw that the container was filled to capacity with dark orange vials with thick white tops, lined in perfect rows five stacks high. She drew out one of the vials and read the typed labeling.

"Oxyline," she breathed, excited and nervous. I've got to get this bin down to my car, she thought. But I need something to disguise the container. Her eyes circled the room, and instantly she knew what to do.

Two minutes later, the heavy vault door opened slowly. Angel's head appeared from inside. Good...still no sign of Stan anywhere. Could this really be my lucky day? Angel emerged from the vault with a small wheeled dolly in tow. At the base of the dolly, a white medium-sized cardboard box sat with a tall stack of outdated Washington Post newspapers piled high across the top. At first glance, the box and pile of newspapers looked like something headed for the recyclable waste bin.

Angel strolled down the corridor and dropped the clipboard back in the drawer without breaking stride. Less than thirty seconds later she was riding the elevator down to the garage, sporting a big Kool-Aid grin that stretched from ear to ear.

Chapter Four

"Law 39: Stir up Waters to Catch Fish"
"Put your enemies' off-balance: Find the chink in their vanity through which you can rattle them and you hold the
strings."
48 Laws of Power

A day after the hit on the GHG territory, Bad Ass
called a meeting at the Petworth safe house. Bad Ass, Loso,
Midnight, Nightmare, and Tommy Gunz had gathered in the
small living room.

Instinctively, as if Loso had pushed a hot-button,
Bad Ass's stare frosted over. He regarded his comrade with
sheer animosity.

"Why?" Bad Ass grunted, his broad back facing Loso as he peered out of the window looking angry and perturbed. Just beyond the front porch, Lamont Street was on
full blast: trap stars trolling the rip, while their look-outs
crisscrossed Lamont non-stop and gathered up drug sales
like the activity was legal.

Bad Ass turned away from the window. "Why the
fuck did you have to start shooting, Lo? You supposed to
stick to the muthafuckin' script, nigga, you know that
muthafuckin' shit!" he hissed, mean-mugging Loso.
Feeling the heat, Loso wanted to defuse the situation as
quickly as possible. "Man..." Loso leaned back on the black
leather sofa. "I couldn't help it. I'm sick. You know I gotta
problem. Once I get that joint in my hand, I gotta bust
something, Cuz. It wouldn't feel right if I didn't."

Bad Ass held his gaze on Loso, teeth grinding, jaw
muscles pulsating aggressively. "Don't give me that dumb-
ass shit!" he snarled loudly. "What's your damn problem?
You trying to fuck up my master plan? And you of all peo-

ple...you know how long I've been putting this shit together!"

Nightmare cut in. "C'mon, Bad Ass, you weren't there, boss man. Plans change and shit happens." the cock-eyed, oversized brute quipped, attempting to be diplomatic about the situation.

Bad Ass gave Nightmare a twisted screw-face and snapped, "Slim, was I talking to you? Say something else and I'ma slap your ass to sleep!" Bad Ass fumed, eager to make good on his word and make Nightmare a prime example of his wrath. He covered the men in the room with a gaze, sharp like a hawk, as he walked across the floor and sat down in his brown leather wing chair – his throne, as Bad Ass called it.

"Anybody else got a fuckin' problem with what I just said?" he snapped with his top lip turned up in a threatening sneer, ready to pounce on any man dumb enough to challenge him. A split second later, Bad Ass turned his anger back toward Loso, berating him. "Like I was fucking saying, Lo...what you trying to do? Sabotage my muthafuckin' plan or what? Cuz that's what the fuck it looks like to me! You know for this lick to come off right, it's gonna take the whole squad, maybe more!"

Tommy Gunz looked suddenly confused. "Maybe more?" he mumbled aloud, and then added, "Hold up, playa. If that's the case, why I'm rolling dolo? C'mon, playa, you know I'm an action junky, I'm tryin' get in where I fit in and put holes in a bamma's ass!" The more Tommy Gunz spoke about violence, the more excited he became.

Stroking his chin with an imperious look, Bad Ass simply said, "OG, we not going there. I've explained the situation. Each man has a specific part to play in this caper, and there will be no deviating from the script. This bitch is already set in stone, so you just play your part...capisce?"

That conversation transpired yesterday...

The master caper was scheduled to jump off at 12 noon sharp today.

Georgetown at noon: a human gridlock as usual all along DC's entertainment and fashion corridor on Wisconsin Avenue.

Strolling westbound on Dumbarton Street was a man wearing an oversized dark gray Georgetown hoody, sweats, and a matching backpack slung over his shoulder. He was moving with purpose, bouncing along the empty side street, heading toward Wisconsin Avenue.

It didn't take the hooded man long to reach Wisconsin. At the corner of Wisconsin and Dumbarton, he strode past the Bank of America, turned right on Wisconsin, and headed northbound, slinking against the heavy surge of human traffic moving to and fro. The hooded man walked right up to the double-glassed entrance of the Jewelry Exchange. He seemed to hesitate briefly before going inside – either pondering his next move or mustering up the nerve to carry it out.

With an air of nonchalance, his shoulders rose and fell in dramatic fashion and the hooded character took a deep sigh. He lifted his head slowly. A dark grin jumped on his lips as Tommy Gunz saw his reflection in the glass. He gave himself a knowing wink and then walked inside.

The International Jewelry Exchange was a mega jewelry establishment comprised of multiple independent jewelers all operating under one roof. Tommy Gunz stood at the door, his cold, calculating eyes bounced from counter to counter to counter, scrutinizing the collage of strange faces – men and women, jewelers and patrons – in the midst of either buying, selling, window-shopping, or haggling over prices.

"Humph..." Tommy Gunz smirked as he slithered through the jumble of patrons standing in his path.

"Hello! How may I help you today?" a jeweler by the name of Ishmael spoke up. His thick Middle Eastern accent was unmistakable.

Tommy Gunz stopped at the glass counter located directly at the center of the exchange. He looked the jeweler up and down, studying his dark olive complexion and polished head. "What's up?" Tommy Gunz answered in a slick tone as he placed his backpack on the floor against the base of the counter.

Ishmael rubbed his hands together and flashed a big cheesy grin. "My friend, is there something special you have in mind that I could help you with? Any special cut, karat, or gem?"

Sucking his teeth, Tommy Gunz said with a sneer, "As a matter of fact, there is." He lingered, peering into the glass enclosure. "That yellow diamond cross," he said, indicating a sizable cross charm displayed on a rich black velvet canvas. "The ice on that joint...are those rocks legit? Official canary joints, right, Akmed?"

"Excuse me?" Ishmael retorted dryly. His expression showed apprehension now. "My name is not Akmed...it's Ishmael. Okay?"

Tommy Gunz responded with a wounded chuckle. "Yeah...right. Whatever you say, Cuz." He glanced at his G-shock watch and changed course. "Matter of fact, why don't you hold that thought. I'm a little short on cash, so let me run outside and grab some extra dough out of my ride. I'll be right back," Tommy Gunz told Ishmael and turned his back on him.

The jeweler immediately regretted allowing his emotions to get in the way of making money. "I'll be right back," Ishmael grumbled under his breath with a look of disgust. He'd heard those words too many times to remember, and the customer never came back.

Ishmael was pushing the door shut on the jewelry case when he noticed the man had forgotten his backpack. *Maybe he is coming back!* He entertained the thought for all of two seconds before dismissing the idea. *I shouldn't say a word, but then again...*

"Excuse me, sir!" he called out to the hooded man, waving both arms in the air. "You left your backpack, sir!"

Tommy Gunz heard the jeweler but didn't bother to stop or look back. "Will you move the fuck out my way, la-dy?" Tommy Gunz was rude and didn't give a fuck as he pushed and jostled his way toward the exit.

The moment he reached the door, Tommy Gunz glanced over his shoulder and made eye contact with Ish-mael. He gave the jeweler a short nod and a smirk before walking out.

That's odd, Ishmael thought to himself. *What's in the backpack?* He wondered, moving around the counter to investigate. Ishmael placed the bag atop the counter, pulled back the zipper, and opened the top flap. Tears instantly jumped in his eyes and his heart sank when he laid eyes on the crude-looking explosive device inside of the backpack.

"Allah u Akbar..." Ishmael was able to utter the be-ginning of the Islamic prayer a split second before detona-tion.

Outside, Tommy Gunz marched straight to the cor-ner and did an about-face. A small cell phone appeared in his right hand and a second later he pressed the detonation key. A nanosecond before pandemonium, Tommy Gunz felt the pavement tremble beneath his feet as powerful shock waves penetrated the surface.

Kaboom!

Tommy Gunz felt his heart skip a beat and his body cringed as he watched the plate-glass entrance explode suddenly, sending a cloud of glass, smoke, and fire billowing

across Wisconsin Avenue and engulfing the stream of innocent passersby walking by the Jewelry Exchange.

"Fuck me!" Tommy Gunz stammered in awe when
he realized the severity and degree of destruction he'd
caused. "Bad Ass is one crazy-ass muthafucka!" Tommy
Gunz spoke aloud before turning on his heels and marching
back up Dumbarton Street.

####

Meanwhile, on the opposite end of Wisconsin Avenue in the posh upper NW Friendship Heights community,
CIX were on the move. Three separate robbery squads were
posted up at different intervals along Wisconsin Avenue,
starting just inside the D.C./MD borderline.

Squad Three: Midnight, Nightmare, and Threat
were the armed trio waiting inside of a shiny black Dodge
Hemi-Charger with black tinted windows. Each man had a
loaded Tec-9 laying across his lap. Squad Three had their
sights locked on the upscale jewelry boutique at the corner
called the Bulgaria.

Approximately six blocks away, southbound, was
Squad Two. Murder, Cut Throat, and Screw sat incognito
inside a steel gray Hemi-Charger with smoke gray tinted
windows. The car's interior was dead silent except for the
echo of metal clicking in place, each man quietly loading
slugs into the magazine for the automatic DPMS-308 positioned in their laps. The look in each man's eye was contemplative and fierce. In the back of their minds they
visualized the imminent robbery they were about to commit on the exquisite jewelry establishment called the Boc-
cacci.

Moving further south another three blocks was
Squad One: Bad Ass, Loso, New Menace, Big World,
Brawny, Quick, and Agile, a beast of a man with an ex-
tremely intense and aggressive nature. At 6'8" and 420

pounds, his torso was solid and armor-plated, his forearms the size of car doors.

Loso steered the pearl-black Dodge Hemi-Magnum with the smoke black windows. He pulled to the curb and came to rest a foot behind the rear bumper of a sunny yellow Range Rover.

"What I tell you, Bad Ass?" Loso grinned slyly and glanced down at his Baume & Mercier timepiece. "Just like clockwork, Cuz. We right on time."

Bad Ass didn't bother to respond right away. He was deep in thought, loading armor-piercing rounds in the magazine for his 5.7mm cop killer pistol. His steely gaze focused like a laser beam out the window, eyes locked on their target – the extravagant Italian jewelry emporium, Calabria.

Without batting an eye, Bad Ass said in a low monotone, "Lo, get an update on the squads. Make sure everybody in position and send a reminder - no verbal communication; text only." Bad Ass peeked over his shoulder. "Big World, you good back there? Everything a'ight? You ready to rock and roll, G?"

The big fella grunted. "I'm good, Bad Ass, just say the word. I'm ready to get this thing crackin', ya heard me?" Big World finished saying. He held up his .45 caliber Heckler & Koch, slammed a fully-loaded clip in the weapon, and chambered a slug. "Let's do this!"

"Bad Ass," Loso spoke up suddenly, "all squads locked and loaded, ready to jump off. They're waiting for us to give 'em the word."

Bad Ass looked over at Loso. "Well then," he huffed, "what you waiting for? Hit that bamma Tommy Gunz and see what's the deal."

"I'm already on it," Loso answered easily while texting Tommy Gunz. Halfway through his text, the Pro-10000 portable police scanner lying on the center console squawked loudly.

"Attention! All available units! Red Hot – 911 – Georgetown, 1300 block Wisconsin Avenue, The International Jewelry Exchange! Be informed, building explosion, mass casualties on scene! All units respond, ASAP!"

"Oh shit!" Loso was both tickled and elated when he heard the police dispatcher. The sound of police sirens blaring in the distance was music to their ears.

Bad Ass felt his heartbeat and pulse rate accelerate. "Awright, Lo, cut the bullshit and get on your job. Pass the word, G! It's takedown time!"

Black ski-masked up, wearing black hoodies and black sweats and armed with big black choppers, Squad One hopped out of the Magnum, charged across the pavement, and stormed the Calabria Jewelry Emporium. Horror and anxiety seized the atmosphere inside of the Calabria. Customers and employees watched in stunned silence as the armed trio of hooded bandits rushed through the door.

Brrraack! Brraack! Brraack! Automatic gunfire ripped the air like a loud chainsaw.
"Awright, muthafuckas!" Loso barked venomously, his gloved hands wrapped tightly around the Colt-M4, anxious to let off more rounds. "You know what time it is! You seen it on TV! Get that ass down. Now!" he ordered, looking wild and angry.

Calabria's manager stood poised in the center aisle between two glass-enclosed counters. He was a stocky Italian dude with coal black hair that he wore slicked-back, and he sported a sharp navy Armani suit and gold-tinted Armani frames. His name was Vinny, and his body language gave the impression of a man looking for trouble.

Bad Ass smiled inwardly and voiced to himself, That has to be the bamma Vinny I heard about. Without uttering a word, Bad Ass causally walked up to the beefy Italian dude and cracked him in the face with the butt of his gun. Vinny's right knee buckled from the force of the blow and he stumbled backwards, groaning in pain and cupping his right hand under his nose to catch the sudden flow of blood gushing from his now-disfigured nose.

"You heard what the fuck he said!" Bad Ass snarled with spit flying from his mouth. "Get your ass down on the floor before I knock your ass on it! And believe me, you don't want that in your life."

Vinny wiped the blood from his nose with the back of his sleeve and looked around at his employees, who were all cowering on the floor. Next, he turned his attention back toward Bad Ass and spoke with contempt. "You don't know who you fucking with!" Vinny paused and shook his head. "But you will, and very soon."

Bad Ass's gaze sparkled, deadly. He snickered before placing the barrel of his pistol on the bridge of Vinny's nose. "Fuck you!" he sneered and then he pumped three slugs into his face at point-blank range.

The back of Vinny's head exploded in a mess of blood and brain matter. The crimson muck splattered the white wall behind him as Vinny teetered backward, dead on his feet, and then collapsed on the floor.

A contemptuous smirk danced across Bad Ass's face when he turned to his men and said, "What y'all bammas waiting for?" His voice was gruff. "Let's get this money!"

With two long strides, Big World's gargantuan frame loomed over the glass counter like an eclipse. He peered down at the colorful array of diamonds sparkling inside and a sinister grin spread on his face. Big World gripped his H-K and lifted his huge hand in the air above the counter, his hand so large that it resembled a bowling ball. With one mighty blow, Big World shattered the glass counter into a thousand pieces.

The towering behemoth then proceeded to the adjacent glass case, smashed it open, and moved on to the next one. For the next thirty-five seconds, the sound of breaking glass dominated the store. A few steps behind World, Loso was aggressively scouring the jewelry cases with a large handheld vacuum, leaving behind nothing but the velvety terrain and the backdrop.

"Three minutes and counting!" barked Bad Ass, sounding like a military drill sergeant.

The moment Big World finished demolishing every glass structure in the store, he rushed over to Bad Ass. "I got this, big dawg," he expressed in a low, breathy voice. "You go ahead and handle your business in the back."

Before moving off, Bad Ass checked the time on his diamond-studded Rolex. "Two minutes, twenty-five seconds and counting!" Bad Ass gave Big World an affirmative nod before rushing off toward the back office.

Three blocks to the north, inside of the Boccaccio, Squad Two was in the midst of emptying the last few jewelry cases. Standing strong and erect at the forefront of the store, Murder was keeping lookout and shouting out the time every thirty seconds. Cut Throat moved from case to case, methodically smashing the glass enclosures with the butt of his chopper. Anchoring the rear, Screw followed with a vacuum, sucking up every piece of jewelry in sight.

"Two minutes men and counting!" Murder shouted. Suddenly, he jerked his head to the left when his peripheral vision detected movement. "Keep still!" Murder growled, directing his anger toward a heavyset Italian dude in a navy suit. Bad Ass warned me to keep an eye on the bamma in the navy suit. He said that bamma was running the show and I would have to deal with him.

"Awright, Cuz!" Murder snapped, indicating Cut Throat as he watched him smash in the last case. "Hit the back office and see what's up. We got one minute and thirty seconds," Murder ordered, moving from his spot on the floor. He stood over the Italian. "You gotta fuckin' problem, Cuz?" Murder asked and then he spit on the man's mousse-spiked hair. "C'mon with it," he dared, hope beaming in his eye. "You gotta problem...well, I'm gonna solve that bitch for you. Yeah, I'm the problem solver, muthafucka!" Murder placed the barrel of his chopper an inch above the Italian's head. His eyes glazed over, simmering with hate. "Fuckin' dago!" Murder spat angrily as he pulled the trigger.

Boom!

Three blocks to the north, the pilfering of Bulgaria was underway. Squad Three was tearing up the jewelry joint like a band of rogue maniacs.

Midnight had just finished kicking the hell out of a dark-skinned Italian dude named Eddie, who also wore a navy Armani suit. Midnight wasn't feeling the vibe Eddie gave off. Bad Ass said to watch the bamma in the dark blue suit and to slump the bamma as soon as the job was finished!

Midnight had a crazed look about him. His yellow-tinted eyes absorbed the scene, the atmosphere, the aura. "One minute!" he bellowed, his jaw clenched violently beneath his black ski mask. "Hands on your fuckin' head, lady!" Midnight commanded in a voice brewing with irritation.

The Italian dude, Eddie, was squirming and moaning on the floor in obvious pain. Midnight got a kick out of seeing him suffer. He looked to Nightmare with a devious smirk and barked, "If you don't shut the fuck up!" The hostility Midnight felt for the dago was stout. He showed disdain and animosity for the Italian. "I'm not playing, muthafucka!" he growled, kneeling beside the Italian's head. "Open your mouth!" He placed the barrel of his Tec-9 against his bloody mouth. "Here, suck on this, bitch!" he taunted, and then he jammed the barrel between Eddie's busted, bloody lips.

"Please...don't do that!" an aged silvery-haired woman of Greek descent pleaded for her boss. "Take what you want, but let us be...please!"

Midnight's head whipped around. "Why don't you mind your goddamn business, old lady!" he remarked snidely, "Before I come over there and deal with you. It won't be pleasant, believe you me."

Shock and dread flashed in the old woman's face. All around the store the same expression was mirrored on the faces of her five co-workers. With the crazy look in the big gorilla's yellow-tinted eyes and the devilry emanating from his aura, Granny looked hesitant.
She better take heed and shut the hell up. Midnight glanced down at his Movado sport watch. "Thirty seconds!" he shouted as Threat appeared from the rear office. "You good, Cuz?" Midnight looked Threat in the eye. He responded with an affirmative mug.

"Baby boy." Midnight was eyeing Nightmare now. "You good, you ready to dip?" Another affirmative mug. Midnight sucked his teeth and looked the dark-skinned Italian in the eye. Tears were flowing openly now. "C'mon, Slim, don't go out like no li'l bitch boy! You're supposed to be soldier material, dawg. Man up and go out like a soldier!"
Emotions got the better of Eddie. The young Italian folded. He cried, wept, and sobbed all at the same time.

"Thirty seconds up!" Threat yelled, lugging a large black duffle bag weighted down with the expensive loot. "What'cha waitin' for? The boss gave the order on the bamma in the blue suit. Slump that ass and let's bounce!" he told him flat out.

Midnight's reaction was emotionless. He shrugged his wide shoulders. "Oh well. Pray, my nigga," Midnight said before he pulled the trigger and blew Eddie's brain out the back of his head.

An agonizingly shrill scream erupted from the old Greek lady. "Lord, no! Please forgive these men, for they know not what they do!"

Blocks away on the pedestrian-filled sidewalk right outside of the Calabria, passersby stopped and stared. They were startled and looking on in disbelief as the menacing trio emerged out onto the sidewalk, toting heavy black leather duffle bags and big black assault rifles.

Rolling south along Wisconsin, Nadia and Mecca's dark gray Charger was en route to the Georgetown explosion when the car cruised by the Calabria and something disturbing caught Mecca's eye.

"Oh shit!" Mecca blurted, surprised. "Nadia, pull over! Look - a robbery in progress!" She whipped out her Glock-21 and snatched up the radio. "Unit 244...Detective Tomay requesting assistance...armed robbery in progress, three armed suspects on the scene. Address..."

Crack! Crack! Crack! Crack!
Mecca's upper torso crouched in the seat for cover when a volley of gunfire shredded the upper edge of the windshield. "Oh shit!" Mecca gasped. "Those bitches fired on us, unprovoked!"

"Don't sweat it, girl!" Nadia grunted, taking evasive maneuvers. "I got these bitches!" She mashed the gas pedal and whipped the wheel hard to the left and right. The Charger lurched forward, wheels screeching.

Bad Ass spotted the unmarked cruiser and on impulse, he slipped between the Magnum and Range Rover and took up a defensive position.

"A couple of broads," Bad Ass groaned under his breath. He lifted his pistol up to eye level and bucked off five rounds. A large Metro transit bus zipped right across his gunsight. "Suck my dick!" he hissed, disgruntled.

Bock! Bock! Bock!

"Oh shit!" Bad Ass ducked as he felt a slight breeze from a pair of slugs zip by his head. "That was too close!" He shuddered.

The Magnum's engine revved loud and hard.

"C'mon! Let's go, Champ!" Loso yelled, taking aim. Brraack! Brraack! He unleashed another volley on the detectives' cruiser, pinning them down for the moment.

Bad Ass took three short breaths.

One...two...three...He sprang to his feet, pistol in hand and finger on the trigger. Bad Ass popped out from behind the Range Rover and fired five more shots before ducking and running for cover.

"C'mon, let's get the fuck outta here!" he ordered, scrambling inside the car and slamming the door shut behind him.

Bock! Bock! Bock!

Big World was giving cover fire from the rear seat. "Yeah, let's boogie! You know back-up is on the way!" he shouted emphatically.

"I got this," Loso muttered. He yanked the steering wheel hard to the left and stomped his foot on the gas pedal. The Magnum leaped from the curb. Loso snatched the wheel to the right and then quickly straightened up.

Bock! Bock! Bock!

Big World let off three more shots and laughed like an overzealous hyena. "Those bitches can't fuck with us!"

The Magnum thundered down Wisconsin, darting left to right, moving in and around vehicles like a bat out of hell.

Nadia gave a valiant effort in pursuing the robbery suspects, but the Charger's tires and windshield had sustained major damage in the shootout. Nadia could barely steer or see through the shattered glass. A moment later, she pulled the cruiser over and said to hell with it.

"Nadia! What are you doing?" Mecca stammered, looking both anxious and perplexed as she watched the assailants drift off into the distance and disappear in the confusion of traffic clutter. "Damn, Nadia!" She stomped her foot and slapped the dash, on the verge of having a temper tantrum. "You didn't have to stop the pursuit! We could've caught those bitches! What's your problem?"

Nadia didn't answer right away. She sat there stewing for a minute, a stoic frown etched in her face as if to say, Bitch, you must've lost your damn mind! "Mecca, they shot the fuckin' tires and the windshield!" Nadia huffed. "If you think you can drive this car in this condition, here, be my guest!" She sat back and folded her arms defiantly.

Mecca looked on apologetically and replied, "My bad." She grabbed the radio and announced, "Unit 244...vehicle disabled! Suspects last seen heading southbound on Wisconsin near UDC/Vaness campus, driving a late model black Dodge Magnum with tinted windows. Proceed with caution...suspects are armed and dangerous..." She let the radio fall from her grasp and simply said to Nadia, "I'm sorry; I was caught up in the moment. You know how it goes."

Mecca proceeded to brush her long hair off her face and she leaned back on the headrest. She felt stupid and jittery and tired all at once. She sighed and tried to calm herself and her nerves.

Chapter Five

Downtown DC: Metropolitan Police Headquarters - 24 hours later

Upstairs on the 3rd floor, situated halfway along the east wing's corridor, inside of a dimly-lit conference room, the special gang task force was in session. Lieutenant Rich Louis stood toward the rear of the room, busy operating a slide projector, while giving a brief narrative about the persons appearing on the white wall-mounted screen positioned directly in front of the room.

"After reviewing out investigative report..." Lt. Louis's voice echoed in the room like a college professor giving a lecture to his class. "We've been able to ascertain a timeline for which the Leonardi Crime Family began to infiltrate the DC region." Louis paused when he noticed Lt. Nubie shifting uncomfortably in his seat. "Please, gentlemen, allow me to finish before asking any questions."

Louis turned his attention back on the screen. "Like I was saying...approximately twelve years ago, we can pinpoint some form of a start line for activity involving constituents representing interests on behalf of the Leonardi syndicate. Keep in mind, that's what we are able to pinpoint. It's not an exact science by any means."
Louis pressed the remote to advance the slide frame.

"What you are looking at, gentlemen, is the man himself." Louis's tone sharpened. "This individual on the screen is the crime boss for the Leonardi Crime Syndicate - the infamous Caesar Leonardi, a.k.a. Caesar Leo."

The dark Italian character shown on the screen was an extremely powerful and sinister man. Caesar Leo was tall, dark, and handsome with striking facial features, slick wavy black hair, a strong square chin and frosty black eyes.

In the image gazing back at you from the screen, you could feel the sheer enmity personified in this dark and diabolical man. Caesar Leo lived a flamboyant lifestyle, a life he purposefully duplicated following in the footsteps of his infamous Mafioso heroes – Lucky Luciano and the Teflon Don himself, John Gotti.

Louis continued, saying, "This crime boss isn't your quintessential quote-unquote, normal run-of-the-mill crime boss. Caesar Leo operates along the fringe of moral boundary lines, maneuvering back and forth from legal to illegal monetary ventures."

Lieutenant Maruchan couldn't wait any longer. "Excuse me," he interrupted, "but how does any of this tie in with the executions and big jewelry heist along Wisconsin Avenue? Crime boss and jewelry store murders? What are you insinuating, Louis, that Caesar Leo has a hand in this mess?" he inquired, giving a quizzical smirk.

Louis returned the look and shook his head. "No, Lieutenant Maruchan," he answered, staring him down. "In this particular instance, Caesar Leo isn't the culprit; he's the indirect victim. The three jewelers on upper Wisconsin - the Calabria, the Boccaccio, and the Bulgaria? The listed owner/proprietor for all three jewelry establishments..." He paused for a second, his brow crinkled, deep and shrewd.

"The Leonardi Crime Family is the controlling shareholder for all three." The revelation caused a slight hesitation in the room, like the air being sucked out.

Lieutenant Nubie spoke up. "What about the jewelry exchange in Georgetown? Do the Leonardi's own that also?" He scratched his head, waiting.

Lieutenant Barnhart rose from his seat at the large pine wood table that ran the length of the room. His upper torso was illuminated by the stream of light beaming from the projector. Now that he was the center of attention, Barnhart moved to the front of the room. "No, Detective."

His voice was firm. "The explosion was a diversionary tactic, employed to distract law enforcement from their intended target."

"Yes, and it worked like a charm," Maruchan chimed in smartly.

"Well then," Lt. Nubie interjected, standing. His long, dark form moved away from his chair. "If that's the case," he said, reaching for the light switch, "then we're back at square one and the primary focus of our investigation." Nubie flicked on the light. "Now those fools are not only targeting other rival gangs, but they're going after Mafia interests?" His left eyebrow rose to a sharp point.

"Allow me to infer..." Maruchan lifted a pointed finger in the air. "If this is correct and our suspect has shifted position, then there's something else at play here and we're missing the boat. Our suspect and his cohorts are moving around like a vaporous force. They attack and then disappear, much like a guerrilla force, staying on the move and in constant motion. They've attacked the A-Team, the GHG's, and now the Leonardi's. Where's the common variable? Where's the connection between these groups? And believe me, there is one."

Louis looked around the room. He hesitated and cleared his throat. "Detective Nubie," Louis cut in. "Lights, please." Louis waited for Nubie to turn off the light. "I don't know what the connection is, if there's one to be made. But we do have a face to focus our energy on." Louis aimed the remote and the projector moved forward five frames before coming to a stop. "This is a video clip from the jewelry exchange in Georgetown just before the explosion, and we're pretty certain the image on the screen is the guy who set off the explosion," Louis professed carefully. The face on the screen gave him chills.

The image on the screen was slightly blurred, but if you studied the frame closely, made some minor adjustments to the angle and clarity, the grainy image on the screen suddenly came into view. Tommy Gunz's hardened face beneath a gray hoody seemed to leap off of the screen.

Chapter Six

The Leonardi estate resided just beyond the border of the C&O canal on a prized piece of real estate, which was a private luxurious ten acre swath of rolling green hills tucked away in a nice quiet corner of Georgetown.

Inside of the Leonardi estate, on the first level in the corner of the west wing, the double mahogany wood doors to a private study were closed, but you could hear the silky smooth voice of Ronald Isley echoing from within.

The study was enormous, its décor exquisite. Rembrandt and Renoir paintings decorated the walls and hung between vast collections of books that ran the length of the study from floor to ceiling and filled the walled bookshelves to capacity like a labyrinth of literary tapestry. This was Caesar Leo's sanctuary, his preferred space within the estate. He was relaxing inside – hands folded behind his head, leaned back on the headrest of his rich burgundy leather chair, feet propped leisurely atop his expensive red mahogany executive desk.

Suddenly, the heavy mahogany door to the study began to creak open. The abrupt sound infringed on the calm, meditative state Caesar was relishing. Instantly, his head popped up off the headrest. Caesar's cold stare targeted the intruder trudging through the doorway.

"Okay, Danny, this better be damn good," Caesar warned, giving the man a disgusted look as he watched him wobble across the thick, padded, designer Dalian carpet.\ The husky overweight panda donning the light gray pinstriped suit and dark shades was one of the Don's most trusted confidants, Danny Boy.

A moment later, Danny's short, double-wide frame stood in front of Caesar's desk. "If I got the balls to interrupt your Isley Brother jam session, you should know it's all good," Danny replied boldly as he placed a manila envelope in the center of the desk. "Check out what I just received - special delivery, I might add."

"Special delivery?" Caesar muttered, incoherent. He hesitated and gave Danny a skeptical glare, and then leaned forward and swiped the envelope off the desk.

"What's this here?" Caesar grumbled, leaning back in his chair. He took a peek in the envelope and produced three glossy 8x10 color photographs. His brow grew intense. "Okay, Danny Boy, who the fuck is this supposed to be?" Caesar's thick, gutter Italian accent swelled with angst.

Caution was evident in Danny's facial expression. "Well, boss, from what I was informed, the man in the picture is one of the suspects. No, let me rephrase that: you're looking at the one and only suspect in the Leonardi jewelry store robbery and murder spree."

"What the fuck are you saying?" Caesar snapped, staring hard at the photograph. "The establishment in this picture has no affiliation with Leonardi interests!"

Danny gave a slight nod and agreed. "No it does not, boss. That's the Jewelry Exchange in Georgetown just before it exploded, and that man is suspected of causing the explosion which drew every available pig in the area of Wisconsin Avenue so the heist could be pulled off with virtually no interference."

The astounding revelation caused Caesar's blood to boil. He reacted from a place of profound hatred and loathing. His dark bushy eyebrows merged as one and the veins in his neck bulged unnaturally.

Caesar growled, "I want his name, and then I want the names of every swinging dick that played a part with him!" The Don's voice dripped with venom when he added, "Then I want their heads handed to me on a fucking platter with their balls stuffed in their mouth!" The expression on Caesar Leo's face was totally demented now.

Chapter Seven

"G-Unit, we in here, we can get the drummer poppin', we don't care.

It's goin' down, cuz I'm around, 50 Cent, you know how I gets down!

What up, blood? What up, Cuz? What up, gangsta!"

"Ka-ching!" Loso exclaimed, loud and obnoxious. His outburst drew a sideways look from Bad Ass as he guided the glossy cranberry Cadillac Escalade into the vacant curbside parking space outside of the Luxe Lounge at the corner of New York Avenue and 7th Street.

"Yeah! CIX stars ballin' in the muthafuckin' house tonight!" Loso was amped up – fist pumping in the air, head bobbing side to side to the banger "What Up Gangsta" by 50 Cent.

A blinged-out Bad Ass stepped out of the Escalade looking frosty. A big dumb platinum and diamond Jesus piece draped his neck, he had a chunky ice bracelet freezing his wrist and a rich black tailor-made fitted suit gave Bad Ass that smooth thug swag. He had donned his Louis lens, iced out with the black diamonds, and bopped across the sidewalk like he was Tha Man! Following close behind Bad Ass were his CIX assassins. Loso, Monster, Killa, and Big World were maxin' in all black attire and sparkling jewels.

A matching cranberry Escalade quickly filled the empty space behind Bad Ass's ride, and Murder crawled from behind the wheel. He stood erect, his disposition powerful as he scrutinized the jumbling, jostling crowd lined up outside Luxe. Murder's red-tinted eyes circled the Escalade. Cut Throat, Midnight, Nightmare, and Threat all alighted from the SUV. Together these men were an extremely potent entourage dressed in expensive black suits.

The Cadillacs' security systems sounded simultaneously as the lights flashed, signaling the automobiles' alarms were engaged.

The potent entourage moved as one and descended on the club. Seconds later, they caught up with Bad Ass and the first squad hovering at the entrance. A wide and burly doorman by the name of Touché greeted the men upon arrival.

"Right this way, big dawg!" Touché said as he removed the velvet rope. "You and your men enjoy yourselves tonight!" He flashed a broad grin and nodded to the entourage as they breezed by him, trailing Bad Ass inside the club.

The last man in, bringing up the rear, was Threat. The moment he strode by, Touché immediately hung the velvet rope back in place, folded his bulky arms over his chest, wiped the grin off his piggy face, and stood at the VIP entrance like a super-sized, overbearing mannequin looking for trouble.

On the opposite side of New York Avenue, a charcoal-colored Charger was hidden amongst a jumble of cars parked outside of Mirrors nightclub. Seated behind the Charger's dark-covered windows, Nadia and Mecca were busy surveying the scene outside the Luxe Lounge. Friday nights at the Luxe Lounge were a haven for D.C.'s underworld power players. They partied, they flaunted their wealth, and they corralled women by the handfuls. Tonight would provide Nadia and Mecca with a plethora of underworld figures to add to their list of viable suspects.

"What do we have here?" Mecca snorted, peering through the telephoto lens of a 35mm camera. Its shutter snapped non-stop when the occupants of both Escalades emerged from their vehicles and disappeared inside of the club.

"They look like a bunch of serious prospects to me," commented Nadia with a powerful pair of binoculars hinged to the bridge of her nose. "So make sure you get some good pictures, girlfriend. The way they rollin', they gotta know somebody who knows somebody who knows something."

The sound of Cool Out blasted the airwaves inside Luxe Lounge. The mood was all good up on the 3rd floor. The atmosphere was live and carefree, bubbling with a high dose of energy and excitement. Hot and hip music pumped from the speakers while the grown and sexy crowd danced, mingled, laughed, and drank until their hearts were content.

Sounds of giddy laughter bellowed from the far left corner of the room where Angel, Dee Dee, Nina, and Renee had staked claim to a comfy red leather lounge sofa situated beneath a large glass window that overlooked New York Avenue.

"Daaamn, Renee!" Dee Dee blurted with a look of wild amazement sparkling in her eyes. Without hesitation, she reached over Nina and snatched the pink crocodile handbag lying on the sofa between Nina and Renee. "Eat me out!" Dee Dee stammered with an envious spark in her eye. "Look what our bitch rockin' tonight! A goddamn Lady Dior bag!"

The moment Renee stepped foot in the lounge, Angel recognized the exclusive one of a kind designer handbag, but she kept her cool. Besides, she figured someone like Dee Dee would put the croc bag on blast, so she waited.

That was Angel's cue. "Lady Dior!" she exclaimed in delight at the sight of the coveted showpiece. "Sis, you working it, girl, with the Lady Dior!"

Nina emptied her glass of Patron before responding. "What? I don't get it," she said, twisting her upper lip.

"Why y'all acting all fruity over a goddamn pink purse? I mean, really, who does that?" Nina rolled her eyes and blew them off with a dismissive wave. "Shit, the way y'all bitches acting, you'd think the bag was worth some real money, and when I say real money, I'm talking twenty thousand dollar type of bag. Feel me?" she finished with a roll of her heavy head. She leaned forward, snatched up the bottle of Patron, and refilled her glass to the rim. "What?" Nina paused, holding the glass to her mouth. "Did I say something wrong?" she muttered and took a big gulp.

"Ms. Know-Everything," Dee Dee retorted, "but don't know shit!"

"Yeah, Dee!" Angel chimed in, instigating. "Tell Nina to shut it up, because that Lady Dior bag is the top of the line! That bag cost every bit of twenty thousand dollars. Ain't that right, Sis?"

Nina choked and spilled her drink. "Suck my pussy! Twenty thousand! For real, Renee?" Skepticism showed in Nina's face.

A smug grin creased the corner of Renee's cherry red lips as she peered into the half-filled glass of champagne that she held so nonchalantly. "Nina, you heard my sister," Renee answered casually. "And you already know Angel don't front for nobody. Besides, for a woman of my caliber, $20,000? Girlfriend, that's a drop in the bucket. I'm surprised at you, Nina."

Suddenly, an uptick of chatter surged in the room and all eyes were drawn to the sharply-dressed entourage making their way across the floor. It was quite apparent to everyone paying attention who the leader of this dark and vicious pack was. The way Bad Ass moved, he seemed to float in an imaginary bubble of superiority as if he was Mr. Untouchable.

CIX swept through the 3rd floor lounge and laid claim to their reserved VIP section, leaving in their wake a swirl of gasps and whispers, as a number of men and women alike expressed their idolization and reverence – especially toward Bad Ass.

Bad Ass didn't take a seat like the rest of his team. Instead, he removed a chilled bottle of Spade from the ice bucket, popped the cork, and took the bottle straight to the head. A minute later, he was like a hawk prowling the floor for prey. His deep dark gaze probed, prodded, and seduced the collection of hot slinky prospects spread out like a heard of horny sheep, just waiting to be chosen by yours truly.

It wasn't long before Bad Ass zeroed in on tonight's sexual conquest. He tossed Loso a wink and a nod and then strode off without hesitation.

"Don't look now," said Dee Dee, beaming with a look of hopefulness and desire, "but isn't that Chevar?"

No one uttered a word. The women all looked at once to the spot on the floor where Dee Dee was staring. Instantaneously, a sparkling gleam of adoration and lust shone in their starstruck gazes. They were like a bunch of young school girls in the school cafeteria fawning over a handsome new boy just starting class for the very first time.

The women watched as Mr. Smooth drifted across the floor toward them. A massive dose of masculinity and confidence exuded in his swagger as Bad Ass made his way through the room, and his chunky rocks glistened on his frame like a magnificent light show.

Angel's brow deepened. What in the hell? His face looks so familiar…but where do I know him from? she quietly pondered. Slowly, gradually, her head started to spin, as if an acute onset of vertigo was suddenly upon her. Images of rapture creep into Angel's head, the juices between her legs got hectic, her pussy simmering now. Before she could react, she realized her panties were soaked, and her conscious mind was sinking hard and fast into that deep black mental space where she dreaded going.

"Hello, ladies," Bad Ass said,, greeting the women with a sleek grin. "You look beautiful tonight, all of you." He hesitated briefly, making eye contact with Renee, and went straight at her. "And you, Renee, with your super sexy self!" Bad Ass leaned in her ear, and his deep voice and Ferragamo scent made Renee weak at the knees. "You're looking extra scrumptious this evening. Mmph, mmph, mmph! The last time you and I were together, we got so down and dirty, those bammas at the Ritz Carlton had to ban us from the premises. Remember that, huh, baby girl?"

Just mentioning the Ritz Carlton gave Renee goosebumps. Happy memories of their sexcapades began reeling through her mind and made her smile all over. Renee's soft china-red complexion flushed slightly. "Chevar," she whispered, feeling a tinge of excitement. "That's enough, boy!" Renee gave him a playful slap on his shoulder. Damn! She gasped quietly when she felt his rock hard shoulder and muscles bulging under his suit. "What I tell you, Chevar?

That's our business, so keep it that way." She tried to sound discreet.

Bad Ass snickered. "That's not a problem, baby girl," he said, eyeing her lustfully as he placed his palms together and started sucking his teeth. His eyes twinkled gleefully as lewd images of her perfect derriere floated in his head. "Hmmm. I'm loving your new hairstyle," Bad Ass told her, licking his lips. "That's real talk, baby," he added, admiring her long, curly blonde tresses. "I want a good view of your new hairstyle from the back...feel me?" He winked slyly.

Dee Dee nudged Nina in the ribs. "You hear that? Back shot," she remarked in a hushed voice.
Renee grimaced. "What did I just tell you?" she said, making a weak attempt at chiding him. Her demeanor and tone

lacked any form of conviction. Renee shook her head and reached across Nina to retrieve her bag. She proceeded to open her croc bag and take out a stick of Bobbie Brown rouge lipstick.

"Say hi to my sister," Renee urged, rising to her feet. "Angel, meet Chevar. Chevar, this is my sister, Angel.

You know Dee Dee and Nina. I'll be right back. I'm going to the powder room." She blew him a kiss before trotting off.

"Sister?" Bad Ass emphasized, giving Angel a hard, studious look. "Well it's nice to make your acquaintance...Angel?" He scratched his head while searching her face. "Damn, baby, I swear I know you from somewhere. Have we met before? You look so familiar."

Natasha fixed him with an adamant stare and her tone hardened instantly. "Excuse me?" she quipped and shot him a harsh scowl. "But I'm not your baby, and I would appreciate if you would address me appropriately."

"What?" Bad Ass thought seriously about telling her to fuck off, but the repercussions... Smashing Renee tonight would be out of the question. He looked her in the eye, sighed, and shrugged. "Whatever you say. Have it your way...baby," he concluded, flashing a shady grin.

Natasha gave him an evil scowl and pursed her lips. Inside she was fighting for control. "Oh, I get it. You're one of those types?" she said, being purposefully vague.
Bad Ass stared at her with a question mark look on his face.

"Those types?" he replied uneasily. "Okay, you got me, what is that supposed to mean?" He leaned back, waiting.

Natasha paused and gave him an icicle stare, and then she turned to Dee Dee and Nina. Both women were all ears. "Damn, bitch! Why don't you and Nina go fuck this piece of shit-ass nigga!" Natasha lashed out aggressively. Her hazel eyes turned frosty brown. She stood up abruptly, adjusted her tan Chanel pants suit. "Move the fuck out of my way!" she hissed and stomped off.

"Bourgie-ass bitch!" Bad Ass cursed loudly, but not loudly enough for Angel to hear.

"I'll be goddamned," Dee Dee murmured in a subdued voice, her expression was incredulous. "Angel still ain't right," she conceded, shaking her head.

Nina answered, sounding indifferent. "Girlfriend, that ain't the half of it. That bitch is seriously fucked up in the head!"

A minute later, Renee came prancing through the crowd with a happy-go-lucky face. "Where Angel rushing off to? She was moving so fast, she didn't even hear me calling her name." When Renee noticed the puzzled faces staring back at her, she paused and her attitude changed immediately. "Okay, Chevar, what did you say to my sister?" She stood back, hands plastered on her hips, looking defiant.

"C'mon now, baby girl," Bad Ass said charmingly, displaying his lady killer smile. "You should know me by now. I'm about having fun and making my woman feel like she's on top of the world." He flashed a toothy canine, looking just like a sly fox.

"He's right, Renee," Dee Dee spoke up. "Chevar ain't do a damn thing to Angel. She nutted up on us once again."

Nina snorted and filled her glass for the umpteenth time. "Nutted up ain't the word. If you ask me, I'd say our girl Angel has lost her fucking mind! Yeah, that's right, the bitch cuckoo for Cocoa Puffs!" Nina said flatly as she guzzled her drink.

While the women were busy going back and forth, Bad Ass had his sights set on Renee. She was fly – effortlessly. The low-cut pink silk Chanel dress she wore was breathtaking. He couldn't take his eyes off her perky breasts, which were bubbling over like she was a sexy glass of Rose Moet. Bad Ass eased up behind Renee, placed his hands around her slim waistline, and breathed lightly on the nape of her neck.

"What up, shawty?" His tone was slick and slippery now. "Why you trippin' cuz I'm limpin' when I'm walkin' and pimpin' when I'm talkin', huh?"

"What in the world did you just say to me?" Renee laughed pleasantly.

Bad Ass didn't speak. He touched his lips to her neck, and he knew she was ripe when he felt her shudder under his embrace. She was his instrument and he was the master musician ready to make sweet music. Bad Ass's hands fell from her hips. "It's time we got our party started, wouldn't you agree?" He knew the answer without her saying. He took Renee's right hand in his and moved off prematurely. He glanced over his shoulder and gave Dee Dee and Nina a wink as they departed.

Far off in the right corner, just beyond the 3rd floor entrance, Natasha was silently fuming, her face a mask of twisted anger and hatred and suffering. She watched the couple walk hand in hand across the floor and out the door without so much as a look over their shoulder. The image was too much for Natasha to bear. She was totally vexed, so disturbed that she didn't notice the tears streaming down her cheeks.

Downstairs, Mecca was making her way in the front entrance. The Thai beauty's swagger was distinct – sexy and sophisticated. She had styled her silky hair back in a playful, genie-like ponytail and she had donned a slim, cropped emerald halter by Oscar de la Renta with matching four-inch stilettos heels. Mecca recognized the man wearing the black diamond Louis shades and the gorgeous redbone supermodel he led like she was a little puppy.

Nadia appeared at Mecca's side, and baby was no slouch. Her dark cocoa complexion was complemented by Donna Karen's platinum pants suit and matching eyewear. She bumped into Mecca's backside when she stopped suddenly.

"What is it?" Nadia asked, snapping her fingers and bobbing her head in rhythm to the music. She was definitely feeling the vibe.

"Look!" Mecca indicated Bad Ass and Renee walking down the stairs. "One of our suspects has scored already, and he's leaving the premises."

Both women eyed the attractive couple as discreetly as possible - but not discreetly enough.

Behind his Louis lens, the left corner of Bad Ass's eyelid jerked suddenly. Po-po! The warning echoed in his head. Bad Ass had this keen ability to detect the police from a mile away. Tonight was no different. The provocative pair standing just inside the entrance drew his attention.

Bad Ass slowed his gait, but not noticeably, as he approached the exit with Renee in tow. He focused intently on the women's facial features. Bad Ass had an uncanny photogenic memory. He pulled a fresh Tootsie pop from his pants pocket, unwrapped it, and popped the sucker in his mouth. Bad Ass gave the lady detectives a smug face and a slight nod when he passed.

"You two lovelies have a good night," he said with a devious smirk as he paused in the doorway to allow Renee to pass. Before exiting, Bad Ass pivoted on his heels. He knew the women were watching, so he turned and blew them a kiss and mouthed "I want that". Before either woman could respond, he grinned and walked out the door.

"He's a bold sonofabitch," Mecca hissed, watching him leave.

"Yes, he is," Nadia chimed in with a concerned expression. "Why do I have a bad feeling about him? Like he did that to let us know that he knows our cover?"

Mecca smacked her lips and rolled her eyes. "Girl, stop assuming. You know what they say about that?" She spun around and her gaze moved across the floor. "He's gone, but the rest of his crew still remains on the premises. All we got a do is find the weak link." Mecca expressed their plight as though it were a foregone conclusion.

Nadia tapped Mecca on the shoulder. "I heard the big boys hang out up on the 3rd floor. That's where the VIP is located." She smiled when Mecca looked over her shoulder. "What you waiting on? The big boys are awaiting our arrival."

Mecca blinked suddenly. "Damn, Nadia, girlfriend is fly! Look how she wearing that bad-ass Chanel suit!" Mecca admired openly.

"Go ahead," Nadia waved the comment off when she realized that Mecca was referring to the woman coming down the stairs. She wore the exact same Chanel suit that Mecca owned.

"Girlfriend..." Mecca stepped in Natasha's path.

"You are killing 'em in that Chanel! I just had to give you your props!"

The scowl Natasha wore softened slightly as she looked from Mecca to Nadia and back to Mecca again.

"Shit," Natasha muttered, eyeing both women from head to toe. "The way y'all hoes look, it's no wonder why our men sniffing behind your ass!" She spat in a tone laced with acid, then pushed by them, leaving both women slack-jawed and staring at her back.

"Fucking bitch!" Mecca snapped as she flipped her off. "She's lucky I chilled out. Any other time, I would've ran her ass down and gave that bitch a good beat-down!"

Nadia shook her head in disbelief. "Girlfriend, that bitch ain't right," she said, pressing her hand against her chest. For some strange reason, Nadia couldn't take her eyes off the doorway. A cold chill raced through her body. She shuddered and gave herself a hug. "Mecca, did you see her eyes? I could feel the hate in her eyes. I swear that woman has the devil in her, as if she's possessed."

Mecca couldn't help but laugh. "Nadia, if you don't go ahead with that crazy-ass devil bullshit." Mecca gave Nadia a playful nudge. "What are you trying to say? The devil getting her groove on tonight? C'mon, Nadia," she said, moving toward the stairs. "We got some bad boys that need attending to."

Nadia lingered for a minute, and then she held her breath and sighed heavily. "Yeah, I know, duty calls." She sounded reluctant as she traipsed off after Mecca.

Natasha walked outside and spotted Chevar and Renee locked in a passionate kiss, leaning against the passenger side of Renee's shiny new fuchsia-colored Lotus Elise.

If looks could kill, they'd both be dead on the spot. So that's how you want to play this game, you inadequate excuse for a man! Natasha voiced cryptically. We gonna see how much blood your bitch ass can really handle! She vowed passionately. She strode off up the sidewalk without attracting any unwanted attention.

Chapter Eight

Later on that night...

In uptown DC at the intersection of Georgia Avenue and Pine Branch Road, the usual bustle of traffic slowed considerably during the late night hour, especially along the quiet Piney Branch corridor. The sparkling white Mercedes coupe made a hard right turn off Georgia onto Piney Branch. A half mile from the intersection, the expensive coupe cruised the deserted stretch of Piney Branch until the vehicle came upon Renee's impressive ride, parked at the curb out in front of a three-story red brick Colonial.

The coupe slowed to a crawl, made another right turn onto Baxter, and disappeared in the dark shadow of a large oak tree. Inside the Mercedes-Benz, Natasha quickly stripped off the Chanel suit, reached behind the seat, and pulled out a brown Louis duffle bag. She pulled the gold Louis zipper open and produced a pre-arranged all-black hook-up. At the very bottom of the bag, a black satin cloth sat all alone. Natasha retrieved the satin cloth from the bag and placed it on the passenger seat. An eerie glow of excitement beamed in her eyes as she unwrapped the prized possession.

Natasha licked her lips, malicious delight glittering in her eyes as she admired her razor sharp chrome machete – her preferred weapon of death and destruction.

R & B singer Miguel's slow sensual groove "Adorn" permeated the dark shadowy interior on the first floor which was illuminated by the soft glow of candles dancing and swaying noiselessly throughout the spacious living room. Renee lit the last candle and placed it on the empty windowsill facing the front porch. Her hips swayed effortlessly to the music, slow and sensual and enticing, side to side like a belly dancer. She raised both arms in the air above her head and glanced over her shoulder and gave Bad Ass her naughty girl grin.

It didn't take him but a second to get the hint. He eased up on Renee's backside and placed his hands gently against the nape of her neck. Slow. Tender. Sensual. He ran the tips of his fingers along her soft, unblemished skin, enjoying the feel of her small delicate shoulders and the tiny goose-bumps bubbling up on her arms. Bad Ass paused when he reached Renee's slender waist. He tightened his grip and started to grind against her luscious backside, savoring the erotic sensation as the sudden rush of blood engorged his fuck stick.

Renee pursed her lips in a naughty way. "Ooooh!" she responded, a pleasant purr oozing from her mouth.

"From that big bulge I feel in your pants. I can tell I'm not the only one that's getting aroused."

"You a sexy red bitch and you know it, don't'cha, baby-girl?" Bad Ass whispered in her ear, his lips tense with excitement. He spun Renee around, aggressive, the way she liked, and slipped his right hand around her throat and began to squeeze. He put his lips to Renee's ear, so close she could feel his hot breath on her earlobe. "This what you want, ain't that right, bitch?" he growled, nibbling on her earlobe. "You want me to bend that pretty ass over and punish that pretty red pussy, ain't that right, bitch?" He hissed as he slathered the right side of her face with his long serpent tongue.

"Come here, bitch," Bad Ass snarled with his hand still firmly in place around her throat. He forced Renee to move backward, directing her toward the royal blue suede chaise lounge at the center of the room. He forced her down on the sofa. "Here, this what you want," he said, unfastening his pants.

Renee looked up at him and bit her bottom lip. "No," she uttered in a breathy tone, and reached out to stop him. "Let me handle that for you," she demanded. She took it upon herself to complete the task of undoing his pants. Seconds later, she had his Armani boxers down while she savored the sight of his pulsating meat dangling between his rock-hard thighs.

Exasperation flashed on Renee's face and she gasped at the thought of Chevar pounding her pussy into submission with his untamed piece of meat. Renee licked her lips slowly and breathed, "You know this is my specialty here...licking that big lollipop of yours." She arched her head back and cast a naughty look up at Chevar.

He caught the mischievous twinkle in her eye before she lowered her head and took hold of his elongated organ with both hands. Slowly, caringly, and tentatively, Renee began to devour him – inch by inch by inch...

"Wow!" Bad Ass breathed, utter fascination swimming in his facial expression as he watched Renee go to work on him.

A few feet away in the dimly-lit dining room, something dark moved in the shadows and startled Bad Ass.

"What the fuck?" he mumbled, straining to see. Renee moaned and took him deeper, causing Bad Ass to gasp and shudder in delight. It distracted him from the movement in the dining room. "Oh fuck!" he muttered, grabbing a fist full of hair. "Yeah, that's it, bitch, swallow all that dick," he grunted with a seedy grin.

Suddenly, right in the heat of the moment, just when Bad Ass felt the tenseness rise up inside his body and his breath skipped a couple of beats and all the built-up momentum and excitement and sensation collided at once to overwhelm his conscious mind, a wicked bone-chilling scream shattered the moment in the worse way imaginable.

"Dirty stinkin' whore!" Natasha lambasted, charging across the living room like a deranged lunatic, wielding the chrome machete above her head with both hands.

Without thinking, Renee spit Chevar's penis out and whirled around. Bad Ass was flash frozen in place like a deer caught in headlights. The sight of a crazed Natasha streaking across the floor with the machete in her hand surprised them both.

Natasha brought the blade down with a powerful, lightning fast, swooping arc and connected with the right side of Renee's face. The razor-sharp blade sliced down her cheek and through her jugular. Renee's hand instinctively grabbed at the deep gash in her throat and tried in vain to stem the gush of blood spewing from the wound. She toppled off the edge of the sofa, choking on her own blood, as she hit the carpeted floor, rolled over on her back, and stared up with crying eyes, galvanized by the sight of her attacker.

"An...gel?" Renee gasped, her voice strained and gurgling unintelligibly. "But...why?" she choked and cried, a look of sheer horror and inconceivability raging in her eyes.

A look of dark fulfillment exuded from Natasha's form as she stood there and watched the blood bubble out of Renee's throat, down the side of her neck, and into the plush burgundy carpet.

Bad Ass couldn't believe his eyes. He felt like a bundle of chaotic impulses, standing there amidst some sort of wicked and demented love triangle he wanted no parts of. Natasha! This crazy bitch is off the chain! Bad Ass silently conceded while keeping a close eye on her.

Natasha stood there relishing the dark moment before death extracted Renee's dying soul. A moment later, she looked his way and gave him a contemptuous look.

"What did I tell you, Chevar?" Natasha muttered, fire burning in her eyes. Her disposition billowed heavily with cynicism. "Once you put your dick in me...that thing belongs to me!" she stated vehemently, eyes flashing and teeth bared in a wicked Cheshire grin.

Although the situation was obscene, even to a man with Bad Ass's insidious nature, he was totally aware of this woman's power and treachery. He could sense her vindictive core surging like a diabolical beacon. This was something completely new to him. He didn't expect a woman to be as supremely nasty as she! Damn, this bitch is a monster! A bona fide psycho-bitch! he realized. Natasha's dark, titillating appeal wowed his manhood and sent a jolt of euphoria through his body.

Sometimes your whole life boils down to one insane moment. Bad Ass's mind flowed at a feverish pace. The deeper he thought about this dangerous and complicated situation, the more he saw connections and had a sudden epiphany. This impelled his hunger to know more, dig deeper. Who is Natasha?

"What the hell is your problem?" Bad Ass spoke up, sounding shocked but standing firm now. "You didn't have to kill her! It's not that serious!"

Natasha pointed the machete. "Don't go there," she warned, aiming the tip of the blade at the limp organ hanging between his thighs. "You see, this is what happens when you try to fuck over a bitch like me. Bitches die and niggas get their dicks confiscated," she told him point blank.

A wave of caution crept on Bad Ass's face. Natasha's glib response made him clearly uncomfortable.

"What? What the fuck are you trying to say, huh?" Bad Ass sounded gruff and full of skepticism.
Natasha moved around the sofa to the spot where Renee lay bleeding to death. She looked upon her with an evil gaze and laughed mockingly.

"Chevar, you don't want none of this. Fuck with me and you'll be leaking and missing parts of your anatomy," she told him as she knelt down beside Renee. Slowly, she began to stroke Renee's hair with a weird, sinister look beaming in her eyes. She placed the chrome machete on the carpet, and two seconds later a pearl-handled straight razor appeared in her right hand.

"You shouldn't cry," Natasha said to Renee, the cadence in her voice both creepy and gentle. "You were destined to die by my hands. Don't you know, bitches like you don't deserve life." She placed the razor at the base of Renee's throat, dead center. "Whore..." she breathed and began to chant some sort of cryptically-moving chorus as she pushed the razor two inches deep in the pit of Renee's neck.

Renee felt the life blood seeping from her body. She summoned the last vestige of her soul, and then she kicked and fought until the bitter end.

The expression on Natasha's face was absolute madness. Sick. Twisted. Demented. She meticulously and methodically carved open Renee's upper torso, focusing mainly on the region around her heart. The chanting ceased abruptly and a squashy, sticky, sucking sound drifted in the air while in the background the slow groove melody continued to play. Natasha raised both arms in the air above her head, triumphant, one fist totally immersed in fresh warm blood, the other fist holding a warm, bloody heart.
Utter astonishment exploded on Bad Ass's face and an icy chill gripped his spine as he stared at the gory sight and felt his heartbeat grow erratic.

Natasha twisted around on the floor, a wild, animalistic scowl etched in her face. "Chevar...are you feeling me now, baby? Or must I continue and do more damage?" she asked and then laughed obnoxiously. Her laugh was wicked and maniacal; a sound that captivated the room with pure evilness.

Bad Ass forced himself to smile. His cold black eyes glistened, but not with eagerness, for he had to smother the wariness he felt growing inside. He had definitely found his match in Natasha, but to what extent and what perils would he be willing to push the envelope? What sacrifices would he have to make in order to co-exist with a woman with such a diabolical nature?

Chapter Nine

Meanwhile, on the opposite end of the city; the stocky, chinky-eyed Dabo was behind the wheel of a glossy black BMW M-5, racing up the exit ramp for Kenilworth Avenue. He bent the corner and made a hard left onto Eastern Avenue and then accelerated.

"Goddamn, Slim!" Trouble gasped and choked, looking tense and grim with his right hand locked in place on the passenger door, bracing himself as Dabo whipped the car, changed lanes, and dipped around vehicles like a fool. "You ain't gotta go that hard, Dabo! I ain't trying to die tonight!" Trouble protested adamantly, his dusty, pimple-ridden face locked in a strained grimace as if he was a split second from having an epileptic seizure.

A raspy-sounding Tommy Gunz chuckled in the backseat and said, "Go ahead with that scared-ass shit, Trouble! Let baby boy do his thing! Ha! Ha!" Tommy Gunz belted out a coarse laugh and took a couple of hard long pulls on a fat marijuana blunt, and then added with a cough, "Shit, I'm getting a rush out of this shit!"
Seconds later, the black BMW went thundering by a decrepit shell of a building that used to house Melvin's Crab House. A few blocks later at the intersection of Eastern and Division Avenues, Dabo slowed down, whipped the wheel hard to the right, and steered the BMW into a 7-Eleven parking lot.

Dabo glanced up at the rearview mirror and said, "I'm gonna cop some more Dutches. Those freaks over in Seat Pleasant love to smoke!"

Tommy Gunz grinned and blew smoke in the air. "Hey...get some Red Bulls while you're in there!" he replied.

Dabo was busy tucking his platinum and diamond chain beneath his navy blue Washington Nationals jersey. He cut his slanted eye over his right shoulder and sneered.

"No problem, OG, I got you." A moment later, he emerged from the car and made eye contact with a young skinny bamma on a BMX beside a trashcan. He watched him take out his walkie-talkie and point towards the BMW before he turned and walked inside of the store.

Minutes before the BMW had pulled into the 7-Eleven parking lot, bammas had already started to clique up at least fifteen deep across the street in front of the liquor store. You didn't need to see any guns to know these bammas were strapped.

Back inside the car, Trouble hit the blunt a few times and passed it back to Tommy Gunz.

"Shit, I'm jive hungry, Slim. I'm gonna go grab me a couple slices of pizza." Trouble twisted in his seat. "You want something, OG?"

Tommy Gunz closed his eyes, leaned back against the seat, and arched his head toward the ceiling. He exhaled and a thick cloud of grayish-white smoke spewed from his mouth like a gusher and spread across the soft upholstery that covered the BMW's ceiling. Tommy Gunz hesitated. "Nah, baby boy, I'm good." His tone was nonchalant.

"You and your man need to hurry up though, for real, cuz I'm tryin' get my dick wet pronto, ya dig?" he suggested while watching Trouble climb out of the car.

A few minutes passed before Tommy Gunz started to get impatient. He leaned forward and peered through the windshield and tried to catch a glimpse of either Dabo or Trouble inside the 7-Eleven. "Those bammas starting to get on my damn nerves, for real!" he hissed. He took a couple more tokes on the blunt before he decided to step outside.

When Tommy Gunz hopped out of the car, a little bamma no bigger than a buck twenty soaking wet stuck a .45 in the middle of his back. Shit got thick real quick! Tommy Gunz reacted without thinking. He gripped and whipped. A pretty P-94 appeared in his hand out of no-where.

Pop! Pop! Pop! Pop!

Blood and brain matter splashed across the rear of the BMW and the asphalt. Tommy Gunz hit the young bamma up before he got a shot off and blew out the back of his head. Young'un was dead before he ever hit the ground.

A twisted, beastly grin jumped off Tommy Gunz's face as he savored his kill, but it was only for a mere second as another volley of gunfire crackled in the distance. The abrupt sound of gunfire sent the OG diving for cover behind the BMW.

"Here they come!" Tommy Gunz muttered, exasperated and ready for battle. From his vantage point, he could see the crew mobbed up in front of the liquor store.

"A'ight, let's do this!" he grunted and then whipped out another gun, this one a .40 caliber Desert Eagle with the laser beam sight.

Tommy Gunz popped up from behind the BMW, fire spitting from both guns, his facial expression intense as he roared loud and fierce like a male lion protecting his territory from intruders.

Chapter Ten

The following evening inside of Angel's Clarksville residence, Mariah Carey's soft, mesmerizing vocals caressed the atmosphere with her heartfelt ballad "My All".

"I'm thinking of you...in my sleepless solitude tonight, If it's wrong to love you...then my heart just won't let me be right, because I'm drowning in you, and I won't pull through without you by my side—I'd give my all to have...just one more night with you; I'd risk my life to feel...your body next to mine, because I can't go on..."

Tranquility soared in the family room as the melody's soothing ambiance gently resonated off the walls and ceiling. Lounging in her strawberry velour short set, Angel was in the midst of enjoying some much needed "her time", relaxing on her chestnut leather recliner. She cuddled up with herself – both knees drawn to her chest. A bottle of Spanish wine and a half-filled glass sat on the edge of a glass-topped end table. Angel's right arm danced in the air, moving to and fro, her index finger pointing skyward as if she were sky-writing while she lip-synched Mariah's lyrics.

A hesitant look flickered in Angel's eye when she reached for the wine glass and suddenly she remembered the pink floral envelope lying in the center of the end table. Instead of the wine glass, Angel decided on the envelope. She plucked it off the table and held it in the air toward the light. The envelope was addressed to "My Heavenly Angel".

Angel carefully peeled open the adhesive seal and removed a silk laminated fuchsia-colored Hallmark card with a beautiful dancing angel captured in a pirouette with a glittering halo floating above her head. She opened the card and smiled.

The Hallmark card was handwritten and titled "Let Love Have Its Way".

My Dearest Angel;

    My soulmate beyond all that man can envision. My beautiful crowned royal honor of love. Let me begin by expressing that you are the seed of my heart and the rock of my soul. Never has there been a touch, a feeling, or an emotion that has elevated my spirit to such an extensive level as you have me at this time. I know expression, because you give me a reason to convey my thoughts in a special way. I open the window of all that I am in a plight to secure a greater and more profound experience of you. I have more to give. Will you accept me into your world of wonder? I can only pray. I do not doubt all that we are, and all that we can be to one another. I just crave more of which can be gained and obtained through the vastness of true belief in one another.

    When our hands touch, I never want to let go. I always want to be there to give and to feed all that you may desire and want. There need not be a moment in time that you should ask, for I am that giver of what you were made to receive. I am made for you and you for me. Together all that is, is; and all that will be is in honor of our union. Let us come together as one and share in a love that has no boundaries or limitations – and let our hearts be alone, together..."

Faithfully Yours,
Shane Holt

    By the time Angel finished reading the emotional and heartfelt words, she had to physically place her hand against her chest. Angel's heart did the love thump on her chest. Angel couldn't hide the sudden tide of emotions she felt. Her facial expressions showed obvious signs of astonishment and confusion. Is it the music, the wine, the written words, or a combination of all three? she silently wondered. One thing was for certain: Mr. Shane Holt was doing one helluva number on Angel's mind, body, and soul. The phone rang and shattered the moment. With a reluctant smirk, she bounced off the recliner, took three quick steps, and scooped the cordless phone off the base. Angel glared at the digital phone screen. Private number? "Hello? Who's calling?" she huffed, sounding agitated.

A man cleared his throat and replied, "And how are you this evening, Nurse Rising? This is Stan the man. Remember me? I work the security detail for the disposal unit? You know, I missed you on your last visit and I've been meaning to catch up with you. You see, there's a little discrepancy in the vault's inventory. You wouldn't by any chance know anything about a stash of missing Oxyline pills, now would you?" Her silence spurred Stan on. "What's the matter? Is there a problem, Nurse Rising? In that case, why don't we meet for drinks and discuss this painstaking problem before it gets out of hand. Because for real, I'm not tripping off the missing pills. I could care less.

But I would like to, uh, get this matter out of the way. We could keep this between you and me, ya know...it'll be our little secret. All I want in return is a little taste of your sweet honey, and I'll forget all about this Oxyline nonsense, feel me? Just think about this as sort of a proposition that we both will gain something from. You'll have your pain meds, and I'll have a little piece of you to enjoy. While you're thinking about what I said, think about a time and place we can get our little rendezvous on. Oh yeah, I'm sort of anxious to see you again, so try and make it sometime tomorrow, would you please? I'll give you a call in the morning. Good night, Nurse Rising."

The phone went dead in her ear. Angel sat there blinking back the tears in a state of utter shock and bewilderment. The sound of Stan's voice echoed eerily over and over in her head, as if he was in some far off distance. "You wouldn't by any chance know anything about a stash of missing Oxyline pills, now would you?" After that, it was as if Stan was speaking a foreign language – "blah, blah, blah..." Nothing he said made sense.

A moment later, the music stopped and the darkness seized her mind.

Chapter Eleven

The white Mercedes-Benz coupe pounded the rain slick asphalt, headed for the elegant Palms restaurant located on 19th Street in downtown D.C.

Stan had arrived thirty minutes early for their planned rendezvous. By the time Angel had arrived, Stan was sitting at a corner table knocking down his third mojito. He was in the midst of people-watching when, suddenly, he laid his sights on a gorgeous vixen strutting into the establishment wearing a jet black pants suit. Instantly, Stan was fixated on her, enthralled by the mere presence of her. Stan smiled so hard, his pudgy cheeks were about to break.

Behind the podium stood the maître d', a statuesque Australian woman with long, curly auburn hair and sparkling blue eyes. The brass nameplate she wore said her name was Valerie.

"Welcome to the Palms," Valerie said with an easygoing smile and bubbly personality. "Your name, please? I'll have Mary escort you to your reserved table." Valerie paused briefly, admiring the woman's jet black pants suit and matching stilettos.

The woman seemed preoccupied at the moment. Her crystal blue eyes wandered the dining room, searching for that one familiar face.

Natasha's evil gaze intensified when she caught sight of the short, dumpy, freckle-faced man sitting alone at a table in the far right corner. Her long toothy canines appeared like fangs and she slung her long blonde mane over her shoulder. She gallivanted across the room like a woman with an objective.

Seconds later, she stood beside the table. The smile she wore was so fake and plastic, it was comical. Stan thought she was actually happy to see him. He was the poster child for a typical delusional pervert.

Stan was so overwhelmed. He began drooling at the mouth with excitement. Natasha heard him slurp the spit seeping from the corner of his mouth and cringed. She was disgusted when she watched him wipe it away with the back of the sleeve of his oversized navy and yellow rugby-style Polo shirt.

Stan clapped his fat hands together and remarked off-handedly, "Nurse Rising? Wow! You look very different this evening! My, my, my...there truly is a God, and he's shining down on me!" He licked his blubbery lips and un-dressed her with his eyes. "Please!" Stan rose to his feet, beaming like a nervous school boy. "Have a seat, Nurse Rising," he offered, coming around the table to pull out the chair for her.

Natasha cringed. Her genuine reaction was enough to draw Stan's perverted eye. He focused on her 36DD breasts as they rose and fell in dramatic fashion.
Damn, she's fine! Stan commented to himself.

"Thank you, Stan," Natasha said, stepping in between the table and chair, and then she added before placing her rear end on the seat, "I see you still haven't gotten a firm handle on your weight issue, huh, Stan?" She snickered and gave him a cunning grin.

Stan was sensitive to her devious nuance. "God help me," he laughed and grabbed her rough around the waist. "No, not quite yet." His brown eyes darkened. "But I'm sure you can understand, the process of losing weight is slow and gradual," he said in a voice coarser than low-grade sandpaper.

Natasha hesitated briefly, and then said, "Slow and gradual, huh? I'll give you slow and gradual."
Stan missed the sharpness in her voice. "Is that a fact?" he muttered curiously and sat down in the seat across from

her. "I'll tell you what - you can give me whatever you want." He stopped short and wiped the drool forming in the corner of his mouth. He continued with an obnoxious snort. "As long as you promise me them draws gonna fall!" Violent forces were uncorked the moment she laid eyes on his perverted fat ass. Right now, Natasha was struggling to control the overwhelming urge to strike him down on the spot. "You have the audacity to speak to me in that vulgar tongue!" she whispered harshly, eyes blazing, hateful.

"You're a sick, filthy-ass whore just like the rest of them, and I hope you all rot in hell!" Natasha's voice trembled slightly with rage.

Stan was oblivious to the fact that he was looking at the residue of pure evil. He felt the tinge of death staring him right in the eye, and he laughed.

A vivid image of her hands ripping out Stan's windpipe flashed in Natasha's mind and made her smile. Stan reached across the table and took her gently by the hand.

"You're too pretty to be talking like that," he claimed facetiously, and then he smeared the back of her hand with his cold, wet, blubbery lips.

She wanted to vomit when he touched her skin with his lips. "Have you lost your goddamn mind!" she scolded him quietly and yanked her hand away.

Stan's eyes popped open. "No...have you lost your mind?" he retorted in a defensive tone. "I'm not here to pussyfoot around with you, so get that straight. You broke the law, Nurse Rising, not me. You can make this situation a learning experience and enjoy the ride, or you can make this situation into one vicious scandal that will undoubtedly bring you and your career in the medical field crashing to the ground." Stan paused and turned up his nose. "Huh? You make the call."

Natasha looked him in the eye and studied him for a moment before allowing the hatred and anger she felt for him to subside. She batted her long eye lashes and smiled.

"You've made your point, Stan, and you're right. Let's stop pussyfooting around and do what we came here to do. Matter of fact, I'm not hungry, so we can get out of here."

Stan rubbed his fleshy hands together and chuckled. "Okay now, that's more like it. Where would you like to go so that we can get this party started?"

Chapter Twelve

"Law 28 – Enter Action with Boldness"
" If you are unsure of a course of action, do not attempt it.
Your doubts and hesitations will infect your execution. Ti-
midity is dangerous: Better to enter with boldness. Any
mistakes you commit through audacity are easily corrected
with more audacity. Everyone admires the bold; no one
honors the timid."
48 Laws of Power

Early Wednesday morning while sitting at a traffic light, Bad Ass had a moment of reflection. Surrounded by darkness in the middle of Rock Creek Park, the only illumination was a low cast beam from the fog lights on Renee's Lotus. Bad Ass watched as the bloody ax blade hovered for a split second in the air and then plunged downward. A dull thud echoed in the air when the blade connected with skin and bones and severed Renee's patella (the kneecap) from her thigh in a crude display of violence.

Pure evil surged from Natasha's form like a dark and deadly physical force. Bad Ass noticed the icy gleam in her eye. She is a cold-blooded, cold hearted killer! he surmised. She glanced up at him, her upper lip curled in a nasty sneer. He watched her take the back of her hand and casually flicked away tiny beads of blood and sweat that dotted her brow.

Seconds later, Natasha stood erect. Her chilled blue eyes slowly rove the blood soaked wooded terrain and rejoiced in the devastation she had caused. Renee's bloody, dismembered corpse was strewn across the dark landscape as if she were preparing to celebrate some type of grotesque satanic ritual.

While Natasha was busy dismantling the corpse limb by limb, Bad Ass went about the task of digging up a number of gravesites in which to bury Renee's scattered remains.

One particular analogy Natasha expressed seemed to have struck a nerve in him, and Bad Ass couldn't for the life in him figure out why.

"Don't you know, baby," Natasha said, standing in the wasteland of her own making. "You and I are alike. It's in our nature to kill." The wicked look in her eyes was un-natural, he recalled, and it gave him the willies.

A subtle vibration on his hip-side whisked Bad Ass back to the present, and without thinking, he ripped his cell phone from his waist clip. "Yeah, what up?" Bad Ass's tone was low and lazy.

"What up with you, young killer?" a familiar voice replied easily. "Is the coast clear? Can we talk?"
The voice on the other end must've given Bad Ass a jolt of energy, because he perked right up. "Yeah, Slim!" Bad Ass sat up straight, his deep set eyes wide and alert now. "It's all good! It's all gravy! What's good with you? You got something for me?"

There was a brief pause. "Do I have something for you? That's an understatement, young killer. I wouldn't risk calling you if I didn't have some serious shit to drop on you." The voice on the phone was cool, calm, and arrogant, strictly business. "Check this, young killer. I just got the word from one of my turncoats that Caesar Leo has called for a meet today with his two drug crews."

Bad Ass's facial expression cracked. "What?" he sneered, aggressive, and mashed the gas pedal.

"I ain't stutter. Caesar is meeting with the GHG's and the muthafuckin' A Team, today! So what does that tell me, huh? Evidently, you and your crew have failed. If you can't exterminate a crew like the A Team, how the fuck do you think you can take on the muthafuckin' Mob!"

Bad Ass gunned the engine. "Man fuck that shit!" he snarled, grinding his teeth. "You ain't sayin' nothing! Tell me where the meet going down at and I'll scratch all those bitch muthafuckas with one head-shot!"

Apparently, the voice on the phone found Bad Ass's testy outburst amusing. A light, hearty chuckle emanated from the cell phone's speaker.

"I hear that shit, young killer. You'll get another chance to prove your worth, but that won't be today," the voice expressed, point-blank. "Our focus today is that two-hundred-plus pounds of yayo. Yeah, that's right. While that dago muthafucka dickin' around with his drug buddies, I want you and your crew to take off their cocaine stash. It's time. You think you can do that without fucking that up?"

The insinuating remark only served to piss Bad Ass off that much more. He could feel pulses of thunder throbbing against his temples as the weight of the words penetrated his thoughts.

"So that's where we at now, big brother?" Bad Ass replied through clenched teeth. "You really feeling yourself, huh, Slim? That position really starting to go to your fuckin' head, and I think you better check yourself before you wreck yourself. Feel me?"

A light, hearty chuckle sounded again. "Yeah...I hear that bullshit," the voice answered with disregard. "I got my game on lock. You just make sure you handle your business on your end and make sure you get that money!"
Before Bad Ass could respond, the line went dead in his ear.

On impulse, his hand clamped down hard on his cell phone with such force that he was surprised when the phone didn't crack or break in his hand.

"Mothafucker!" Bad Ass spat and slammed the phone down on the passenger seat. "Get this money..." he spoke aloud to himself. "Yeah, I'm gonna get the money and the power and your bitch! Then we'll see who's the man!" He was in deep thought as he sped along the East Capital freeway, money on his mind and his mind on his money!

###

Later on in the evening, the meet took place at the rear of the Leonardi estate, outside on the palatial stone granite patio.

Power suit. Power tie. Power stare. The boss of the Leonardi Crime family was the epitome of power.

"Fuck him!" Caesar Leo lambasted. "Up against me, that muthafucka is infantile and weak! Bad Ass? Never heard of him. Huh, he sounds like a fuckin' joke!" Caesar Leo had a stilted air about him as he turned and leaned over the dark granite railing. He stared out over the sprawling green acreage spread out like a lush green ocean.

Lounging in the background on an expensive earth-tone sofa, drinking glasses of straight Belvedere, a dark and brawny-looking dude was totally out of place, like some flashy peacock amongst lions, dressed in a colorful lavender silk suit with matching fedora and alligator boots. The flashy dude also sported a thick, beaded beard, dark Ray Ban shades, and he was holding a gold eagle's head cane. Behind the colorful character, guarding the glass doorway, a pair of oversized suited goons stood guard like a couple of intimidating statues.

The glass doors suddenly parted, and the movement drew harsh stares from the two goons until they recognized who was walking outside.

It was the overweight panda, Danny Boy. He wobbled out on the patio escorting two of Caesar's most dangerous and power-hungry kingpins. The first man bringing up the rear was the little big man in charge of the GHG's,

Lucius. The last man out the door was the new leader for the A Team, Santana's older brother, Severe.

"What the fuck?" Severe's tall athletic frame came to a sudden halt and his smooth, hairless face twisted into a shocked, grimacing look. His surprised gaze was unwavering, as if the man in the lavender suit was inflicted with a bad case of leprosy. "Goldie? Slim, we thought your ass was dead!"

Hours earlier, the CIX were summoned to the Petworth safehouse. In no time, CIX crew members had gathered in the basement conference room, where each man was seated at the big round table. A buzz of chatter filled the room with all eyes gradually converging on Bad Ass. He sat at the head of the table like a Don and looked supremely dangerous and sinister, clad in an all-black Armani outfit.

Black shades covered Bad Ass's eyes as he leaned back, lounging on his black leather high back chair, legs crossed – left over right. He peered around the table at the anxious faces looking back at him. With a reflective glean in his eye, he studied each face while stroking the fine hairs on his chin. There wasn't a doubt in his mind that these men he'd hand-picked were more than willing to do his bidding and take a life. Bad Ass looked to his right where his second in command Loso sat in his designated seat. He leaned over and whispered something in Loso's ear.

The seating arrangement at the round table followed from right to left: Loso, Midnight, Nightmare, Threat, Dabo, Screw, Trouble, Big World, Cut Throat, and Murder.

Bad Ass straightened up in his seat. "Alright, men." His voice was strong, demanding everyone's undivided attention. "It's time. This is the moment we've all been waiting for. A few hours from now, Caesar Leo will be meeting with the bosses from the GHG's and A Team." He lingered for a moment, allowing his words to sink in. He noticed the surprised looks spreading on their faces.

Bad Ass tilted his head forward. His expression was cool and cerebral.

"Don't look so surprised," he said, peering over the top of his Armani frames. "We all know the deal. Severe is a cold bamma! Fake-ass fugazy bitch! And his bitch-ass been hiding with his head between his ass the whole time! But I figured he'd show up once he was able to regroup and get some balls. So don't sweat it, because we gonna show his bitch ass how real gangstas get down!" Bad Ass rose to his feet, clasped his hands behind his back, and stepped away from the table.

"You see, men," he went on, "we're dealing with a different breed of bammas. In order for us as a whole to be successful, we must act like a lion a fox and a lamb." Bad Ass had his strategic wits about him. He employed them with the kind of strength and passion that spoke to the hearts of the diabolical men under his direction.

"When we are the lion, we act aggressive and direct, going straight for the jugular. At other times, we have to be the fox—getting our way through crafty finagling that disguises our aggression. Lastly, we must know when to play the lamb—the meek, deferential, and good creature. The lamb is bad in the right way. You see, men, the lamb is calibrated to the situation and careful to make his actions look justified," Bad Ass concluded, looking around at the faces, gauging his words' effectiveness.

Loso chimed in, absentmindedly, "Okay, so who are we today?"

Bad Ass whipped his head around. His eyes trained on Loso. "Who the fuck do you think we are?" he snarled, shrewd and decisive.

A hushed reverence swept the room; all eyes were glued to Bad Ass. An uncomfortable pause seemed to stretch out endlessly, before Bad Ass finally cracked a dark grin – his razor-sharp teeth glinting like diamonds.

"Today, we the muthafuckin' lion, and we going medieval on that ass!" Bad Ass expressed forcefully as he repositioned himself at the head of the round table. "While Caesar and his bamma-ass crew are participating in their fake-ass meeting, we're going to use this golden opportunity to take down their stash house." Bad Ass's dark pupils sparkled as he licked his lips and rubbed his palms together. "A hundred plus bricks just waiting for us," he uttered, sounding distant.

"Well, let's get it crackin'!" Murder exclaimed.

"Yeah, the sooner the better!" Monster spoke up, entering the room with his twin brother Killa in tow. "Cuz, we ready for twelve rounds and no less," added Killa with a shady look.

"Twelve rounds?" Bad Ass remarked snidely. "Psst! Slim, we train for fifteen!" The sound of laughter gradually filled the conference room, as if every man at the round table was waiting for the moment when something light-hearted broke the tension in the room.

Bad Ass gazed around the table. "Now that everyone is finally here, it's time to get down to business." He turned to Loso and said flatly, "Lo, I want you to get one of those chicken heads you be fuckin' with. We gonna need shorty, like right now. Feel me?"

A couple of giggles and snickers cracked the air.

Loso looked up and a splash of agitation covered his face. "Chicken head? Check out my cell, Cuz. I gots nothing but supermodels on my speed dial. Keep it real!" He glared at the table. "What the fuck y'all bammas laughing at, huh?"

Bad Ass glanced down at Loso. "Yeah, G, if you say so," he snickered before continuing. "Alright, we need your supermodel chicken head ASAP!" Laughter and chuckles erupted. "She needs to get in the joint and set the stage, feel me? That's her job."

###

The stash house was a three-story red brick Victorian-style home located on the corner of Rhode Island and South Dakota Avenue in the Woodridge section of NE, D.C.

Ding! Dong! The sound of the doorbell interrupted a serious smoking session going down in the living room.

"Who the fuck is that at the door?" a young, dusty-looking dude snarled dryly. He had short, twisted, spiked hair and went by the name of Pin Head. "Ay, Ugly!" he said to his dark-skinned, beady-headed and extremely unattractive homeboy. "Gimme the blunt and go see who that is at the door," he ordered, reaching for the half of a blunt perched between Ugly's black, ashen lips.

Ugly shot Pin Head a resentful look when he snatched the smoking blunt from his mouth. "Why couldn't you get the damn door?" Ugly complained, standing. He paused and then turned to another homeboy, a stocky dude with a low and tight Caesar cut. "Hey Alpo!" Ugly snorted. "You need to holler at your man, Slim. I don't know what dudes problem is?"

The doorbell sounded again. "Slim, if you don't get the fuckin' door..." Pin Head warned. He shot Ugly a harsh stare before he took two long drags on the blunt and passed it off to Alpo. "Yeah, Cuz," he spoke easily to Alpo. "That there is that killa weed!" Pin Head walked over to the front window and pulled the curtain aside. "I'll be god-damned!" he gasped when he laid eyes on the curvy young lady standing on the porch. "Hey Alpo! Take a look at shorty. Baby girl got it going on, for real!"

The moment Ugly opened the front door, he was blown away by the woman with the ultra-thick body standing before him. "What up, shorty? You lost or something?"

Ugly asked, eyeing her delicious physique and licking his lips like the big bad wolf about to pounce on his prey.

The woman standing at the front door went by the name Dimples. She was hot, fresh, and sprightly, and she was an absolute delight to the eyes in her incredibly skin-tight, hot pink short outfit that hugged her curves extra tight. Dimples's thick, high-yellow frame gave you an instant erection.

She looked Ugly in the face and gave him the most innocent but indignant sneer. "Lost? No, I'm not lost. I'm here to see my baby Nasty. If you're rollin' like that and you get down like that, then your black sexy ass can hit this later on." She looked him in the eye and lied with a straight face.

Ugly looked hesitant for a split second. Oh yeah! Is this little bitch for real? he wondered to himself until the sight of her nipples protruding through her blouse rattled his brain.

"Goddamn!" Ugly blurted unintentionally.

Dimples paused. "What you say?"

"Huh?" Ugly shook his head while gathering his thoughts. "Oh, you're here to see Nasty? Okay, shorty, c'mon in."

A guilty grin parted Dimples's lips. "I thought you'd never ask."

Damn, she's a beast! Ugly conceded as he shrugged off the warning he felt nudging him in the gut. Instead, he waved her inside, drew the blinds shut, and slammed the front door. "Mmph, mmph, mmph...look at all that ass!" he voiced under his breath.

Dimples felt his eyes on her backside. She didn't walk; she strutted. Her plump posterior jiggled with hypnotic effect. A few feet down the hallway, she moved past the living room on her left, and instantly her nostrils filled with the pungent aroma of marijuana smoke. She hesitated and caught a glimpse of the two dudes lounging on the sofa, blowing O's in the air.

"Hey, baby girl!" Pin Head couldn't help himself. "You trying to puff on something?" He snickered. "And I'm not talking about weed," Pin Head mumbled under his breath as he tossed Alpo a sly wink.

"Damn, who shorty here to see?" asked Alpo, looking curious.

Pin Head hunched his shoulders and replied casually, "Hell if I know. She's probably one of Nasty's hoes."

The dining room was Dimples's main concern. Ugly said the second door on the right was the bathroom, so she purposely stopped at the door on the left and turned the knob.

Her brown eyes lit up with excitement. "Oh shit!" Dimples stammered when she laid eyes on the huge stacks of rubber-banded bills spread across a chrome and glass coffee table. "Is that real money?" she asked with an astonished look frozen on her face.

"Hey! Who's the little bitch?" a giant Jabba the Hut look-alike sneered, hopping to his feet. "Pin Head! Ugly!" Nasty roared. "Come get your bitch!" he ordered, slamming the door in her face.

Dimples quickly spun around and darted off in the bathroom. She locked the bathroom door and made a bee-line for the window. A moment later, Dimples unlatched the window and carefully raised the frame, not making a sound. When the window was halfway open, she reached outside with her right hand and pulled in a black metal contraption. She paused and took a breath and carefully looked around the bathroom, her heart beating wild and erratic in her chest. She took another deep breath and calmed her nerves before positioning the black metal contraption in the small space between the window and the window frame. Dimples glanced around the bathroom, held her breath, and pulled the window shut, slow and deliberate. When her business was done, Dimples proceeded to the toilet, flushed the bowl, washed her hands in the sink, gazed at her reflection in the mirror, and took a long, deep sigh.

A minute later, Dimples stood at the bathroom door. She took a couple of deep breaths to gather herself, and then she pulled open the door and walked out.

"I don't know this hoe!" Nasty blasted in her face when she stepped back into the hallway. "Bitch! What kind of games you playing?" He snatched her by the collar. "Ugly! Get this hoe out of here now!"

Nasty burst in the bathroom and glanced around. Nothing looked out of place or out of the ordinary, so he turned off the light and pulled the door shut.

Exactly fifteen minutes after Dimples was tossed out of the stash house, the window inside of the bathroom began to open. Someone outside was repositioning the black metal wedge, operating slow and meticulously. He watched in glee as the window frame began to rise.

Across the hall in the dining room, Nasty's bad attitude was on front street. His gigantic black frame hovered above the automatic money counter. His huge hands were busy shoveling thick stacks of 100's into the machine's automated hopper. Once the bills were whizzed through the machine, Nasty scooped the counted bills from the base.

"Man, that bamma Ugly better get his shit right. Who the fuck does that? Any broad with a phat ass he just let 'em in the joint," Nasty grunted while stacking the counted bills on a small card table sitting to his right. His short and cocky comrade with the big square head and curved spine was named Lump. He was busy straightening out the counted stacks, binding them with thick beige rubber bands and then writing the exact amount across the top.

"Nasty, ain't that your man?" Lump replied without breaking stride. "If you got a problem with Ugly, it shouldn't be nothing for you to holler at him and get that bullshit squared away, know what I'm saying?"

The last comrade in the room was Earthquake. He was a big muscle-bound brute with a pointed nose and chin and a head that was too small for his bulky frame. He sat perched atop a burgundy bar stool in front of a 32-inch flat screen, gawking at an X-rated sex video. On the shaggy green carpet beside his right foot, Earthquake's fully loaded AK-47 lay undisturbed.

"Lump giving you some real talk," Earthquake injected his two cents into the conversation. "You need to, uh, listen up and take heed to what that brother saying."

Earthquake had one of those awkward sounding voices, somewhere between a lisp and stutter. When Earthquake spoke, his clumsy tone caused Nasty to cringe.

Nasty's head snapped back. "What the fuck you say?" he barked aggressively. "Ain't nobody ask your bamma ass jack shit! So do what bammas do and stay the fuck out of my business!"

Even Lump could feel the sting left hanging in the air by the harshness in Nasty's words. He thought about speaking up for his big, mentally-challenged comrade. But one look at Nasty killed the thought in its infancy stage.

Earthquake glanced around the room, a strained, dumbfounded expression etched on his face. It was clear by the way his body language swelled with combativeness that Earthquake was on the verge of lashing out.

A pause settled over the room for a split second, and then all hell broke loose.

Bam!

Loso was the catalyst leading the violent charge. His size 12 boot kicked in the dining room door a second before he rushed in strong with a large Street Sweeper clutched firmly in hand.

Nasty, Lump, and Earthquake were stunned. The men's hearts flash froze in their chests when they caught sight of the menacing gun barrel ready to unleash death.

What seemed like an eternity amounted to a split nanosecond. The sudden appearance of a black-dressed Loso brandishing the Street Sweeper sucked the air and life out of the room.

Earthquake's compulsive nature prompted his reaction. In the back of his mind, he told himself, It wouldn't be right if I go out without making a play for my AK. So he did just that.

Boom!

The Street Sweeper exploded. The first blast was a crippling gut shot, so powerful it punched a gaping hole through Earthquake's back.

Boom!

The second blast was mortal, a wicked throat shot that totally obliterated the entire left side of Earthquake's throat. The lumbering brute teetered blindly atop the stool with massive amounts of blood gushing from the crater in his throat. A moment later, Earthquake's hefty frame toppled over and hit the shag carpet with a dull thud.

Nasty's huge physique was surprisingly agile. The giant Jabba the Hut lurched over the table, the money counter, and the pile of money in a single bound.

Boom!

The third blast caught Nasty's right ass-cheek as he hurled through the air. He landed hard on the floor, howling like an injured hyena in pain.

Loso caught Lump flinching.

Boom!

The fourth blast was a deadly head shot. It blew off the entire right side of Lump's face. His body slumped over on the card table and the rubber-banded bundles of money. Lump's decimated body jerked and twitched a couple of times, blood and brain matter oozing profusely from the gaping head wound. A moment later, he lay perfectly still.

Two men down! Without thinking, Loso rushed across the floor with the Street Sweeper leading the way. He quickly side stepped around the table and appeared before Nasty's eyes.

"Say your prayers, Slim," Loso sneered with his finger poised on the trigger.

Nasty stared him in the eye and hissed defiantly, "Muthafuck you, bitch!"

Loso took aim and said, "Naw...it's fuck you!"

Boom! Boom! Boom!

The final three blasts were horrible face shots. Large, deep, bloody craters ripped Nasty's face apart. His face was a mangled mess of shredded bloody flesh and splintered bones.

A moment after Loso had kicked in the door, Murder and Cut Throat stormed the living room.

"Surprise, muthafuckas!" Murder loomed large in the doorway like the Grim Reaper, his Heckler & Koch-MP5 locked, loaded, and ready to spit.

Alpo looked astonished as he frantically searched the room for an escape route. There was none. Without warning, a shot rang out and a hole the size of a quarter appeared in Alpo's summer-white Solbriato pull-over. He gasped and his 6'2", 233 pound frame wilted like a dying flower.

Seconds later, Cut Throat dashed to the front door, flipped the key on five deadbolt locks, and pulled the door wide.

Midnight, Nightmare, Threat, Dabo, and Big World rushed inside while Cut Throat stepped out on the porch and took a quick survey up and down Rhode Island and South Dakota Avenue. Everything looks good, he told himself before he walked back inside, secured the door, and eagerly joined his comrades in murder.

Inside of the Woodridge drug den, the men left a trail of human wreckage – CIX's signature calling card.

Chapter Thirteen

It was days later at the D.C. Metropolitan Police Headquarters. The door leading into Chief Holt's office was off-limits. Inside, a secret meeting was underway with members of the covert Black Hole Operation: Chief Holt, Inspector Woo, and both detectives, Nadia and Mecca. They were busy poring over the mounting evidence spread out on the chief's wide oak desk and papers and photographs pinned to the soft-framed bulletin board.

Tony Woo's disposition was stout as always, a total contrast to the dark, wrinkled, throw-back Pierre Cardin suit he wore.

"Concerning the murder of D.C. businesswoman Bambi..." Woo said, peering up at the gruesome murder photos and detailed status report posted on the board. "Earlier that day, she was found unconscious in a restaurant ladies' room, where she had been assaulted." Woo stopped short, folded his short stubby arms over his chest, and made eye contact with the chief, who was busy taking notes and observing the procedure, step by step. Woo went on to say, "Afterwards, Bambi was rushed to the hospital - "

Mecca interrupted, finishing Woo's thoughts. "And following the assault at the Georgetown restaurant, the perp doubles back to finish the job? That's what you were insinuating, isn't that right, Inspector?" Mecca struck a pose with both hands hinged on her hips. The gorgeous Thai model looked surprisingly dainty, dressed in a baby-blue blouse and skirt set with matching stilettos.

"That would indicate that our perp was involved in some extremely risky stalking with this victim, as if this was something personal," added Nadia in a matter-of-fact way. She stood erect, straightened her bright white blouse, and then stepped in front of the bulletin board. "We need to examine the extent of his journey," Nadia said, looking over her shoulder. "The perp went from the Peacock in Georgetown, and then traveled to George Washington Hospital, and finally over to Bambi's friend Paris's house, where he waited outside in the park for Bambi to finally show up."

Tony Woo stood off to the side listening closely as both detectives critiqued the evidence and worked the angles to fit their hypothesis, while at the same time Woo's intuitive receptors were tingling. He sensed a peculiar vibe coming from the chief. In the midst of watching the detectives dissect the evidence, Woo sensed something else at play, especially when the conversation moved to the newest wrinkle in their investigation – the vicious murder of NIH security personnel, Stanley Hanes.

Woo noticed an abrupt emotional swing in the chief's demeanor. He watched him go from a calm, self-absorbed mood while they were discussing the Stanley Hanes murder to instant discomfort the moment they began to focus on the Bambi homicide. Woo couldn't put a finger on it, but he knew without a shadow of a doubt there was something seriously out of place and flawed.

Tony Woo focused on Nadia and Mecca. "Okay, ladies, the Hanes homicide is all yours. Why don't you two ladies take a ride out to the NIH facility and see what you can dig up, probe into Mr. Hanes's work environment? Ask yourselves why our perp chose to take out a man in this manner? He's never before actually targeted a man. He's murdered a male witness before, but that was because he was an eyewitness, and our perp leaves no witnesses. The way he murdered Mr. Hanes...our perp took his time and made him suffer. You ladies need to find out why," Woo suggested wearing a scrutinizing grimace etched in his face. He concluded by stating, "The victimology in this slaying is totally abstract and extremely disturbing, to say the least."

Woo glanced back at the chief. His body was there, but it was plain to see by the chief's far-off gaze that he was pondering something that was in totally out of sync to what they were focused on.

###

"Don't nobody fuck with my Angel!" Natasha growled, baring her teeth a moment before she chomped down on Stanley's erect penis. The sadistic infliction of pain gave her instant satisfaction. Stan's horrified shrill scream cut the air and she looked up into his piggy face. Stan's expression was stricken with grief and horror and disbelief. He watched his blood spill from her lips and run down the side of her chin. Stan's eyes popped out of their sockets when Natasha opened her mouth and he could see the mangled head of his penis rolling around on her tongue like a piece of fleshy hard candy.

Stan grabbed hold of his mangled, bloody penis and stumbled backward, his mind completely overwhelmed by the searing pain that consumed his entire body.

Slowly, Natasha rose to her feet; the aura she embodied was dark, unaffected, lacking humanity. A chrome straight razor sparkled in her right hand.

"Where do you think you're going, Stanley?" Natasha's tone was wicked. "We're just getting started. Don't you wanna fuck around some more? Huh, Stan? Ha! Ha!"

With every fiber in his being, Stan tried to get away from this demented woman, but the wound she inflicted on his groin was too grave to overcome. A moment later, when Stan stumbled and lost his footing and hit the floor, he saw his life flash before his eyes and he realized at that moment that his life was over. The sound of wicked laughter resonated from every direction and seemed to rain down on him as Natasha descended with merciless intent.

Natasha watched him struggle and squirm across the floor before she casually reached down and raked the sharp blade through the back of Stan's left ankle, ripping his Achilles tendon in half, crippling him.

Stan wailed like a dog in mourning.

"Now, now, Stanley…" Natasha gloated as she kneeled beside him. \"You sound like a little bitch, and we can't have all that screaming," she scolded him as she smothered his screams with her free hand. She gripped the straight razor and rammed the blade deep inside his scrotum, twisting and turning and pushing the razor to the hilt, as deep inside his bowels as she could possibly go.

When Natasha was done, she stood over him, gloating at the sadistic piece of work she'd created. The pig-faced man lay dead on the floor, wide, terrified eyes frozen on a face gripped in blood-chilling agony. Natasha took Stan's lacerated penis and testicles and crammed them into his mouth.

Suddenly, Angel sprang wide awake and stared around the office, a troubled and bewildered expression stricken on her face. She hesitated, then heaved a deep sigh of relief and pressed her hand against her chest when she realized the disturbing images were only a dream.

Angel paused for a moment before she decided to stand. There was something amiss, something creepy she felt in the back of her mind. When she finally stood up, she felt a little lightheaded, so she leaned on the edge of the desk. She braced herself and then lowered her head to her chest and inhaled, slow and measured breaths. As she glanced down, her gaze fell upon the front page of the Washington Post newspaper and she froze, startled by the cover story:

Sadistic Serial Killer on the Loose in D.C.
Mutilated Body Discovered In Dumpster – Male Genitals Missing From Corpse!

A touch of nervous anxiety seized Angel's mind and she started to feel the walls closing in on her. Suddenly, the air inside of the office was unbearable – stale and stifling hot. Angel started to choke and cough uncontrollably, and the room started to spin. She needed air, and she needed out of the office - immediately!

Right outside of the office, the doorknob rattled and instantly caught Diana's attention a split second before the door abruptly swung open and Angel staggered out, coughing and struggling to catch her breathe. It didn't take long for Angel to gather her composure, and in no time, she quickly adjusted her cream Donna Karen blouse, stood erect, turned, and strode off in the opposite direction without ever looking Diana's way.

"6th floor...7th floor...8th floor..." Angel stood at the elevator and quietly mouthed the numbers lighting up above the elevator doors while wringing her sweaty palms looking nervous and agitated. Every two or three seconds she would glance over her shoulder and peer down the hallway, as if she was expecting someone to jump out and stop her at any moment.

The elevator finally arrived with a wisp of air echoing from the slight space around the elevator's chrome doors when they parted, and a polite little Mexican maintenance man named Jose emerged from the mechanical platform. "Hola, Nurse Rising," Jose greeted Angel with his usual happy-go-lucky smile. "Buenos dias!" He immediately jumped to the side to avoid being run over by her when she rushed on the elevator in such a hurry.

Jose's words didn't register or elicit a single response from Angel. She was totally consumed by the alarming images playing over and over in her head, and she barely noticed the little Mexican when she rushed on the elevator. She had a weird feeling, as if she was losing touch with herself and reality.

Angel hovered at the front of the elevator and peered down at the floor, looking lost and confused and completely unaware of her surroundings. She was so consumed with the disturbing images swirling in her head that Angel didn't realize she wasn't alone in the elevator. Two feet away stood a paralyzed and absolutely frightened Dr. Saint. The moment Angel stepped foot on the elevator, he was instantly shaken by her presence.

Dr. Saints's memory flashed back in time to the day when that terrible and unnerving encounter happened on this exact elevator. Unconsciously, the Doctor's hand moved to the spot on his chest where the permanent teeth marks served as a constant reminder to him. The incident scarred Dr. Saint so deeply. It gave him a new perspective on dealing with women. The arrogance he had formerly displayed was all but gone now.

Dr. Saint stood behind Angel and held his breath, completely silent, and didn't make a move. An air of caution and fear radiated in his demeanor and the mere presence of her made his blood run cold. Dr. Saint was totally fearful of her now, for he realized she was very unstable and was capable of untold violence.

Suddenly, the doctor leaped across the elevator and mashed the "hold" button so fast that he jumped clear out of his loafers. His abrupt movement startled Angel and caused her to rear back and glare at him with a perplexed look.

"What is it, Dr. Saint? Is there a problem?" she asked, sounding annoyed.

Dr. Saint shook his head adamantly. "What? Me, have a problem with you? Oh no, Nurse Rising. I think it would be best - well, wiser of me to, um, give you your space, that's all," he said, stumbling over his words. He quickly leaned down, snatched up his loafers, and darted off the elevator. "You have a nice day, Nurse Rising," he expressed. He gave her a curt wave goodbye as he watched the doors glide shut and took a deep sigh of relief.

Seconds later, the elevator reached the main floor lobby. Ding! The doors opened and Nadia and Mecca were startled when Angel blew by them as if they were invisible. Mecca jumped. "What in the hell is her problem?" she complained, glaring at the woman's back.

Nadia glanced over her shoulder. A fleeting glimmer of recognition sparked her eye as she stepped on the elevator. "Damn, I think I know her from somewhere," Nadia said with a vague look in her eye.

Mecca pushed the button for the Disposal Unit and then turned to face Nadia. Both women locked eyes and suddenly a jolt sparked the air between them.

"The Luxe Lounge!" they both blurted in unison, just as the elevator doors sealed shut.

Chapter Fourteen

Later on that evening at D.C.'s five star party venue, Ibiza Nightclub, the VIP was platinum-coated with D.C.'s underworld juggernaut. Bad Ass sat poised with not a care in the world, but primed for anything. At the moment, his lustful gaze were fixated on a hot new prospect, an Ethiopian and Puerto Rican hybrid named Ayanna who possessed that innocent man-eater appeal, an attractive, pretty face and a salacious hooker's body.

Oh yeah...shorty is definitely a winner! Bad Ass declared inwardly as he undressed her with his eyes. Ayanna exemplified sexiness and class to the tenth power. Her exotic features and plentiful curves set her apart from the rest of the women in her group.

Bad Ass's thoughts were abruptly broken when he caught a glimpse of the police chief and his drop-dead-gorgeous arm candy.

When Shane and Angel stepped in the room together, they were explosive as a couple. Shane was ultra-handsome and debonair in his tailored raven black designer Gucci suit. The way his date Angel represented, she literally took your breath away. Angel dazzled the senses with her hourglass figure caressed by a skintight, chili-red Diane Von Furstenberg wrap dress, a magenta pashmina, and metallic-gold stilettos.

Loso casually followed Bad Ass's gaze when he noticed his attention was suddenly consumed by the sexy couple entering the VIP. He leaned forward on the edge of the sofa.

"What up, Champ?" Loso asked, sounding interested. "Look like you plotting on dude's pussy. Want me to run interference so you can cop that?"

Bad Ass tightened his jaw. "When and if I need you, you won't have to ask, Slim, because I'll let you know without hesitation," he advised in a tone filled with sarcasm. Bad Ass's penetrating stare never wavered from the couple.

Loso fixed him with a sincere gaze. "You got it, big dawg, just be careful with that one."

Bad Ass tone turned sharp with Loso. "Who the fuck you think you talking to, Slim?" He hopped up off the sofa, gave Loso a sharp look, and then pulled his hater-blockers – Jacob shades – down over his eyes. "Don't fuck with me tonight, Lo, I'm not in the mood." \He adjusted the heavy platinum link laced with quarter carat black diamonds, and then turned and stepped off.

Loso glared disbelievingly but he didn't utter a word in response; he just watched Bad Ass maneuver through the crowd. Bad Ass's intense but arrogant charisma seemed to encompass his form like a pulsating force field as he directed his path straight for the Chief of Police. The moment their paths crossed, Bad Ass and Shane made eye contact, knowing looks exchanged in the twinkling of an eye, with neither man breaking stride.

Shane escorted Angel arm in arm and deposited her on a sofa where Dee Dee, Nina, Ronnie, and their male companions were accompanying them. Shane smiled to himself. He gave Angel an innocent wink and apologized with a light kiss on her forehead before sliding off back into the crowd.

Upstairs on the second level, Bad Ass was seated alone at a corner table, twirling a fresh cherry Tootsie Pop between his lips. His deep gaze swept the crowded room while his mind quietly reflected on his past.

"Discipline is your honor!" Bad Ass recalled his Uncle Broody saying. Bad Ass referred to him as his mentor – the wisest, most crafty street slickster in the world. Uncle

Broody preached with passion, "Chevar, you must defend your honor at all costs, because as a man, a strong black man living in the hood, all you have is your honor, your word, and your balls! And you best not break not a one if you plan on being a successful figure in the hood!"

Bad Ass learned to employ the kind of mental discipline that would catapult him beyond the normal boundaries of other gang bosses. His discipline served as the foundation for his strength — his sole base of power.

His focus suddenly shattered when he noticed the Chief of Police moving his way. Bad Ass didn't move an inch. He sat there and watched him for a moment before acknowledging him with a curt nod of his head. A second later, he greeted Shane with a lazy smile. "Well look who's here," Bad Ass spoke in a sly tone and flashed his canines in a mischievous grin. "It's the Commander and Chief of Pimpin'!" He laughed obnoxiously.

Shane was sharp, quick, and witty. His usual confidence beamed out. "What? Chief of Pimpin'?" he remarked, wearing a fake smile as he sat down at the table opposite Bad Ass. "I'm hearing a lot of nonsense on the streets, and you know when them flies be singing, them rats be listening. And right now you got the city on your back," Shane said with a serious mug. "You know that, right? The hit on the Leonardi's sent the Mafia an ambiguous fucking message. So don't let those dago sons-of-bitches catch you slipping."

"Catch me slippin'?" Bad Ass grumbled, shaking his head. "Slim, we've been on the grind too long for me to let some dumb shit like that go down." He took a breath before saying, "Look around you." He swept his arms around the lounge. "Can't nobody in this bitch fuck with me. You see those big gorilla-looking muthafuckas standing over there?"

Shane twisted in his seat and spotted three behemoths – Big World, Killa and Monster – posted up by the railing. Where did they come from? They weren't there a minute ago...

"Yeah, that's right," Bad Ass boasted, staring over the top of his hater-blockers. "When I move, my team moving in the shadows."

Shane decided to humor him. He sighed and responded, "Yeah, I hear you, young killer. It's all fine and good while you're eating. Everybody riding your dick right now, but you better keep your eye on the prize, because you are invulnerable to true regret, and I got too much riding on your ass."

Bad Ass scrunched up his nose and snickered. "I'll be goddamned! Look at my big brother! I think you've been hanging out with me too much. I think some of my ways are starting to rub off on you. The way you're talking now...damn, you remind me of myself. What you think, you the King of DC? Big brah, you're not me!" Bad Ass pounded his chest for emphasis. "You could never be me. You can't teach a cat dog tricks. Yeah, I got the city on my back and that's how I thrive. The hood knows when it's blood in the air, and so do I because I'm a fuckin' shark! I lives for this shit! So you better stop talking out the side of your neck. I did what I'm supposed to do. I fulfilled my end of the deal.

Now it's time for you to give some reciprocity. You all laid back and shit with your feet kicked up, feeling yourself now because you the top dawg of the DC police force. You better bring your bad ass back down to earth, Cuz!" The passion in Bad Ass's words was evident.

Shane was thoroughly convinced now; his younger brother was slowly but surely getting crazier by the day. The depth of his cynicism and callousness was far below the human threshold. Shane sucked his lower lip. "Get it

straight. nigga. Your success depends on my position. Without me, there would be no you!"

Arrogance covered Bad Ass's face like a thick, pulsating crust. "Without you there would be no me?" He
leaned over the table, sharpened his tone to a point. "Slim,
you got shit twisted and misconstrued, because I've been
here from the start. Uncle Broody...remember him?"

A look of concern flashed briefly across Shane's
face. He took a slight breath and said, "Look, let's cut out
the bullshit. Where did you stash the cocaine?" His expression was salty now.

Back in the VIP, the drinks were flowing and the
people were happy. Dee Dee was bopping her head in
rhythm to the music and sipping champagne.

"Girlfriend..." She smacked her lips extra loud and
scooted closer to Angel, as if being discreet. "That shit
about Renee blew the hell out of me. She's missing and nobody knows a damn thing about where she is! Can you believe that shit?" She smacked her lips again and rolled her
eyes.

As soon as Dee Dee mentioned Renee's situation,
Angel's look of excitement withered away. Angel cringed,
thinking, I want to have fun tonight! She quickly realized
that adding Dee Dee to the mix was a bad idea. She had a
reputation for being a total killjoy.

Before responding, Angel turned up the cocktail
glass to her mouth and took a healthy gulp of cognac.

"Oooops!" She gasped when she felt liquid trickling
down the side of her chin, and immediately snatched a
napkin off the table and caught the spill dead in its tracks
before it could make its way anywhere near her dress.

Angel glanced down at the red fabric, gave it a
quick once-over and sighed when she realized no damage
was done. Next, she set the glass down on the table, turned
to Dee Dee, and placed her left hand on Dee Dee's knee.

"Dee, girl...I was so upset when I got the news that my sister was missing. I got sick to my stomach," Angel told her and dropped her head in defeat.

Nina's meaty paw appeared out of nowhere and grabbed the bottle of Remy. "That's a shame," she uttered, twisting her upper lip. "I hope girlfriend is okay, even though I really don't know her all that well," Nina whiffled as she filled her glass to the rim. She licked and smacked her thick, red-glazed lips happily and added, "It would hurt my heart if something really bad happened to Renee." With that said, Nina concentrated on the glass of Remy as if the elixir was calling her name. She pulled the glass toward her mouth. Her alcoholic taste buds popped and spasmed with excited anticipation until contact was made. Nina slurped loudly and obnoxiously like a thirsty horse drinking from a trough.

A few feet away, Ronnie looked on with disgust when she noticed Nina and her rude, uncouth behavior. She quickly excused herself and stepped away from the trio of men that was busy talking her ears off. She was fabulous in the floaty silk peach number she wore as she eased down on the sofa beside Angel.

"Don't let this thing with Renee get you down, Angel," Ronnie said, looking Angel straight in the eye. The tone in her voice was both calm and comforting. Ronnie's bright eyes sparkled when she said, "Rest assured, the Lord is watching over our girl, and when we fall prey to worry and distress, that's the devil working his witchery on our lives." A broad grin spread on her face. "Guess who I learned that from?"

"You learned that from me," Angel whispered, her eyes glassy now. She sighed and smiled inside when she felt the genuine goodness and honesty flowing through Ronnie, especially when Ronnie took her by the hand. Angel could feel the warm radiance streaming from Ronnie's form like a spirited beacon of light washing over her.

In the background, Angel could sense a cold vibe coming from Dee Dee, prompting her to look. She cut her eyes to the left and was struck by the chilly expression etched in Dee Dee's face. Dee Dee looked startled when she noticed Angel looking her way. She wiped the look off her face and bounced up off the sofa.

"Excuse me, ladies," Dee Dee spoke casually. "I'm going to the ladies' room. Anyone care to join me?" She cackled as she walked away. Her flashy gold leopard print pants shimmied from side to side as she tossed her hips and pranced through the lounge, drawing lewd, excited looks from every Neanderthal within eyeshot.

Meanwhile, the meeting on the second level was drawing to a close. Bad Ass's domineering personality and combative nature were on full blast.

"I'm a fucking monster! That bamma Caesar ain't got nothing coming! I'm going at that bamma off the muscle. Fuck him and the Mafia!"

Shane laced his fingers together on the table and sat up straight and rigid. A cool, studious gaze swimming in his eyes.

"You know what?" Bad Ass leaned forward, his stare intense, his palms pressed forcefully on the table.

"This partnership you and I got going, we could run this city. Who could stop us? Not a fucking soul! You wanted to get rich; we there. Fuck getting rich, Slim. I'm talking about being wealthy!" he declared greedily.

Shane lowered his head. His confidant look wavered now with concern. "Young killer," he began, stroking his chin. "That shit you spitting sounds good, but the fact of the matter still remains...this shit right here ain't meant to last. It's the nature of the business. You see, you and I, we have a legitimate objective behind our actions, so the laws of karma are stacked in our favor. But you start going off half-cocked being greedy, that shit gonna fuck up the game." Shane hesitated, glanced left then right before going on. "Let me drop this jewel on you. People as a whole are innately jealous, and greed breeds greed. Shit, one of the members on your team could take you out and you'd never see it coming. Just a little food for thought, li'l brother."

"Man, fuck that shit you talking!" Bad Ass fired back assertively. "Greedy is good! Especially the way shit goes in my line of work. One day you're on top of the world, the next, well, ya know..." He shrugged. "Shit turns on a dime in this business, you know that."

Shane could see the madness in his brother's eye. He snorted, "You're one crazy sonofabitch, you know that? What is it with you? You got a death wish?"

"Crazy?" Bad Ass voiced impatiently. "Figures you'd say some dumb shit like that." He bit down on his Tootsie Pop. "Now let me drop a jewel on your ass." His black pupils sparkled when he leaned in closer. "Ain't a damn thing crazy about me, G...but it's the nature of man to confuse genius with insanity." He paused for a brief second in thought.

"Do I have a death wish? Nah, I wouldn't say that. I'm just psychotic, that's all. And when it comes down to life or death, kill or be killed, I'm like fuck it, I ain't got a damn thing to lose. Because I was dead the day I was born..."

Minutes later when Shane finally departed company with his brother, he could actually feel the weighted pressure lift off his chest.

Damn...my little brother has that kind of effect on me? Shane pondered deeply with a troubling sense gnawing at his conscience as he reemerged on the first level.

"Oh, there you are!" Dee Dee burst through the crowd and accosted him. "My dark and sexy stallion...I've been looking for you!" She looped her right arm around his and gave Shane a hot, frisky leer that needed no words. I want to fuck! flashed boldly in her eyes.

Dee Dee's unexpected and brazen antics caught Shane totally by surprise. He could see right through the charade. She's stroking my vanity in order to gain some-thing...but what? he wondered.

"You know, I miss our naughty little rendezvous," whispered Dee Dee with a devilish grin. "And I know you miss how I slob that knob and sink my teeth in that dark chocolate ass of yours." She smiled openly when she recog-nized the sudden look of alarm on his face.

Angel appeared out of nowhere and all hell broke loose. "Get your dirty hands off of my man! You nasty hoe!" she blazed, spit firing from her mouth like she was insane.

Shane jumped, rattled and shocked. He could see the raw rage burning in Angel's eyes. Her grim expression was so intense, it made his legs weak.

Dee Dee looked on, ready to rumble. She had a reputation also and was known to whoop ass! "Who the hell you calling a hoe? Hoe!" Dee Dee hissed aggressively. "This nigga ain't your fucking man! Stop dick-claiming, bitch! Nigga tap that ass a couple times and you dick-whipped? You dumb bitch!"

Shane felt compelled to intervene when he sensed the violent tension brewing between the two women. He put up his hands in a submissive gesture. "C'mon on now, ladies, this isn't the - "

"Fuck you, bitch!" Angel hurled a glass straight at Dee Dee's head.

In the heat of the moment, the lines became blurred. Angel bared her teeth and charged across the floor. Dee Dee didn't back down, and they both collided head-on. The violent scene brought to mind a pair of lion-esses squaring off in a heated battle – sharp canines and claws bared as they brawled to the death.

A few feet away, Bad Ass moved past the melee and confusion going on in front of the bar and snaked through the wall of curious onlookers. He reached his preferred section and plopped down in his reserved spot on the sofa. "Hey, what's going on over there?" Bad Ass looked to Loso for an answer.

Loso was busy trying to get his freak on with a hot chocolate shorty, his lips pressed against her ear, communicating all his lewd intentions. He paused briefly, gave a nonchalant shrug, and muttered, "I think a couple broads going at it."

Big World's oversized mittens caught Bad Ass's eye when he reached across the table and plucked a bottle of Ace of Spades from the ice bucket. "Yeah, that's all it is, big dawg," Big World's heavy rumbling baritone cut the air. "A couple of bettys going at it...nothing major," he concluded and let out a big hearty chuckle.

The rest of the crew took turns adding their two cents to the mix, each man trying to get a laugh, until a pleasant interruption invaded their space.

"Hi, handsome." Ayanna's soft, feathery voice was music to Bad Ass's ears, her gentle tone appealed to his manly senses. Instantly he turned toward the voice and the allure of her smile charmed him. "I was wondering if I could keep you company for a while? Would that be alright?"

Smiling cheerily, Bad Ass replied, "Keep me company for a while?" He hesitated, turned to Murder, and shooed him away. "As pretty as you are, baby, how about we concentrate on making this a long term venture. How does that sound?"

Ayanna eased her salacious hooker body on the sofa next to him, tossed her long black hair over her shoulder, and giggled playfully.

"Okay, Mr. Handsome," Ayanna purred. "How do we go about making this a long term venture? I'm anxious to know all about that." She smothered the sly grin tickling the corner of her mouth and batted her almond-shaped eyes slowly. She watched and listened as the flamboyant gangster's dominant persona captivated her womanhood. Oh yeah...he's definitely a manly man! she quietly declared.

Chapter Fifteen

Later on after the club...

The sparkling black Cadillac Escalade raced around the bend on New York Avenue, careening at breakneck speed.

"Angel, have you lost your goddamn mind?" Shane scolded her. "What's gotten into you? Fighting in the goddamn club like a couple of juvenile delinquents! I thought you had more class than that!"

Angel wasn't paying him any mind. Her far off gaze was plastered to the passenger window and the sea of blackness blanketing the landscape in every direction. Suddenly out of the blackness, the Escalade's halogen headlights splashed across a reflective road sign. Baltimore/Washington Parkway whizzed by in a blur of green and white, then swiftly faded to black.

Angel cut her eyes to the corner, never moving her head an inch, and when she spoke, the cadence in her voice was so soft and subtle. It was unnerving. "I'm used to dealing with real men, Shane." She totally disregarded his comment and pursued her own agenda. "A real man does what he says and says what he means."

Shane's intuitive nature was on heightened alert now, and he knew the remark she made was aimed directly for his ego. With that in mind, Shane figured he'd best proceed with caution and tread lightly. "Now why you gotta go there, huh?" He couldn't resist the bait Angel had tossed out. "This real man is in love with you girl," he skillfully imposed his own objective. "From the first moment I saw you, like in a novel, I knew. Just like when I look you in the eyes, I get so emotional inside. I've never experienced a feeling like this before in my life. Angel, this shit is real!"

Slowly, Angel turned her face from the window. When she faced him, it was clear to see she was touched by his words. Her graceful eyes were softly radiant and emotional, swooning soulfully, searching out Shane's true feelings, the sincerity in his heart.

"In love with me?" Angel responded with a smirking grin and skeptical eye. "To love me is to know me, and to know me is to accept me as the individual woman that I am - all of me."

"What?" Shane detected trickery in her statement. "What are you saying, baby? If I say I love you, then that goes without saying. Of course I love all of you. How else would it be?" He peered through the windshield as more questions swirled in his head.

"So you actually believe that you're ready to be serious and deep and monogamously involved with a woman like me?" Angel inquired, studying him closely — the quirk in his brow and cheek, the slightest twitch of his eye, and every movement and expression his mouth made — almost like she were choreographing an emotional map of his facial features.

Shane gripped the wheel firmly and glanced over at her. "Baby, check this out," he said, licking his bottom lip. A dead serious look fell on his face. "I'm not gonna sit here and claim to be this perfect man, because that I'm not - not by a long shot. The fact of the matter is, I'm actually an imperfect man with a whole slew of issues that I need to work on myself. With that said, does that make me incapable of loving you? Or treating you like the precious gem of a woman that I know you to be? Will I be able to shower you with all the love, the affection and the attention that you desire? Will I exalt you over all others, especially those of your gender?" Shane exhaled deeply and looked her right in the eye. "If you'd be my woman...you're damn skippy!"

The confidence he exuded was emotional – the lies and lust were a rush.

Without warning, the light in Angel's eye grew dim.

"Humph," she snorted, giving him a villainous sneer. The hazy look in her eyes swelled with contempt and animosity. "Okay, Shane, tell me this: to what do I owe this sudden act of emotional out-pouring?" Natasha cracked a smile, but the essence of her smile was pure evil.

It was in the wee hours of the night. Nadia and Mecca were patiently waiting inside their mobile unit, both women's eyes glued to a glowing laptop monitor with a digitally enhanced street map of Washington, DC. The detectives were paying close attention to a flashing red dot that sat idle right outside of an address on Lamont Street.

Nadia's right index finger tap danced across her lower lip as she sat gazing at the screen.

"Our boy has been in there for over an hour now," Nadia voiced her concern casually. "Are you thinking what I'm thinking?" She cut her eyes at Mecca.

Mecca turned to face her. "What...primary residence? I sure hope so. You know I've been going over those files with those serial killers, Jovan and Ray. And you know what? These two characters seem to be exhibiting the same behavior as those serial killers. They're mimicking their pattern almost to a tee. I mean, think about it, Nadia.

These two spend the majority of their leisure time together. They're constantly prowling the clubs for attractive promiscuous women and they come out late at night to play." A look of concern seized Mecca's brow.

Nadia responded with a daunting huff. "These two and every other street player and hustler in the city and beyond. You know, I would want nothing more than for what you said to be confirmed as absolutely correct." Nadia turned from the computer screen so they were face to face.

"But my doubts seem to outweigh your reasoning. I say that because remember that night at Luxe when you met Loso? His partner Bad Ass had already left the club with a woman. After that, neither man hooked back up that night. Look where Loso took you: the Radisson. For Christ sake, Mecca, he paid for five-star accommodations just to get a piece of your five-star ass. Which you say you didn't give him." Nadia grinned and looked at Mecca sideways.

Mecca playfully swatted her hand. "I beg your pardon," she retorted. "Five-star? That's a damn insult. All this junk I'm hauling is priceless. If he is really serious about getting a piece of this, he'd better put together a two-week itinerary for an exotic port with all-inclusive amenities."

"Two weeks?" Nadia smirked. "Girl please!"

"Okay," Mecca giggled. "I'd go for a week's stay, but the accommodations better be diamond, nothing less!"

Both women cracked up laughing together.

It was about 7:30 in the morning when a Capitol Cab rolled up in front of the Lamont Street safe house. Seconds later, the gorgeous Ayanna emerged from inside the house. A great big Kool-Aid smile stretched across her face as she trotted down the front walkway and out the gate and then hopped in the rear of the awaiting cab.

"Don't forget to call me later on!" Ayanna shouted before closing the cab door.

Bad Ass didn't respond. He stood at the door in his black Ralph Lauren robe and black silk boxers and watched the cab pull off. The moment the cab was out of sight, he turned his attention toward the pair of black Suburban SUVs parked at the curb in front the house. Bad Ass gave a slight head nod, acknowledging his soldiers – Fats, Trouble, Killa and Monster. The men were lounging incognito behind the SUV's blacked-out windows. A horn sounded in response, which was the signal that everything was all good. Satisfied, Bad Ass turned and moseyed back inside the house.

Bad Ass walked down the hall and into the kitchen. "Man that pretty bitch suck a mean dick!" Bad Ass boasted, entering the kitchen.

Loso was standing in front of the refrigerator chugging a carton of orange juice nonstop like he hadn't had a drink in days. "Ahhhhh!" he finished. He let out a loud burp before he slammed the door shut, took two steps, spun on his heels, and shot a three-point jumper. "Swoosh!" he exclaimed when the empty container ricocheted off the corner wall and bounced into the trash can.

"Hey, Lo, why don't you make yourself useful," Bad Ass said, pulling a box of Frosted Flakes from the wooden cabinet. "Grab the milk out of the icebox for me."

Bad Ass sat down at the kitchen table and immediately began to devour a large bowl of Frosted Flakes. A minute later, he was interrupted by the blaring ringtone on his iPhone – Drake's "From the Bottom to the Top" was his new anthem.

Multi-tasking, Bad Ass continued to shovel spoonfuls of cereal in his mouth. "Yeah, talk to me," he answered. "What? Caesar want a sit-down...with me? That bamma don't know me!"

Suddenly, out of nowhere, a hail of automatic gunfire shattered the early morning calm. It sounded like chainsaws ripping the air.

The initial burst of fire brought Bad Ass and Loso to their feet. Their instincts were tingling and they were both super amped-up from a fresh adrenaline rush as they bolted for the front door and snatched up a chopper – Bad Ass armed with a sawed-off and Loso the Street Sweeper.

Without breaking stride, they stormed outside and blasted on anything moving across their path.

A navy blue Lincoln LS thundered through the block, guns blazing the air from every window, including the sunroof, where the shooter had an AK spitting fire like a maniac.

The sleek automobile raced through the block at top speed, and the fat-faced dago behind the wheel didn't touch the brake pedal until the sedan was less than ten feet from entering the intersection at Lamont and Sherman Avenue. The car's low-profile tires lost traction and skidded — a high pitch scream raked the air as the driver regrouped and floored it. Thick rubber tread burned the asphalt before the tires gained traction and propelled the sedan through the intersection like a motorized projectile on wheels.

In the background, Killa and Monster were relentless, charging down the middle of Lamont, flames leaping from their Mac-11's like the barrels were on fire.

Bad Ass and Loso opened fire from the front yard, looking flustered and angry as they watched the Lincoln flee the scene. Moments later, the sudden wave of war and chaos dissipated as abruptly as it began, replaced by an eerie sense of calm that hung heavy in the air with the pungent aroma of burnt cordite.

"Awww man!" Loso agonized when he realized that neither Fats nor Trouble was moving inside of the Suburban, which had sustained major damage to the front windshield and cockpit.

A feeling of grief galvanized Bad Ass's heart when he laid eyes on the bullet-riddled SUV. He shook his head and huffed. "C'mon Lo!" he ordered and bolted for the vehicle.

Bad Ass paused at the passenger door and stared in the window at the bloody, bullet-riddled corpses lying inside. A dark jolt shot through Bad Ass when he saw Fats lying disfigured in the driver seat, half his head blown clear off, and Trouble's body slumped in the passenger seat. He'd sustained traumatic injury to his upper chest, where a number of gaping wounds zigzagged across his chest and leaked huge amounts of blood.

The grief Bad Ass felt morphed instantaneously. His eyes glistened dangerously, like black crystal, and his entire being quivered inside with the force of a violent volcano erupting.

The sound of sirens descending on the area snapped Bad Ass to attention, just as Killa and Monster came rushing up to the vehicle.

"Fuck!" Killa cursed angrily when he noticed his dead comrades. "Let's handle those bitches! It was the Mafia! I got a good look at the bamma hanging out the sunroof. No doubt, the bamma was a fuckin' dago!" Monster's head bobbed up and down in agreement.

Bad Ass groaned. "Yeah, I thought so," he said looking Loso in the eye. "First up, Killa, you and Monster get these bodies out of here. Hit me on my cell the second you got everything squared away. Alright?"

"That's a bet," Killa grunted as he jumped in the rear seat. "C'mon, Monster, pass me the bodies! We have to get low before five-O gets here!"

Bad Ass turned to Loso. "Lo, that bamma Caesar wants a meet. We gonna give them dago bitches a meet they'll never forget!" The dark, ominous sparkle in Bad Ass's gaze and the finality in his words were strong and emphatic.

Loso watched, listened, and hurried to catch up with him as he strode up the walkway leading into the house.

The completion to CIX's so called Road-to-Riches puzzle was coming to a head faster than anticipated. Bad Ass would boast how he was the master of adaptation.

Pressure situations and fluid situations brought out the best in him.

"It's like a chess game," Bad Ass would preach to his team. "Every subtle move is vital; you can't afford to waste a single move." He loved to expand on his logic, his mental street war philosophy on how to conquer the hood and its legions of followers.

Chapter Sixteen

By six o'clock that evening, CIX had learned the whereabouts of the Mafia members involved in the drive-by. Bad Ass gave the word. "Scratch 'em all...except one!"

"It's the next alley coming up on the left!" A bloody Threat leaned over the back seat, looking hysterical.

"C'mon, Murder! Hurry the fuck up! Screw losing too much blood! He's bleeding all over the fucking place!" Threat cringed when he looked down at his fallen comrade.

"That's it...hold on, Screw!" Threat sounded anxious as he continued to apply pressure to a gaping hole in the side of Screw's neck with a blood-soaked white tee. "We'll be there in a minute, just hold tight!"

The Pirelli tires on the gold Lexus sedan squealed when Murder whipped the luxury sedan into an alley with a burgundy Denali following close on its bumper.

Midway through the alley, the Lexus skidded to a halt outside of a worn, dilapidated garage, and the doors instantly flew open. Murder and Threat sprang into action, hoisted the wounded Screw up in their arms, and immediately rushed him inside of the garage. The Denali pulled up and Cut Throat hopped out from behind the wheel.

"Let's go, muthafucka!" ordered Midnight, emerging from the rear of the Denali. He turned, reached back inside, and pulled a bloody and beaten dago across the seat.

"Move your ass!" Nightmare barked as he shoved his size 16 Polo boot up his ass.

"Where's Bad Ass? Where's Loso? Are they here yet?" Cut Throat asked, strolling into the garage.

Murder stuck his head outside. "C'mon, soldiers, get in here," he directed, peering up and down the narrow stretch of alley. "I got Loso on my cell now. They're both on the way. Be here in five minutes!"

The mention of Bad Ass prompted the crew to move with urgency. In mere seconds, the alley was cleared and the steel gray garage door came sliding shut. A loud clamor echoed along the vacant alley in their wake.

Fifteen minutes later, a sparkling cranberry Cadillac Escalade blew through the busy intersection at Florida and New York Avenue. The SUV drove three more blocks, slowed down, made a left turn off Florida, and cruised through a vacant industrial warehouse district.

Within seconds, the Escalade was parked behind the Denali and Bad Ass was strolling in the garage, his head slung low, black eyes fierce, scrutinizing the faces of his men. Bad Ass moved across the concrete floor. His noxious swag made him look like a venomous snake itching to strike. Suddenly he paused. His mouth turned grim when he saw his soldier Screw bleeding to death. His limp frame lay withering on a shabby rust colored sofa, his eyelids fluttering weakly as he wheezed and struggled to catch his breath.

The sound of metal chains clinking overhead drew Bad Ass's eye to the nude and bloodied body dangling from the rafters in the center of the garage.

Suspended in midair like a carcass of beef in a slaughter house, the dago's battered and bruised body dangled helplessly from a heavy duty chain that bound his hands and wrist together in a crude, twisted way over his head.

"Dago...you soft pussy muthafucka!" Bad Ass growled as he took a knee beside the sofa and pulled a wooden bat from hiding. He groaned and climbed to his feet and angry sparks leaped from his chilled black eyes. "Yeah, muthafucka...you good as fucked!" he sneered. "CIX warned your bitch ass, didn't we? If you not from DC, you not allowed to conduct business in DC, point blank!" Bad

Ass expressed as he closed the distance on the dago with the baseball bat slung casually over his shoulder. "What, the Mafia thought CIX was fakin'? Thought CIX was soft?"

He grabbed his stomach and laughed aloud to the delight of his team. "Calling Bad Ass soft...ha! Picture that!" He lingered a few inches from the nude body dangling from the rafters. His gaze swept the garage and the faces of his men, who were silently admiring the master at work. Bad Ass glared up at the chains and a mocking grin jumped on his lips when he noticed the chains cutting through the skin around the dago's meaty wrist.

"Right now I bet you're thinking, damn, how in the hell did I get myself into such a fucked up situation?" A cynical grin parted his lips when he heard giggles erupt in the background. "Let's see...what kind of information can you offer me? I'm gonna be straight up with you, Slim. It's a wrap; your ass dying tonight. But you can do yourself some justice. Hold up, that don't sound right." He glanced around the garage and added, "What I meant to say is, you can save your ass some serious suffering. And I'm talking slow and painful suffering, that fucked up shit that makes you wish you were dead, feel me?" He paused. "Ay Lo, toss me a stick of dynamite. Let me show this bamma what I'm talking about."

Dynamite? The dago's eyes bucked white with fright. He couldn't believe his eyes or ears. Are these hoodlum fucks for real?

"You see this?" Bad Ass held the stick of dynamite up to his pudgy face. "You know what this is and you know the damage this muthafucka capable of inflicting on the human body?" He sucked his teeth and went on. "Check this out, dago. You give me what I need and I'll let you choose how you die. Hold up. Damn!" Bad Ass snapped his fingers. "Let me rephrase that. You get to choose where on your body I can strap this stick of dynamite. Ya know...strap it in your mouth, on your chest, strap it to your dick, or stick it up your ass. If it was me, I'd go for a head blast. Although getting your head blown off may seem a bit extreme, you have to look at the bigger picture. It's a quick fix because you'll be dead in the blink of an eye, real talk. Otherwise..." Bad Ass stopped suddenly, dropped the stick of dynamite, and without warning, he reared back with the bad and let loose with a bone-breaking blow to the dago's exposed rib cage.

A painful whimper erupted from his mouth. Terror, shock and grief exploded on his face and a floodgate of tears streaming down his blood smeared face.

The sound of suffering was music to Bad Ass' ears. Devil horns sprouted atop his head when he grinned and said, "So what d'ya say, huh, dago? How you want to die tonight?"

A few feet away, Threat was at the side of his dying comrade. He watched helplessly as Screw took his last breath. Threat reached out, placed his hand over Screw's deadpan eyes, and pulled them shut. At that moment, Threat felt a coldness race through his body. His breath caught in his throat and he grimaced. The loss of Screw hit him harder than he could've imagined. Screw was more than just his comrade and partner in crime. The two were first cousins and had been inseparable since the age of three when they had started daycare together.

"Slump that bitch muthafucka!" Threat snapped, feeling the sting and hurt pierce his insides. He jumped up.

"Here! Let me beat his bitch ass to death!" Threat rushed across the floor, grabbed the bat from Bad Ass, and commenced to swinging.

Whack! Whack! Whack! Whack!

Threat moved from side to side, up and down, con-necting wood to flesh, delivering bone-crushing body blows to the dago's pale, naked, blubbery frame. Bad Ass stood by quietly, cheering Threat on and gloating with a devilish grin. Threat was forced to stop only after one emotionally-charged swing to the torso snapped the wooden bat at the neck.

Satisfied, Bad Ass moved to Threat's side and placed his hand on his shoulder. "You good, soldier? You get it all out? Nothing you do gonna bring our man Screw back. But a little blood spill does make you feel good though." Bad Ass hesitated. "Is he the bamma that shot Screw?"

Threat heaved a deep breath. "Naw." He exhaled and shook his head. "That's not the bamma that hit him up."

"Doesn't matter," Bad Ass said quickly. "He's Mafioso and he's apart of Caesar's entourage," he expressed with a sinister gleam in his eye. Pure hate radiated from Bad Ass's form as he stared straight at the broken, disfigured man dangling from the rafters. Pieces of broken bones had pierced the skin on his legs and gave the dago a sick, unnatural look.

Bad Ass reached out and slapped him across his beer belly. "Wake up, muthafucka! You ain't dead yet." He grunted and whipped out an eight inch hunting knife. "Fuck the information!" he snarled. "I want every man in here to get a piece of your ass, starting with me." Bad Ass tightened his grip on the knife and rammed the sharp blade into the dago's left butt cheek.

The dago squealed like a stuck pig and the entire crew fell out laughing.

At that very moment as Bad Ass stood in the garage, in that spot, he felt powerful and godlike. He realized he possessed the power to control life, to allow a man's life to continue and prosper unimpeded or take away a man's life with a spoken word or stroke of a hand.

That power was euphoric and exhilarating and intoxicating all rolled into one. That awesome feeling had Bad Ass literally salivating at the mouth.

Chapter Seventeen

After the vicious catfight in Ibiza, an uncomfortably tense vibe seemed to captivate the mood on the long drive out to Angel's Clarksville sanctuary. Somehow, the two lovebirds managed to put aside their differences to salvage the rest of their evening and a good portion of the ensuing day.

Beyonce's touching melody "Halo" set the mood inside of Angel's swanky pink love nest:

"Remember those walls I built/Well babe they're tumbling down/And they didn't even put up a fight/They didn't even make a sound/I found a way to let you in/But I never really had a doubt/Standing in the light of your halo/I got my angel now..."

Shane was relaxing in his nakedness, his dark chocolate mound sprawled across pink satiny sheets. His eyes gazed up at the whirling ceiling fan as he drifted in and out of consciousness, his male desires fully satiated and his mind totally relaxed. The sound of running shower water wafted in the background and created a mood of serenity.

The serene atmosphere was abruptly shattered by the loud ringing of Shane's cell phone. Instantly he was rattled from his chilled state. His head twisted toward the nightstand on his right, and with a reluctant grunt, he rolled over and scooped up the phone.

"Yeah, young G." Shane sounded irritated. "What's the deal? It ain't time for the meet yet, so why you hit me up so early? I'm right in the middle of smashing ass. Damn, can I live?"

A light chuckle sounded over the line. "Yeah, I know that's right," Bad Ass answered easily. "Didn't mean to interrupt you gettin' your fuck on. But this fat bird just landed right in my lap, and this fat joint just put a serious bug in my ear."

A slight frown creased Shane's forehead. "Cut to the chase. What's going on?"

"Well," Bad Ass said with an arrogant smirk. He hesitated and glanced up at the half-dead dago, his body battered and mangled and leaking blood from a number of deep gashes and stab wounds. Bad Ass continued, "The shooting on Lamont Street earlier..."

Shane's eyes flashed, startled. "What? Somebody from my force fucking with you? Give me their name and badge number. I'll take care of that; that's nothing."

"Hold up, Slim. There you go jumping the gun." Bad Ass paused when Loso walked up with a stick of dynamite in one hand and a fresh roll of duct tape in the other. Bad Ass looked him in the eye and placed his index finger to his head. Loso acknowledged him with a quick nod, spun around, and ordered Midnight to bring him a stool.

"This ain't got anything to do with your people fucking with me, although, I did peep those two bettys you put on my ass."

"Who? Nadia and Mecca? Don't sweat them broads. I got them running around like two chicken-heads with their heads cut off. I put them on your ass to throw off my robbery task force, feel me?" Shane was being extremely blunt and nonchalant about the whole set-up.

Concern flashed on Bad Ass's face and faded. "Oh yeah?" he smirked. "Well, you just make sure you got them hoes in check and they ain't nowhere around when this meet goes down tonight, or I'm gonna have a serious bone to pick with your ass - brother or no brother."

A dry laugh echoed over the phone. "I hear that dumb shit," Shane replied in a snide manner. "You just worry about handling your business on your end. I got Nadia and Mecca wrapped around my dick. Now what about this fat bird that put a bug in your ear? What's that all about?"

There was a noticeable pause before Bad Ass finally spoke. "I don't know if you got word yet, but my folks caught up with them bammas who rolled through Lamont Street earlier. If you don't already know, there's been blood spill outside the Florida Avenue Grill. Yeah, my folks did that, and in the process, they nabbed a fat dago, live and kickin'. And guess what I was able to learn from his fat ass? Your boy Goldie...that bamma still alive and kicking!"

The revelation caused Shane to bolt straight up in bed. "What? That pimp muthafucka still living?" Shane looked suddenly ill.

"Chill, Slim," Bad Ass told him coolly. "Don't get yourself all worked up and bust a vein. Just add Goldie to the list. You already know that bamma is a dead man walking. I put that on my life. You said that bamma played a part in dad's murder. It's a wrap, Cuz. You can stick a fork in that bamma's ass...he's done!"

Shane dropped the phone and stretched out on the bed. I can't believe Goldie been walking around all this time. He moaned, shaking his head while trying to dispel the uncomfortable knot he felt growing in his gut the moment his brother mentioned that Goldie was still alive. Suddenly he began to feel a throbbing pressure build around his temples – the beginning of a dreaded migraine.

The bathroom door swung open and Angel strutted into the room. Shane gawked at her in silence and watched her sexy water-speckled ass slink sweetly across the plush pink carpet. Her luscious view seemed to take a bit of the edge off of Shane's daunting mood. He enjoyed the view when Angel placed her plump backside on the edge of the bed and proceeded to run a comb through her long silky hair.

Angel arched her head and gave Shane a sideways look. "I've seen guys like you before," she said in a deceptively calm voice. "Quiet, complicated, all types of demons wrapped up in a pretty package." She lingered briefly as the light in her eyes faded and her disposition sharpened. "Who in the hell are Nadia and Mecca? And why in the hell are they on your dick?" She lashed out like she wanted to bite off his nose and spit it in his face.

Shane was completely blindsided by Angel's off-the-wall accusation and the sudden change in her tone. She went from nice, polite, and sassy straight to a seething she-devil in the blink of an eye. Whoa! He exhaled, looking stunned. Really? Are you going there?" Shane smirked and then sat up straight in bed. "I'm not feeling this right now, I think it'll be best that I leave."

On the long, lonely ride back to the city, Shane had a lot on his mind. His thoughts centered on the pimp Goldie and the unstable situation he presented to Shane's well-being. The secret Goldie possessed could destroy everything Shane had worked so hard to build: his name, his impeccable reputation, his coveted position atop the Metropolitan Police Department, and the relationship he had forged with his younger brother Chevar. Goldie held information that could literally dismantle his entire life.

Shane's mind teeter-tottered, back and forth from the predicament with Goldie to the unnerving situation with Angel. It was as if Angel were two totally different people. The image was so vivid in his mind. I witnessed Angel's kind eyes lose their soul, he voiced to himself, replaying it over and over in his mind.

Suddenly, Shane's heart skipped a beat when he had a startling epiphany. "Why didn't I see this before?" he muttered. "Angel's fucked up in the head. She has a split personality!"

###

Later on that evening in the mysterious night sky over Clarksville, dark cloud formations swept across the dark blue skyline and seemed to brush against the glowing white façade that was a full moon. Upstairs on the second floor, a shadowy silhouette hovered in Angel's bedroom window and pure evil glared out over the rolling black landscape that stretched out like an endless black blanket toward the horizon.

Natasha exhaled. "Angel, I'm not going to warn you again," she spoke in a low, husky voice. "I'm running this show, and I make the decision on who stays, who goes, who lives and who dies. So stop fighting me! I know what's best for you!" Darkness surged behind Natasha's cold blue eyes as she peered across the colorless oasis outside the window.

Suddenly, without warning, her entire body went rigid, stiff as a board. Her pupils started to dilate slowly, focusing on a square pane of glass that was inches from her face. The reflection on the window was a wicked image of a blue-eyed, blonde-haired vamp.

A cold shudder rolled down Angel's spine and she clamped down hard on the windowsill with both hands. She gave a powerful thrust and launched herself halfway across the bedroom, stumbling backwards.

"No!" Angel growled, head slung low, upper torso wavering from side to side as she struggled to catch her breath. "Bitch, I know what's best for me! I make my own decisions! Who in the hell?" Suddenly Angel's breath caught in her throat, her eyes rolled up in her head, and her eyelids began to flutter and spasm uncontrollably. A second later, she lurched forward like she was about to vomit.

"Don't fight me, Angel," Natasha hissed through clenched lips. "You can't win. Don't you know who I am? I'm the bitch that don't take no shit! I'm the bitch that you and every other woman want to be, but don't have the nerve or the balls! I'm the bitch that cleans up all the scum in your life! Those whores and the back-biters! I'm you, Angel, but on a darker level!"

Angel's head snapped back in a violent arch and her face twisted in pain. "Nooo!" Her lips quivered when she howled and fought back against the dark forces in her head threatening to consume her. "Those people are my friends! I'm my own woman! What do you want from me?!?"

A powerful jolt rocked her to the core and caused her to double over in pain, fall to the floor, and ball up in the fetal position. Her entire body trembled and jerked as if she were suffering an epileptic seizure. The episode lasted a few moments and then Angel's body went totally limp. The only sign that she was still alive was the rise and fall of her chest. A minute later, her upper torso sprang upright into a seated position. She had a hazy look in her eyes – lucid, strong, and unwavering now.

"Angel, you can't be that gullible," Natasha grumbled, standing. "They aren't your friends. They're nothing but whores!" She moved across the plush carpet on her way to the bathroom. Natasha sat down on the stool in front of the vanity mirror and eyed her reflection in the mirror. Next, she reached for the gold case with the dancing angels, opened the lid, and fished out two pink Oxyline pills.

"My Angel," Natasha said, gazing in the mirror, wearing a dark cryptic grin. "Those type of friends you can do without." She popped both pills in her mouth and then added, "They have lust in their blood. Trust me, Angel, people like that don't deserve life," Natasha concluded, and then she tossed her head back and laughed—a loud, wicked, maniacal cackle that echoed through the house and sounded dark and spooky.

Chapter Eighteen

11:37 p.m.
Michigan Park NE, DC

Dee Dee's powder-blue E-550 Mercedes Benz was parked at the corner of Michigan and South Dakota Avenue, directly in front of her two-story brownstone. Dee Dee resided in a nice quiet section of Michigan Park where tall birch trees lined the sidewalks in full bloom and every lawn was spoiled. At this hour, besides an occasional straggler trotting through the neighborhood every now and then, the streets were virtually empty except for a periodic stream of automobiles whizzing by.

At the top of Dee Dee's porch, dangling from the rafters, a unique ensemble of crystal wind chimes greeted visitors upon their arrival. The chimes waltzed and twirled in the soft late night summer breeze and the delicate symphony resonated in the air. The windows facing the porch on the first floor were pitch black, but upstairs, the trio of windows facing Michigan Avenue were all aglow. Soft flames danced atop honeysuckle-fragranced candles on the windowsill.

The house seemed at piece with itself, but that was a mirage, because downstairs in the first floor hallway, just beyond the kitchen, a subtle squeak of aged wood echoed from behind a dark wood door that led into the basement. Slowly, the doorknob turned 360 degrees and stopped. Something moved against the door and exerted pressure on its frame until it gave way. A low creaking sound drifted along the vacant hallway and a dark shadowy figure emerged from the dark enclosure and moved ghost-like off the basement steps out into the hall.

A dark-cloaked Natasha froze in the center of the hall as her vision and hearing quickly acclimated to her dark surroundings. A moment later she heard it - movement on the floor above her. The ceiling gyrated and the sound of muffled voices resonated in the dark.

Natasha glanced up sharply, her upper lip curled in a wicked sneer. Her nostrils flared as she took a deep whiff of air. Dee Dee's scent filled her nostrils and caused the blood in her veins to run cold as ice. Natasha felt hatred brewing inside of her as she envisioned Dee Dee's death in her head. She quickly removed the machete from a black silk bag, and like a predator on the trail of its prey, she crept stealthily in the dark.

Upstairs, at the far-east end of the long padded hallway was the entrance to Dee Dee's erotic domain resided. She referred to her master bedroom as Dee's Karma Sutra Playpen, which in essence was an exquisite ivory white seductress's lair with a decor dominated by pearly white Asian artifacts and furnishings. The room was quiet inside except for the low, sensual moans and whimpers that echoed from within.

"Ooooh yeah! Suck my pussy, baby! You know how I like it," Dee Dee whispered in a raspy voice, squirming and moaning under her lover's oral embrace. She lifted her head slightly off the white satin pillow and gazed down between her legs, where her lover was feasting diligently. Dee Dee made eye-contact with her lover and the heated suckling stopped. She extended both her arms and gently cupped Nina's face. Both women smiled and gazed at one another, emotional lust burning passionately between them.

Slowly, Nina rose to her feet and stood at the edge of the white satiny bed, her nude hefty frame swelled with excitement as she cast her lustful gaze upon Dee Dee's soft glistening skin. The hot oil Nina slathered on Dee Dee's sexy chocolate physique gave Nina goose bumps. She proceeded to reach down with her right hand and gently place her index finger against Dee Dee's mouth. She eagerly accepted by wrapping her pink -lazed lips around Nina's meaty finger.

A lewd gleam shone in Dee Dee's eye as she began to suckle and molest Nina's digit with vulgar tenacity, prompting Nina to bite down hard on her lower lip and moan with glee.

After a minute of enjoying Dee Dee's oral hand copulation, Nina eased her finger from Dee Dee's mouth and employing a feathery touch, she glided her saliva-coated digit down the center of Dee Dee's chest and in between her breasts. The soft feel of Dee Dee's soft, oiled skin caused Nina to shudder and blush while she continued on her slow and tentative path, descending across Dee Dee's midriff and around her diamond-studded navel piercing. Nina's digit glided to a halt right at the top of Dee Dee's fresh Brazilian-waxed vagina.

Nina licked her lips and drooled. Her facial expression was greedy and obscene as she lusted over the sight of her lover's swollen vagina, which was yearning to be suckled and caressed and filled. Nina reached down and grabbed hold of the eight inch black strap-on dildo she wore. The weight and feel of the swinging prosthesis in her hand gave Nina an overwhelming sense of power over her lover. She lingered for a minute, watching and listening to Dee Dee moan and purr and squirm in anticipation of getting her hot canal pleasured and satisfied.

Yeah...this how men feel right before they punish a good piece of ass - cocky as fuck! Nina surmised, rolling her head and shoulders, as she got into position, dildo grasped firmly in hand. She reached down with her free hand and began to fondle Dee Dee. When she felt that her lover was ready to receive the strap-on organ, Nina gently inserted the lengthy black dildo. A feeling of utter euphoria and domination washed over her as she watched Dee Dee squeeze her eyes shut, arch her back and head, and grab a fistful of satin and then squeal excitedly.

"Yeah, that's it, baby," Nina whispered softly. "Tell me how bad you want this, how bad you want me. You want all this don't you? I know how to please your pussy, don't I, baby? You love how I stroke this pussy. Tell me how much you love me, baby. I love your pretty brown sugar ass." Nina spoke in a low growl while grinding and winding her hips, prompting Dee Dee to cry out in pleasure.

Outside the bedroom, at the very end of the long dark hallway, Natasha's shadowy form hovered silently as she stared down the hallway and listened to the small weeps and moans drifting from the master bedroom. She felt her pulse rate increase, heartbeat soar, and muscles grow tense as she stalked the padded floor.

Back inside the bedroom, Nina was consumed with pleasing her lover—pounding her, kissing her, biting her with aggression. Nothing else mattered at that moment except to pleasure herself and her lover. Both women were in the throes of passion, unaware that ten feet from the bed the doorknob began to turn, and then the door slowly creaked open.

The sound of the door caused a chill to roll down Nina's spine and the hairs on the back of her neck turned rigid. She instantly froze mid stroke and snapped her head around.

Just beyond the open doorway, hidden in the shadows of the hall, Natasha's pupils narrowed to needle points, both hands locked around the black leather handle as if she were a Samurai warrior preparing to strike down its enemy. Natasha screamed – a demented shriek raked the air as she charged in. In three long, swift strides she was on Nina before she could react.

Nina gasped in shock, but it was already too late. Her body was riveted in place. All she could see was a long, silvery streak rushing toward her. Time seemed to stop as the blade plunged deep in her chest, through her heart and out Nina's back.

Absolute horror and disbelief and sorrow galvanized Nina's soul as she stood face to face and stared Satan in the eye. She could barely hear Dee Dee screaming frantically in the background as she felt her body wither. Her breathing went shallow and the light in her eyes dimmed.

Natasha smirked at the damage she'd caused.

"Fucking whore!" she spat. She ripped the blade from Nina's chest and watched her crumble to her knees while Dee Dee was having a hissy fit on the bed.

"Bitch, shut the fuck up!" Natasha scowled, giving Dee Dee an evil look, and then without warning, she spun around 360 degrees with the sharp motion of a swordsman and swung the machete with conviction.

The blade sliced clean through Nina's throat like she wasn't there. Nina's head tumbled to the floor and globs of fresh blood splashed and oozed on the plush white carpet. Her headless torso collapsed on the bed in prayer position. The sight of Nina's headless torso twitching and jerking at the foot of the bed was absolutely hideous, surreal, like a nightmare from a horror movie.

But this was no horror movie; this right here was real! Nina was chop-suey and Dee Dee figured she was next in line. She snapped. The screaming ceased and Dee Dee morphed into survival mode, scampered to her feet butt-naked blonde hair wild and untamed like an uncivilized cavewoman.

Dee Dee bared her teeth in a crooked sneer.

"C'mon, you crazy bitch!" she snarled and then went airborne off the bed like a deadly panther leaping on its prey. She slammed into Natasha full force and knocked her off her feet. They both hit the floor hard.

Natasha landed on her back with the full weight of Dee Dee crash landing on top of her and knocking the wind out of her body. Dazed, discombobulated, and gasping for air, Natasha appeared to be more infuriated than hurt.

Dee Dee wasted no time. She immediately sprang into action and pinned Natasha's arms to the floor with her knees and started pummeling her face with wild and wicked blows. "You crazy bitch! You fucked with the wrong bitch tonight!" Dee Dee shrieked without letting up.
But the blows only stunned Natasha and seemed to bring her around. Suddenly, her blue eyes peered up at Dee Dee.

"Bitch, I'm gonna cut you a new asshole!" Natasha's voice was cryptic, like a woman possessed.

"What?" Dee Dee gasped, startled. "Fuck you, bitch!" she cursed. She bashed Natasha in the face with all her might, drawing blood from a busted lip.

Natasha stared her in the eye, blood lust raging in her expression, but Dee Dee paid her no mind. The sight of blood seemed to incite Dee Dee to violence. She went ballistic on her, pummeling her head and face with a flurry of hard wild punches, slaps, and hammer-blows.

Natasha's right hand flopped around on the floor, attempting to locate the machete. A moment later, she sounded unnatural and beastlike as a sick gurgling roar erupted from her throat. Natasha balled her hands into tight fists and stretched both arms straight out.

Panting and out of breath now, Dee Dee stopped swinging and grabbed Natasha around the throat. She leaned over in Natasha's ear. "This is for my girl Nina," she growled and squeezed with all her might. "You crazy bitch!

I'm gonna cut you a new asshole!" she said, applying more pressure to her windpipe.

Natasha's forearms began to rise off the floor with Dee Dee's full weight upon them. Dee Dee felt the muscles beneath her knees swell and turn hard as bone a second before she felt herself being lifted in the air.

"Oh my God!" Dee Dee shrieked in a panic, and then with every ounce of strength she could muster, Dee Dee tried to strangle the life from Natasha.

But it didn't matter. Natasha was unfazed by the threat Dee Dee posed. Before Dee Dee was able to get her wits about herself and make a defensive stance, Natasha suddenly lurched forward with the strength of five men and tossed Dee Dee off her as if she were tossing a toddler. Dee Dee crashed landed on the floor flush on her back and cried out in pain.

"Bitch, it's my turn now," Natasha muttered, climbing to her feet. She swiped the blood from her nose and mouth and hissed, "I'm gonna carve your ass up real good...cuz bitches like you don't deserve life!"

The threat of death was stifling, like a poisonous cloud descending upon Dee Dee, and she had no way to escape. Lord please help me! the voice in her head screamed as she looked up with tearful eyes. Dee Dee's heart dropped in her chest when she saw Natasha reach down and scoop the machete off the carpet.

"No!" Dee Dee cried out, kicking and screaming and twisting. "You crazy bitch! Leave me alone!"

The look of horror on Dee Dee's face gave Natasha an instant high. She lingered for a minute, marinating in that ominous moment before death. "Don't cry now, bitch!" Natasha laughed and grabbed Dee Dee roughly around the ankle. "I told you I was gonna cut you a new asshole," she said, dragging her kicking and screaming and crying across the bedroom floor.

"Nooooo!!!" Dee Dee cried and kicked as she was dragged into the bathroom.

Once inside of the bathroom, the reflection of candlelight danced silently along the chrome surface of the machete as it dangled from Natasha's right hand. The menacing sight made Dee Dee cringe inside.

A sinister grin flashed on Natasha's face just before she reached back and slammed the door shut.

Bam! Dee Dee's cries echoed along the hall and then evaporated into silence.

Chapter Nineteen

Law 3: Conceal your Intentions
"Keep people off-balance and in the dark by never revealing the purpose behind your actions. If they have no clue what you are up to, they cannot prepare a defense. Guide them far enough down the wrong path, envelope them in enough smoke, and by the time they realize your intentions, it will be too late."
48 Laws of Power

The Meet
11:45 p.m.
New York Avenue NE, DC

A motorcade of glazed black Cadillac's about five cars deep cruised along one of Washington's main thoroughfares, en route to a prearranged destination just off New York Avenue.

Five blocks later, at the corner of New York and Kendale Street, the lead vehicle slowed down and made a right turn on Kendale. The procession continued down a narrow street that was lined with vacant brick warehouses that ran the entire length of the block.

The driver behind the wheel of the lead Cadillac was Freddy G, a lumbering toothpick thin Italian with heavy-moussed spiked hair, big droopy eyes, and a double butt chin. Freddy steered the sedan along the deserted roadway, his gaze instinctively sweeping back and forth across the bleak landscape, darting from one building to the next, scrutinizing the buildings' blank façades.

"Hey Eddie." Freddie spoke up and glanced over at his partner. "How far up ahead is this building we're looking for?" he asked, waiting for a reply.

Eddie was a burly Italian brute with no brains, a super-thick unibrow, and huge elf-like ears. He brought to mind the Incredible Hulk - the extra-terrestrial version.

Peering out of the passenger window, Eddie was caught up in his own thoughts, consumed with the deserted street and empty bank of warehouses. His extra-thick unibrow served as a disguise for the troubling twitch jumping just beneath the hairs. Eddie was accustomed to meetings such as the one they were about to attend, but for some odd reason, this particular meeting gave Eddie a bad feeling in his gut.

Another Italian by the name of Lucky was seated in the back seat. He cocked his .44 Magnum and leaned up front. "Hey Freddie, you see that tractor trailer parked up there on the left?" asked the dark-skinned Italian with the short wavy hair and big green fish eyes. Lucky paused and motioned with his Magnum. "Pull in front of that truck and park. That's the spot," he directed in a heavy Italian accent.

Beep! Beep! Beep! The semi's back-up alarm resonated off the vacant buildings as the semi rolled slowly in reverse and eased its full payload down the newly-paved driveway. The truck driver's arm rested atop the driver's side mirror as he steered the semi. His eyes focused on the muscle bound man in the mirror wearing a bright orange jumper with no shirt.

The man in the jumper was Big World. He stood in the roadway directing the truck driver by giving him hand signals and keeping a watchful eye on the motorcade as they closed the distance. Suddenly, when the vehicle reached a certain point, Big World shifted position. His massive arms rose above his head and formed an X, the hand signal for the truck driver to halt.

Big World watched the trailer come to a complete stop and then he directed the motorcade to proceed around the trailer. He waited for the last sedan to clear the area before continuing on with the truck driver.

The motorcade drove a few yards before turning into an empty parking area situated just beyond a trio of loading bays. The bay door in the middle was the only one open for business.

In seconds, Freddie G, Eddie, and Lucky exited the sedan and maneuvered into position around the Cadillac – each man scanning the perimeter for any signs of danger.

The second vehicle rode up and another trio of Mafia enforcers appeared from their sedan. They quickly moved into position around the third Cadillac when it parked and stood guard at the rear passenger door. A moment later, the rear door opened and a shroud of black umbrellas shielded Caesar Leo from view as the Don emerged from the sedan.

Big World's name flashed on Loso's iPhone. "Hey Cuz, that bitch nigga Caesar is here!" Loso announced and hopped up from a conference table.

Seated at the head of a long redwood conference table, Bad Ass looked shrewd, the corners of his mouth turned down in a harsh smirk. His deep gaze skimmed the table's rich lacquered surface that was covered by a smorgasbord of high powered and high caliber firearms.

At the moment, Bad Ass seemed at peace. His right hand rested atop his personalized 5.7mm cop-killer pistol on top of the table. Suddenly, his gaze shifted from the contents on the table and he made eye contact with Loso.

"CIX hit squad!" Bad Ass's strong voice boomed with authority. His piercing black stare carefully swept around the table, examining the anxious faces of each CIX hitter who sat awaiting the orders to kill.

Murder, Cut Throat, Threat, Dabo, Midnight, Nightmare, Killa, and Monster... The entire CIX squad was geared-up in all black hoodies and sweats and ready to run up a serious body count. The men watched quietly as Bad Ass rose from the table.

"My soldiers ready to show these Mafia bammas who run this city?" Bad Ass posed the question, already knowing the answer.

"Hell yeah!" A charged roar bellowed inside the glass-enclosed conference room as the men turned to one another and relished the feeling of excitement and anticipation.

"My soldiers ready to show these bammas how DC gangstas get-down? What we tell those suckas? If you ain't from DC, you can't conduct business in DC! We not having it! And we're not going to allow no dumb shit like that to go down in our city...not CIX!" Bad Ass paused and took a breath. A second later he gave his men a sharp look, cocked his pistol, and gave the order. "Strap up, soldiers. It's time we do these Mafia bammas!" Bad Ass looked on like a proud father as the men eagerly raided the table.

Outside of the warehouse, Big World watched the Mafia entourage as they made their way inside, and he noticed the trio posted up around the lead car hadn't moved an inch. He figured they were assigned to lookout detail. With that in mind, World fished a wad of bills from his pants pocket and quickly counted out a couple stacks in crisp big-faced Benjamin's, and then he proceeded to the driver's side door.

A big country redneck with an overgrowth of wiry matted hair that protruded from a dry cracked and wrinkled face emerged from the cab and dropped to the pavement.

"Here, Cuz." World handed the driver two stacks.

"Shit about to get thick out here, and it'll be best if

you vacate the area for a while. Come back in about an hour. Shit should be straight by then."

The redneck jumped, disgruntled. "What you say? You want me to leave the trailer like this, blocking the street? What about my cab?" He looked completely stumped and slightly worried.

Big World took a step closer. His massive frame towered over the man by at least a foot and a half. "Your cab...don't worry about that." World chuckled and slapped the wad of bills against the man's chest. "Here, dude, take this loot and get the fuck on like I said." The finality in World's tone was crystal clear.

The redneck's bloodshot eyes grew big like silver dollars. He knew this big black mutha meant business, so he immediately took heed. "Ahhh...okay," he mumbled, sounding nervous and dumbfounded, his disgruntled smirk completely wiped off his dusty face now.

Meanwhile, back inside of the warehouse, the Mafia Don Caesar Leo and his band of Uzi-toting henchmen were making their way through the vacant docking area. It led to an expansive main warehouse floor that was lined with huge brown wooden crates stacked twenty feet high and stretched several aisles wide.

Danny Boy led the entourage, for he held the coveted position as top capo. His hefty frame wobbled down the aisle like a life-size Pillsbury Dough Boy dressed in a black suit and tie.

"Hey boss," Danny Boy grunted over his shoulder. His eyes pointed upward and keyed in on the top edges of the crates. "It's dark up ahead. You sure this is the right aisle?" Danny Boy stared straight ahead toward the end of the aisle. His suspicion and worry grew more pronounced with every step.

"Aw-oh! Sounds to me like somebody's scared of the dark." Bruno, a tall, husky Italian with short curly hair and no neck replied snidely and gave a mocking chuckle.

"Danny Boy, you want to fall back and let me take lead?" he asked, sucking his teeth and rubbing his ashy palms together. He shrugged and then glanced left and right at the two men under his direction – Mike and Paul.

The remark Bruno had made was an infringement upon Danny Boy's authority. Bruno was second capo in command, and every man in attendance was fully aware that he was itching for the chance to take over the coveted lead capo position.

Directly behind Bruno and his men was the next capo in line, Vito. He brought to mind the Michael Corleone character played by Al Pacino in the Godfather trilogy. He was short in stature with a heart as fearless as a male lion in its prime. Vito moved with a strong, adamant swagger like he was seven feet tall. He was flanked on both sides by two of his crew – Tony and Ray.

Marching in Vito's wake was the Don, Caesar Leo. He was surrounded by his most trusted enforcers – Sammy, Carlo, Fredo, and Tommy.

As they approached the end of the aisle, the men realized there was light up ahead. A dim glow emanated from a small overhead lamp that was suspended from the rafters and hung fifteen feet off the warehouse floor.

Danny Boy reached the end of the aisle and stopped dead in his tracks. Twenty feet away, sitting in a small clearance right below the hanging lamp, Danny could see a black hooded man perched on the edge of a small gray office desk. He noticed there were two other black hooded men standing on either side of the desk like human statuettes.

Suddenly, the man rose off the desk and spoke.

"What up, Slim?" he voiced with an air of nonchalance and arrogance as he tossed both hands in the air. "I'm here to talk mano y mano with Caesar. You other bammas can take a chill pill and stay right where you are. Capisce?"

"Stand aside," a firm voice commanded, and like the parting of the Red Sea, the suited mobsters cleared a path for the Don.

Caesar stepped forward in the clearing and peered straight ahead, his eyes locked on the man standing in the middle. Caesar gave a cursory glance around the floor and surveyed the area, which from his vantage point was dark and empty. Caesar hesitated briefly and then turned to his left and eyed Danny Boy. He looked to his right and found Bruno.

"Danny Boy. Bruno. Let's check out this fugazi and then blow his brains out," Caesar grunted, his lips tight and unmoving.

Racing along Florida Avenue, a navy blue ZR-1 Corvette whizzed past Gallaudet University on the right. Lieutenant Maruchan was focused on his iPhone while his partner Lieutenant Nubie drove the sleek-looking coupe.

"Hey, check this out, Nubie," Lt. Maruchan spoke up suddenly. "I just received an email from one of my C.I.'s saying that Caesar Leo is in a meeting right now with one of his gang bosses, and the meeting is taking place in a warehouse over on Kendale Street." A look of elation jumped in his slanted eyes.

A low whistle sounded from Lieutenant Nubie as he whipped the Corvette from left to right and pushed the sleek coupe in and around a gold Navigator like the SUV was immobile.

Recognition flashed in Lt. Nubie's eye and his dark shiny brows went up simultaneously. "Kendale?" he muttered, looking surprised. "That's right around the corner from Love nightclub." He stomped on the gas pedal. "Call for back up. We'll be there in five minutes." Nubie's tone was bursting with excitement as he watched the needle on the RPM gauge climb steadily.

Maruchan gave him a sideways look and sneered.

"Back up? Yeah right! Fuck 'em, this is our collar. Besides, they'd just fuck it up." Both detectives eyed one another and shared a good laugh.

Meeting mano y mano – face to face with a Mafia Don. This was an extremely dangerous and complicated environment for a gang leader. This was one of those so-called life-altering, life-changing moments—the proverbial fork in the road. Bad Ass was putting it all on the line with this move—his reputation, his life! This was the play that could make him or break him. Bad Ass would be going down in the annals of DC's criminal history as either one of the dumbest and craziest gangsters to ever ride in DC, or one of the best and boldest to ever do it. Yeah...I took on the muthafuckin' mob and won, goddamn it!" Those were the words he dreamed about reciting over and over to his followers, once it was all said and done.

Caesar stood face to face, mano y mano, with the man directly responsible for the transgression against his family's interests. That's what he was led to believe. Wearing a crooked smile, Caesar nodded and offered his hand in greeting. It took every ounce of his resolve to keep from strangling the riff raff standing before him.

"Bad Ass...so you're the man behind the madness. Running around DC making moves on Leonardi interests as if our business was some kind of free-for-all."

Murder gave the Don an iron handshake and stared him right in the eye. "Yeah, right now I'm drinking Kool-Aid and my favorite flavor is Leonardi. So what'cha gonna do about it, huh?"

"What?" Caesar pondered. This guy is either slow and mentally challenged or totally out of his mind. The snide remark seemed to strike a sour note with the Don. It was a mighty task, but Caesar somehow kept his composure.

Instead, Caesar chuckled, but he didn't break eye contact. "What, you trying to hurt my feelings? C'mon now...that little stunt you and your crew pulled, that amounts to petty theft. Leonardi packets run deeper than your little brain could ever imagine." Caesar finally broke eye contact and looked Danny Boy's way. \"Will you boys get a load of this character?" He turned to Bruno. "He can't be serious?"

Bruno sucked his teeth and snorted. "Nah, boss, he's just what you said he was. He's a fuckin' fugazi!"

"A fugazi!" Murder scoffed, aggressive. He glanced left and right. Cut Throat and Dabo were ready to bust off at the slightest provocation. "Muthafucka, who the fuck you callin' fugazi?" Murder spat, standing his ground with his chest puffed out.

A slight snicker fell from Caesar's mouth. "C'mon now, Bad Ass," he spoke in a condescending tone. "That type of talk isn't necessary. I take it you do have some measure of intelligence? Well, that's obvious because you caught my attention. So you should know that kind of disrespectful talk wouldn't be conducive to your well-being, now would it?" A devious gleam flashed in Caesar's eye.

Bad Ass's voice echoed through the Bluetooth device connected to Murder's ear. He was on point, reciting every word Bad Ass spoke, verbatim.

"Check this out," Murder said coolly. "You call the hit on your establishment's petty theft. We call it a warning shot. You do business in our city, you gonna pay the price; that's the bottom line," Murder expressed pointedly. "Now before that little bullshit your boys pulled uptown earlier today, there was a slight possibility that we could've negotiated some type of business arrangement. But that's off the table now." Murder paused and mean-mugged the Don. "Shit about to get thick now. Just ask your son, because that bamma gonna be the first to go," he smirked, sounding vague.

Caesar's head swiveled left and right. "Uptown?" He gave Danny and Bruno a scolding look. "Do either of you know what he's talking about?" Both men shook their heads, hunched their shoulders and mumbled, "No", but their tone lacked any conviction.

Caesar's face was beet-red now. No one made a move without the Don's approval, which was Leonardi law!

"Somebody knows something, and when I get to the bottom of this shit, heads will roll," Caesar warned. Then he refocused his attention on the man standing before him. "So, Bad Ass..." Caesar rolled the name around on his tongue like pronouncing it put a bitter taste in his mouth. "What does my son have to do with our business? He's going to be the first to go where?"

"Ha!" Murder grunted. "Where do you think? To hell, muthafucka!"

A queasy gut feeling suddenly became a harsh reality when Caesar realized he hadn't heard a word from his son all day.

Caesar's eyes shimmered – deep and powerful and cynical. "Let me tell you something, Bad Ass!" His aura was fiery when he spoke, his voice adamant. "I'm not into playing games with street thugs." Out of nowhere, an iPhone appeared in Caesar's hand. He trained the phone lens on Murder's face and went on to say, "Pilfering from my family business is one thing. But you fuck with my flesh and blood...I'll cut off your fucking balls and stuff them down your throat!" Caesar put the phone to his ear. "Well, is He official?"

Outside, huddled in the rear seat of the Don's Cadillac, Goldie stared hard at his iPhone screen, a contemptuous look brewing in his face. "Naw, big dawg," Goldie snorted. "Those bammas playing you cuz I don't know who that bamma right there is. But he sure ain't Bad Ass."

Caesar didn't like being made a fool of by anyone, and add to the equation the fact that CIX had robbed his jewelry stores, murdered his men, and most recently Caesar had been informed that CIX were the sole conspirators behind the robbery and murder at the Woodridge stash house.

In retrospect, CIX had mounted an all-out assault on the Leonardi Crime family. But these street thugs had done it in a way that was so complex and indirect, catching Caesar and his men totally off-guard by the masterful move. But the Don was no fool. CIX had help in pulling off a feat of this magnitude. There was no doubt in his mind. Someone with major connections was pulling strings and Caesar had the wherewithal to know that Bad Ass and his cronies were pawns in a vicious game of chess.

Caesar took a quick look around. He fumed, and then whipped out his chrome-plated .45 from his holster beneath his jacket as he slipped the iPhone in his pocket.

"You got shit really misconstrued!" Caesar growled in a voice dripping with acid. "You actually thought you could pull the wool over my eyes? Do you stupid mutha-fuckas realize who you're dealing with?"

The sight of the chrome pistol made the men cringe. How in the hell did we let this bamma get the drop on us? Each man was mentally kicking himself in the ass.

As soon as Caesar pulled his strap, his men seemed to relax and let down their guard. The Don had the situation by the balls, so the entourage hung back in the aisle – snickering, chuckling and enjoying the Don's antics as he waved his pistol in the air and lambasted the thugs like they were a bunch of low-life wannabes going up against bonafide made men.

Halfway into his verbal tirade, it dawned on Caesar. *If the man standing before me is a fugazi...where in the hell is the real Bad Ass? Is he here somewhere lurking in the shadows, watching and waiting?* Caesar had a sudden epiphany. *If that's the case, that would mean that we have once again miscalculated and underestimated these CIX thugs!* Then it hit him like a ton of bricks. *This meeting is a set-up! We're sitting ducks!*

Something creaked overhead. The unsettling sound seemed to pierce Caesar's confident armor, eclipsed his angry swell of emotions. He paused mid-sentence. His head rotated left then right, gazing intensely, trying to peer into the shadows that dominated the warehouse floor.

Caesar winced. "He's not Bad Ass; he's a fugazi!" Without warning, the Don sprang into action. With the chrome .45 gripped tightly in hand, he pounced on Murder, snatching him around the collar. "Alright, you son of a bitch!" Caesar snapped as he wound his arm tightly around Murder's throat and placed him in a chokehold. "Bad Ass, I know you're out there! Don't be a coward! Show yourself! Let's handle this business like men! You and me...mano y mano...gangsta to gangsta!" Caesar barked, using Murder as a human shield.

The Don's sudden move alarmed his men. They could sense a chink in Caesar's seemingly impenetrable armor, and this was new territory for them. Whatever the situation, Caesar was always even-keeled, unrattled, and ready for anything. But this situation was different. There was obviously something more at play here than he was letting on.

Vito took charge and made a gesture with his hand. The entourage instantly morphed into defense mode. Every finger was on a trigger and ready to pull. In the blink of an eye, Danny Boy and Bruno had their Uzis locked and loaded and aimed at both Cut Throat and Dabo – right between the eyes.

"Just say the word, boss," Bruno said, "because I'm dying to pop this nigga's top." He stared the gorilla looka-like down until Cut Throat submitted and broke eye contact.

"Yeah, that's right." Danny Boy shrugged, sporting a cocky smirk. "Give me a reason and you can kiss your black ass goodbye," he finished saying and blew Dabo a kiss.

The abrupt sound of feet ambling overhead prompted every man on the floor to look up.

"What in the hell?" Vito muttered under his breath, his eyes poised toward the top of the crates, attempting to get a bead on the action twenty feet above.

Laughter erupted suddenly from the shadows and the Mafia team looked rattled and uneasy. Twenty feet away from the action, Bad Ass was holed up inside of a dark utility closet.

"Caesar Leo!" Bad Ass shouted from cover. "Say your prayers, muthafucka, cuz your bitch ass is dying to-night!" His deep voice resonated throughout the ware-house and tensions flared.

A cunning gleam shone in Bad Ass's eyes as he ad-justed his hands on the black rubber-grip handle of a 12-gauge slide-action pump and dislodged the safety. The utili-ty room door opened without a sound. Bad Ass slipped out on the warehouse floor and then eased into a dark corner with his back pressed tight against the wall.

Bad Ass focused with supreme intensity and mum-bled under his breath, "Three...two...one!" He snapped the pump-action and pushed off the wall in one quick motion.

"Bad Ass right here, bitch!" he snarled and pulled the trigger.

Acting off reflex, Danny Boy spun toward the voice and the shadowy silhouette. He saw a flash of fire and caught the full gunshot blast to his chest. Danny Boy lurched backward from the impact. The blast was so powerful that it knocked all 300 pounds of him clear out of his shoes.

The whites in Caesar's eyes sprung wide in shock and his finger yanked the hairpin trigger, more from the impulse of shock than intent.

Boom! Murder's heart exploded from a gaping hole in his chest. He stumbled forward a couple of feet and crashed head first on the floor, landing at Bruno's feet.

For a split second silence captivated the warehouse, and then all hell broke loose. A hair-raising howl erupted from Bruno as he gripped the trigger on his Uzi and cut Dabo in half. Caesar and Cut Throat had a brief face-off until he witnessed his man Dabo get gunned down three feet away. Cut Throat's heart dropped and his adrenaline soared. He went from standing into a vertical swan dive, like a human-sized jackrabbit escaping the clutches of death in a single bound. A volley of gunfire ripped the air around Cut Throat, missing him by a hairsbreadth as he cleared the table, hit the floor, and rolled out of harm's way.

Bad Ass let off two more rounds before Vito and his men opened fire and forced him to get low in a hurry. He was twenty feet above the action, hovering just out of sight along the edge of the crates. CIX were armed to the teeth and ready. On both sides of the aisle, CIX moved silently into attack position like a well-armed tactical squad primed for a covert assassination plot.

Loso crept to the edge and leaned over to get a good look below. He made a hand gesture and whispered, "Three...two...one! Drop theses bammas!"

CIX sprang up on both sides of the aisle and opened fire on the unsuspecting Mafia entourage like an all-out turkey shoot. The abrupt burst of gunfire echoed throughout the entire building and resonated outside.

"Oh shit!" Freddy G gasped and clutched his Uzi.

"Sounds like a goddamn war just broke out in there!"

Eddie was immediately on point. "Ay, Freddie, let's go!" he commanded, waving his Uzi. "We going in. Lucky, you handle lookout."

A twisted cackle sounded in the background and startled the men. "Hey, you fuckin' dagos," Big World hissed and stepped from behind the sedan. "It's CIX, muthafucka!" he spat and let his AK-47 spit fire. World showed no mercy as he mowed them down in a hail of gunfire. He watched them hit the ground and then he let out a triumphant howl as he emptied the entire fifty round magazine. A couple of seconds later, silence reached out and tapped him on the shoulder. Big World glanced around the empty parking lot and then rushed over to examine his work.

Dead as a doornail. He grinned, victorious, and then cuffed the AK under his right arm and ran back across the parking lot. He proceeded across the street and made a beeline for the corner of an adjacent warehouse where a silver Jeep Commander was parked incognito. Big World hurried around to the rear and opened the cargo hatch.

Lying in the cargo area was the naked, bloodied, and duct-taped Italian they had tortured earlier – Caesar Leo Jr. He was still alive, but barely, fading in and out of consciousness with two sticks of dynamite and a wireless detonator strapped to his chest.

Big World listened as another volley of gunfire cracked the air before he pushed aside a duffle bag, snapped up Caesar Jr., and slung him over his shoulder like a sack of potatoes.

"The third Caddy is Caesar's," World said to himself as he rushed around the Cadillac. He stopped at the rear passenger door, grabbed the handle, and pulled it open.

Boom!

A single shot rang out. The violent impact felt like a sledge-hammer slammed into his chest and a look of sheer aston-ishment and pain exploded on Big World's face as he stumbled and rocked back on his heels and strained to keep his balance. Big World stared at the man holding the gun inside of the Cadillac. Suddenly, a deep, agonizing pain seized his heart when he recognized the bearded and burned and disfigured man inside. Goldie? But he's sup-posed to be dead!

"Suck my black dick!" muttered Goldie as he scoot-ed across the seat to get a closer look. "I can't believe you, World. You turned your back on me for these CIX bammas! But why? You were my road dawg," Goldie expressed, feel-ing the sting of betrayal pierce him to the core. He placed his feet firmly on the pavement and rose slowly to his feet without the assistance of his gold-plated cane. "You wanna roll with CIX?" Goldie snorted, wearing a wicked smirk.

"Okay, now your bitch ass can rest in peace with them bammas!" he declared, looking hateful as he lifted his 9mm to eye-level and hesitated. "See your ass in hell, Slim..."

Big World knew his life was over. He could actually feel his soul slipping away, and it saddened him. He wasn't saddened by the fact that he was about to meet his maker.

No, Big World was hurt about the fact that he would be letting his team down, especially Bad Ass. The reality that the man he had given up for dead would be the one to do him in was too much of a burden for him to bear. Big World seized the moment when Goldie hesitated.

It was as if time froze. Big World summoned everything he had. He took a deep breath, held onto Caesar Jr.,
and reached into his pocket.

Soon after the initial wave of gunfire, Bruno rallied
to protect the Don.

"Boss, it's an ambush!" Bruno yelled emphatically
as he watched his Mafioso comrades get outgunned.

"C'mon, boss, follow my lead. We have to get out
of here!" Bruno swore and punctuated his remark with a
wild burst of gunfire as he charged down an adjacent aisle,
swinging his Uzi from side to side, spitting fire nonstop.

Caesar followed right on Bruno's heels. "Move it,
Bruno!" Caesar barked, looking over his shoulder every few
seconds. "These sons of bitches mean business! As soon as
we get out of here, I want you to get every available man
and find Bad Ass immediately. \I'm gonna bury a piece of
his ass in every quadrant across DC! It'll be ten years from
now and they'll still be finding pieces of his ass around the
city. I swear to God!"

Bruno stopped abruptly at the end of the aisle.

"Okay, boss." He bent over, panting and gasping for
air. "That's all good, but first we have to get out of here!"

The sound of gunfire reached a crescendo, echoing
off the wooden rafters and walls and stacked crates. The
nerve-wracking sound rained down on Caesar and Bruno
from every direction. Caesar's eyes bounced from the ceiling to the floor to the crates and up and down the aisle.

The Don looked frustrated, nervous, and jittery all
at once, like a man on the verge of losing his mind.

"Bruno! Why are we standing here?" Caesar
growled and tossed his hands in the air. "Are you fuckin'
crazy? Get me the hell out of here, now!"

Bruno looked hesitant for a brief moment. A fleeting glimpse of irritation showed itself and then evaporated
from Bruno's tense brow. He didn't utter a word. Instead,

he responded with action. Bruno snatched off the empty magazine and slammed in a fully-loaded one.

"Let's go, boss!" He grunted and sprayed a burst of cover fire before moving on. The pair proceeded cautiously, their eyes darting left and right as they moved across the vacant docking area.

"Look, boss, that's our way out," Bruno said with a measure of calmness when he spotted the rear bay door.

"C'mon, boss, we're home free now."

The men instantly put a little pep in their step as they headed for the exit. Bruno eyed the Don and smiled as he leaned against the metal door and forced it open. They both marched outside and froze dead in their tracks.

Pure rage and madness burned in Big World's eye as he stared Goldie down and attempted to project his spirit unto him.

"Muthafucka, you goin' to hell right along with me!" Big World sounded possessed. His nostrils flared violently as he inhaled. His massive form swelled almost to the breaking point. "Aaaarrrgh!" A low, guttural yawl spewed forth, sounded like a demonic beast from hell, as he charged full-steam ahead, knowing he was going to die.

Boom! Goldie fired and caught World in the upper right shoulder. He stumbled and kept coming. Boom! The second shot hit him dead center of his chest and big boy was still coming! Boom! The third shot pierced the heart and sent pieces of World's cardiovascular spewing from a hole in his back. Boom! The fourth shot blew off his chin. World stumbled and then lunged forward with his last dying breath.

"CIX!" Big World managed to say at the moment of impact. He collided head on with Goldie, sort of like a big Mack truck crashing head-on with a passenger vehicle. Goldie fell backward. The back of his head smacked the top of the door frame as he landed on the rear seat with Big

World and Caesar Jr. on top. Big World grinned facetiously and pressed the remote detonator.

Kaboom!

The Cadillac exploded into a mangled metal shell that was totally engulfed in flames.

###

Nubie grimaced when he heard the explosion.

"That was no gunfire," he muttered flatly.

"Yeah, I'd bet the house on that," Maruchan remarked glibly as he pulled out his .44 Magnum and cocked it. "I felt a shockwave, didn't you? Something exploded."

Nubie looked Maruchan in the eye. "Are you thinking what I'm thinking?" he replied. A knowing smirk pinched the corner of his mouth.

Maruchan responded with a quick nod and took the words right out of his mouth. "That was dynamite," he groaned. "The perpetrators behind the murders and robbery used dynamite." He sounded wishful, but confident.

A glint sparkled in Nubie's eye as he glared at the road up ahead. "Damn, if we could be so lucky..." he voiced aloud, speaking mostly to himself.

Back inside of the warehouse, Bad Ass was busy creeping along the wall of the docking area when the explosion outside rocked the foundation. He stopped on a dime.

"Oh shit, that was too soon! What are you doing, World?" Bad Ass felt an overwhelming sense of dread surging inside as he continued toward the exit.

Ten steps later, Bad Ass stopped again. He was surprised to see Caesar and his goon loitering just outside the doorway.

"Your ass is mine now!" Bad Ass was all teeth. He carefully hoisted the pump to eye-level and aimed for his mark. He took a deep breath, paused for a second, and pulled the trigger.

Boom! The back of Bruno's head exploded in a shower of blood and brain fragments. The violent blow-back left Caesar's face drenched in Bruno's blood with the Don standing flash-frozen in place, a dazed and discombob-ulated look swimming in his eyes and a deaf ringing echoing in his ears. The dumbfounded expression he wore was the initial state of shock he was experiencing.

Bad Ass walked right up to Caesar and whacked him in the back of his head with the butt of the pump. He watched the Don wobble and fall to the ground. A second later, gunfire erupted out of nowhere.

"Oh shit!" Bad Ass grunted and dropped to the ground as bullets split the air above his head. "Who the fuck?" he shrieked.

"Bad Ass! Bad Ass!" It was Loso running across the floor of the docking area. "Where are you?"

"I'm over here, just outside the door!" Bad Ass shouted. "Get low; bammas out here bustin' off!" He reached out and grabbed hold of Caesar and tried to pull him inside.

Loso carefully eased over to the doorway and took a quick peek outside. Bam! Bam! Bam! "Muthafuck!" Loso gasped and ducked his head in the nick of time. "C'mon, Cuz, we gotta get low!" Loso's demeanor was wild and jumpy.

Bad Ass huffed, "What the fuck you think I'm do-ing? Help me lift this heavy muthafucka!" Bad Ass paused. His head sprang up like a groundhog surveying the land-scape.

Bam! Bam! Bam!

Bad Ass bobbed and weaved and jumped back in-side. "I peeped two bammas hiding behind a navy Cor-vette," he told Loso as he grabbed him by the arm. "Check this out...all we have to do is make it to the second Caddy. The trailer blocking the street, so we good."

Loso nodded. "Sounds like a plan to me," he agreed. "But where's World? We could use some more firepower."

Bad Ass shook his head and gave a dejected look.

"You see that fucked up Caddy out there on fire? Yeah, our man World went out like a soldier."

"Damn," Loso uttered, sounding somber. "That's fucked up. I guess it's you and me. That's what it is, so let's do this!"

Bad Ass smacked Caesar in the head once more with the butt of the pump for good measure, and then with the help of Loso, he hoisted him onto his shoulder. Loso glanced out of the door and fired two warning shots. Two seconds later, Bad Ass came sprinting outside with Caesar over his shoulder and Loso unleashing hellfire on the Corvette for cover.

Within seconds, Bad Ass reached the car and glanced over his shoulder. Loso was running full speed across the parking lot with his Tec-9 blazing the air as he moved.

Bad Ass didn't waste a second. He tossed Caesar in the back seat and had the Cadillac revved up and in gear.

"Let's get it!" Loso yelled as he dove in the passenger window.

Bad Ass floored the car in reverse, whipped the wheel a couple of times, hit the brake, slammed the gearshift into Drive, and floored it.

The Cadillac left a trail of black tire marks on the pavement as the sedan high-tailed it out of there.

Chapter Twenty

Law 15: Crush your Enemy Totally

" All great leaders since Moses have known that a feared enemy must be crushed completely. (Sometimes they have learned this the hard way.) If one amber is left alight, no matter how dimly it smolders, a fire will eventually break out. More lost through stopping halfway than through total annihilation: The enemy will recover, and will seek re-venge. Crush him, not only in body but in spirit."
48 Laws of Power

Approximately five minutes after escaping the warehouse shootout, the black Cadillac was seen at the intersection of 12th and Saratoga, where the sedan crept into the rear parking lot of the Brentwood Projects. In the Cadillac's rear cockpit, Loso was busy putting the finishing touches on Caesar. He bundled up the Don real nice and tight with a fresh roll of duct tape and smiled to himself, admiring his own handiwork.

Bad Ass parked the car alongside of a black Range Rover and peeped the scene. Not a bamma in sight. Good! he thought to himself. "Alright, Lo, let's do this!" he commanded and jumped out.

In a matter of seconds, the men dumped Caesar in the rear cargo of the Range Rover, hopped in, and were riding out of the projects with the voice of Jay Z filtering into the night as the Range drove on.

"Lucifer, Son of the Morning, I'm gonna chase you out of here

Sing, sing, sing...I'm from the murder capital, will her murder for capitol?

Lucifer...Lucifer. Lord forgive him, he got them dark forces in him, but he also gotta righteous cause for sinning!"

###

Two miles away, Natasha was in the process of annihilating, dissecting, and dismembering Dee Dee, whom she referred to as Angel's adversary. Natasha had transformed Dee Dee's master bathroom into a horrifying slaughter chamber.

The bathroom was bathed in soft candlelight, compliments of Dee Dee's personal scented candle collection – at least thirty. They dominated the bathroom's rose-colored tile.

Natasha looked wicked hovering in front of a body length mirror with a dark expression scrawled on her face. She smeared thick crimson blood on her cheeks, which she had collected from a deep gash in Dee Dee's wrist. She resembled a wicked female version of the Joker villain from Batman. When she finished applying the fiendish war mask, Natasha stood erect and eyed her wicked reflection in the mirror. A moment later, her lips were moving incessantly, mumbling gibberish under her breath—some kind of black magic dialogue that made sense only to her.

Suddenly, the mumbling stopped as abruptly as it had started. Natasha scooped the machete off the counter top and turned from the mirror. Tiny shimmering flames danced in her frosty blue eyes as she cast her evil gaze down upon Dee Dee while she lay unconscious on the bathroom floor with blood oozing profusely from the deep slashes in both her wrists.

The moment the mumbling ceased, Dee Dee began to stir. "Yeah, that's it, bitch," Natasha hissed, fondling her blood-coated lips with her tongue and savoring the pungent tang that was Dee Dee's blood. Natasha quickly moved away from the counter and stood over Dee Dee. "I want you to see and feel everything I'm about to do to your filthy ass!"

Dee Dee's eyelids fluttered weakly as she strained to open them and get her bearings. It took a few seconds, but gradually her vision came into focus, and she squinted.

"What's going on?" Dee Dee muttered nervously while attempting to make out the dark form floating above her like a black ghost. She tried to move her head and winced. "Oh my gosh!" she moaned and ran her tongue along her busted lip and then reached up and felt the huge lump on the back of her head. When she removed her hand, she immediately noticed something thick and sticky was coating her palms.

That's odd, Dee Dee thought as she placed her hand close to her face for further inspection. Blood! She cringed at the sight of fresh blood pulsating from the wounds in her wrist, and then the horrible memory reeled through her mind and galvanized her core. Nina's dead! The ghastly image crashed in her head. Oh my gosh! I remember seeing a crazy-looking albino bitch! It was all starting to come back to her now. Dee Dee glanced up. "Lord, no!" She screamed, terrified, when she realized the crazy woman was standing over her.

Natasha reached down, grabbed a fistful of Dee Dee's hair, and hoisted her clear off the floor. Dee Dee was face to face with pure evil. But there was something else about this crazy woman that she thought she recognized.

No...it's not possible! It couldn't be! Dee Dee thought to herself, examining the woman's facial features up close and personal. Dee Dee raised an eyebrow. "Angel?" She uttered the name aloud without realizing what she had said.

A sharp scowl pierced Natasha's face and her upper lip curled into a vicious sneer. "No, you nasty whore!" she snarled vehemently as she placed the razor's tip against

Dee Dee's navel. "I'm Natasha, bitch!" She rammed the machete into her gut, the force so violent that the entire blade punched clear through her stomach and three razor sharp inches were left protruding sickly from the small of Dee Dee's back.

Dee Dee felt a searing lava flow erupt inside her belly at the same instant she felt a strong ebbing sensation invade her body, and then a moment later she felt herself go airborne. She tried to brace herself for a hard impact, but when she landed there was no hard impact. Instead, there was a clash of flesh when she landed in the Jacuzzi tub on top of a body. She immediately started to thrash and flail around like a fish out of water.

"Lord help me!" Dee Dee gasped in horror when she realized the person lying beneath her was Nina's headless corpse, and the slick, sticky fluid she was slip-sliding in was Nina's blood. She quickly realized there was something else in the tub with her. It was rolling around and bumping up against her feet. Dee Dee paused, held her breath, and looked down.

Nina's decapitated head lie at her feet. Her deadpan eyes gazed up at Dee Dee and seemed to be calling out to her friend and lover in death. That was the moment Dee Dee lost it and spazzed out. When she screamed, the sound she made was inhuman. Dee Dee was so horrified and consumed by the look and feel of Nina's head touching her skin that she never saw the bloodstained silver blade rise up in the air and pause for a second before it came down in a flash, like a deadly lightning strike. It sliced through Dee Dee's throat and separated her head from her torso in one violent stroke.

Natasha hesitated and watched Dee Dee's head tumble over in her lap. She was flat out giddy over her work and the death she had caused. In the aftermath, Natasha stood there for a minute and relished in the moment before the sick, demented cackle burst from her mouth and rose to a raucous roar that resonated throughout the entire house.

Miles up the road, the shiny black Range Rover was exiting Baltimore/Washington Parkway. It proceeded west on Route 32 for another mile before taking the exit ramp for Dorsey Road.

While navigating the back, winding road, Bad Ass quietly reflected on a time long ago when his father would drive down this exact stretch of road with himself and his older brother Shane. This was before Shane Sr. was seriously crippled by a massive stroke, which he succumbed to the following year. Shane Sr. was a major contractor in the Washington/Baltimore region. An industrial area located in Jessup, MD was the location for the company's headquarters for Holt Contractors.

Wow! That shit seem like a lifetime ago, Bad Ass pondered, feeling the grip of reality rush in and yank him back to the present just before he made a hard left turn onto Patuxent Range and then a sharp right into a lengthy parking lot. He rolled straight ahead, far from the roadway and into an obscure wooded area. The parking lot came to a dead end.

Bad Ass stared through the Range windshield and the pitch black wall spread out in front of the vehicle. He knew this area well from the endless hours he and Shane would spend exploring the thick, forested landscape, which stretched for miles.

This is the perfect spot. It's dark, remote, and not a soul for miles around, he surmised, as he rolled to a stop. Fifty feet in front of them was a thick curtain of black trees that was dark and ominous. High above the trees a full moon shimmered in a cloudless night sky, and the moon's eerie glow created a creepy forbidden scenery. The black silhouette of towering tree branches seemed to reach sky-ward toward the heavens, as if the trees were alive.

Outside, the forest was extra quiet except for the occasional owls that were hooting up in the dark canopy and the subtle rustling of crisp leaves in the breeze.

Bad Ass killed the engine and an eerie silence permeated the night. The Range Rover's bright halogen head-lamps continued to illuminate the thick black shroud lurking just beyond the glowing perimeter like a giant black wall.

Bad Ass exhaled. "We're here." He turned to Loso.

"Alright, Lo, let's show this bamma how CIX keep it a thousand and takes no prisoners."

Loso rubbed his palms together. Cynical delight sparkled in his eye. "You the man, Bad Ass, so let's slump this bamma!"

The men dragged Caesar bound and gagged across the grassy terrain and deposited him on a dusty dirt mound ten feet away. Bad Ass gloated and hovered over him as contempt and ill will surged in his heart for this man. "You stupid muthafucka! You still don't know who I am?" Bad Ass spoke through clenched teeth, as if he was grinding rocks between them.

Caesar lay perfectly still on the ground, not moving an inch. Although his mouth was covered with duct tape, he didn't attempt to utter a sound; he just peered up at Bad Ass. A chilly, tempestuous silence radiated deep in his eyes.

"You dago muthafucka!" Bad Ass spat, and out came the pistol. "Remember Holt Contractors? The company's owner, Shane Holt Senior?" Bad Ass squatted down and ripped the tape off his mouth. "I know you remember the business you and your boys cheated and extorted until the owner was under so much stress, he became ill and died!" Bad Ass shifted position and then tightened his grip on his pistol. His eyes sharpened as he took aim.

Boom! The barrel exploded in a flash of fire and thunder cracked the night, followed instantly by the sound of pure agony, as the tip of Caesar's black Ferragamos burst open into a mangled mess of blood, flesh, and bones. The shriek Caesar let out sent chills racing through the air.

Loso watched in silence, transfixed, pulse racing. He could feel the icy chill emanating from Bad Ass as if he were possessed.

"Shut the fuck up, bitch!" Bad Ass snarled before placing the barrel of his 5.7mm between Caesar's quivering lips. "Okay, muthafucka, you remember him now?" His eyes sparkled dangerously and his voice grew louder. "If you don't, I got some shit for your ass that'll make you remember the first words you ever spoke!" Bad Ass told him. He shoved the barrel of his gun in Caesar's mouth so hard that he knocked out the Don's two front teeth.

The strong silent front Caesar had erected was all but gone as he stood there shivering and squirming around in pain.

Bad Ass wondered what thoughts, regrets, and fears were rushing through Caesar's head. Bad Ass wore a facetious, smug grin. A minute later, Bad Ass removed the barrel from Caesar's bloody mouth while the Don shivered like he was on the verge of having fatal convulsions.

Caesar fought though the haze of excruciating pain.

"No!" Caesar fired back, thick-tongued. "You got it fucked up. Somebody fuckin' with your head! Think about it...!" he struggled to say but he continued. "His son, Shane Holt, is the chief of police. How in the hell do you think he got that position? It was because of me. I pulled the strings to get old man Holt's son placed at the top of the police department. Old man Holt did business with my father, not me! So you can shut the fuck up and kill that bullshit!"

Caesar started to speak again, but this time he was cut short by a violent kick to the ribs by Loso. "Shut the fuck up, dago!" Loso spat.

Bad Ass snickered and gave a snappy retort.

"What's that? Yeah, right! Man, fuck what you saying, for real. Don't you get it? What you say doesn't matter now. You need to say your prayers, muthafucka! Look around you and take a good look, because this right here is your eternal resting place. Yeah, that's right...it's dirt nap time for your ass," he expressed nonchalantly.

Caesar could feel the hateful vibe pulsating behind his eyes, and it made him shudder and feel lightheaded all of a sudden. A minute later Caesar's heart jumped in his chest when it dawned on him who his kidnapper was. "Oh shit, "he stammered incoherently. "You're old man Holt's youngest son. But why? What do you want with me?" he asked simply, but the words struck him.

Bad Ass gave him a sideways glance, his grim expression so intense that it made the Don's legs weak. Bad Ass hesitated, took a deep breath, and then jumped on him without provocation. He blasted Caesar in the face with head-shattering hammer punches.

A minute later, after five or six blows to the face, Bad Ass got to his feet. "Grab that bitch!" he ordered Loso.

"Stand him up!" The quick violent beat down had left Caesar fucked up. His nose and mouth were busted and bloody with a deep gash over his left eye that leaked blood like an open faucet. "Yeah, that's it." Bad Ass swung with all his might and crushed Caesar's jaw, destroying the entire bone structure.

"Ooooh shit!" Loso moaned jokingly. "I know that shit gotta hurt something terrible?" His laugh was harsh and psychotic and over-the-top. He glanced at Bad Ass and grinned mischievously when he realized he wasn't finished. Bad Ass tore into Caesar and unleashed the years of hurt and anger that had been eating at him ever since his father's death. He was inexhaustible, pummeling the Don with a merciless barrage of powerful blows to the head and face. A minute later, a loud crack resonated in the night, followed immediately by another.

Boom! Boom! Boom! Boom! Boom! Five more shots rang out in succession, piercing the quiet, and then the sound slowly evaporated into the dark twilight.

"Reap what you sow, muthafucka!" Bad Ass growled acidic. "This right here is for my father, Shane Holt Senior!"

Chapter Twenty-One

A dark cloud hung over Debra Nobles's residence on this brisk and cloudy day. Just beyond her doorsteps law enforcement, first responders and anxious news reporters swarmed the area around Michigan and South Dakota Avenues while overhead, helicopters hovered and crisscrossed the skyline non-stop.

A grave and somber vibe swept the community and cast a dreadful mood over the neighborhood. Crowds began to congregate just beyond the police barricade.

"What's going on? Did somebody die?" asked a little old lady with a concerned look etched in her face when she stepped out onto her porch.

"Mama Josephine," a heavyset woman wearing a pink shower cap responded from the crowd. "C'mon now, you see all these police, paramedics, and news people out here. What else could it be?"

"Shit, maybe it's a big drug bust or they found a bomb inside," offered a frail adolescent boy with a hopeful look swirling on his face.

The nervous chatter swelled when an assortment of people offered their take on the somber situation.

Meanwhile, upstairs on the second floor, a team of CSI techs and one Tony Woo converged on a grisly scene of human devastation that was arranged so neatly, like the geometry of a fateful spider's web. Tony Woo paced the floor like a caged lion, his hands clasped firmly behind his back as he moved to and fro. He paused only when he noticed Chief Holt coming down the hall with Nadia and Mecca close by his side.

"You know, they say Satan comes in all forms," Woo spoke in a voice that was uncharacteristically cold and

emotionless. He stopped in the center of the hall. A poign-
ant glare floated in his slanted eyes.

Chief Holt locked eyes with Woo and answered
pointedly, "So what form has Satan taken on in order to
commit this act?"

"He's a monster!" Woo hissed without breaking eye
contact. "This individual encapsulates all things evil!" He
made an about-face and led the way to the entrance of the
master bedroom.

The stench of decomposition and blood hung heavy
in the air and grew more pronounced as they closed the
distance to the bedroom. Inside was a scene from hell. The
ivory white décor was drenched in blood. Dee Dee's gutted
corpse lay in a twisted heap and rested in the center of the
bed in a thick, gooey pool of blood. Nina's remains were
strewn across the plush blood-soaked carpet. Her shredded
torso and limbs were placed intentionally at different intervals around the room and gave birth to a hideous creation
that only a deranged psychopath was capable of carrying
out.

Tony Woo spread his arms wide in a mocked gesture. "Welcome to hell," he said facetiously. He cut his eyes
toward the Chief when he heard Nadia and Mecca gasp at
once. "Notice how the killer disemboweled both victims,"
Tony Woo continued, and then gestured toward the bed.

"You see the victim on the bed? He carved out her
uterus. But the second victim, her remains he chose to scat-
ter around the perimeter of the floor. Each limb was skillfully disarticulated at the joint. Keep in mind that our perp
disarticulated the body after the kill," he explained with a
cool, detached expression.

Mecca felt nauseous, but she refused to let on that
the horrible scene was weighing on her. She wanted to gag,
but she concealed it with a cough and placed a hand over
her mouth. "Excuse me, Inspector," she said, carefully

choosing her words. "What are we working with here? What's his twisted motivation?" Although the grisly scene made her sick to her stomach, Mecca couldn't look away. She was captivated by the diabolical nature the perp had employed.

Their conversation paused when a short CSI tech in a light blue plastic suit that resembled Saran wrap approached them. He stopped three feet from the doorway and stated, "Inspector Woo, I've never seen anything like this since I've joined the force. This crime cuts so deep to the core! The level of overkill exhibited in these murders shows a killer who's experienced a psychotic break." The tech felt compelled to express his take on the matter.

Tony Woo shook his head slowly and said, "No, Hanes, that's not the case with this killer. We're dealing with a predator, and this predator deliberately, methodically and reflectively murdered these women in an extremely satanic manner for his own perverted purpose. Take my word, Hanes, this was done with premeditation. This was thought out and planned long in advance."

Chief Holt observed and listened for a minute. He had a very disturbed look stretched across his face as he eyed Nadia and Mecca and then finally Woo, and then he exhaled, a long, and exhausted-sounding huff.

Tony Woo picked up on the signal and ordered Hanes back to work, and not a second too soon for the Chief. A reluctant sigh sounded from Chief Holt before he spoke. "Talk about finding the wizard behind the curtain! Shit, in our situation we need to find the killer lurking in the shadows."

Nadia spoke up suddenly. "He's toying with us, taunting us, saying to us, "I can do this and you can't stop me!" She gave Mecca a knowing look.

"If we're to solve this case," Mecca chimed in, "we have to use our logic, common sense, and intuition, and then think outside of the box - far outside the box."

Chief Holt straightened the lapels on his black blazer before responding. "Okay," he breathed with his lips turned down. "That sounds good and all, but I don't need the wordplay. I need results. I got the mayor breathing down my neck, and if something doesn't give very soon, changes will be made, and believe me when I say, no one is exempt." He hesitated and gave the inspector a nod. "Ladies, I will meet with you two downstairs. The Inspector and I need to speak in private."

Tony Woo watched the women head back down the hall.

"I heard our leads are literally wafer-thin. Is that correct, Inspector Woo?" The frown Holt wore deepened when he noticed the stressful look on the Inspector's face, but there was something else on the Inspector's mind. Holt could sense an elusiveness wavering in his disposition and red flags jumped to attention in his head.

"Well, that's true to a point," Woo replied, sounding vague.

"To a point? What's that supposed to mean, Inspector?" Holt's demeanor took on a guarded stance now.

Tony Woo smiled to himself when he noticed the concerned look the chief seemed to be attempting to hold in check. "Well, Chief," he began calmly, "I've just been informed that our serial predator may have some type of connection with his victims, like an inside track that would provide him insider information that would enable our perp to strike out at his targets with optimum advantage." The inspector lingered for a minute, before adding, "That has to be the critical link we've been missing all along. Think about it. How else could he account for such a high kill rate and not a living eyewitness to verify anything?"

The concern on Holt's face suddenly turned shrewd. He carefully stroked his chin and responded, "So that's the motivation behind the killer harvesting body parts." The comment was a statement, not a question.

Tony Woo gave an arrogant retort. "I wouldn't go so far as to state that as fact, because when viewing this whole sordid scenario from my professional vantage point, I can literally separate predator from prey. The difference between a normal individual and a psychotic – the psychotic individual experiences fits of rage or impulses that he's unable to control." He was studying the chief's reaction closely. "A psycho killer feels that murder and mutilation are the same as eating dinner. They have no remorse.

That's not to say a normal individual doesn't have the propensity to, uh...how should I put this...experience some form of debilitating life-altering tragedy that could cause him to have a profound psychotic episode." Woo hesitated, and then moved his wire-frames to the bridge of his nose. "You know, in the field of psychology," he added as an afterthought, "My colleagues and I have this saying: inside all of us, there lurks a dark, malevolent thinker, which we refer to as the shadow. Some of us have to work a lot harder to keep that so-called shadow at bay. Catch my drift, Chief?"

The chief did a double-take. A splash of apprehension seized his facial expression. "What?" The insinuating remark didn't bode well. "Don't pussy-foot around with me, Inspector," he warned. "You're barking up the wrong fucking tree buddy. I'm the one that made your ass, and I am also the one that can break your ass! Catch my drift, Inspector?"

Sergeant Brubaker rushed up the hall and interrupted the exchange. "The owner of the residence is named Debra Noble, sir," he announced.

The Chief made a funny face. "Debra Noble? Dee Dee?" There was a sour note in his tone and a ridiculous smirk plastered on his lips.

The inspector detected a subtle jolt of recognition in the chief's attitude. "So you know the deceased, sir?" Tony Woo's slanted brow had an accusatory arch.

The headless corpses! Holt cringed inwardly. I never inquired about the missing craniums. Fuck! He mentally kicked himself for the slip-up. "Yes, Inspector, I know the owner of this residence," the chief answered, looking both smug and disturbed all at once.

The Inspector pushed his wired frames snug on his round face. "Hmmm, that's odd. You never asked to examine the missing craniums. Why?" His mood was strong with a calculating undertone.

Chief Holt snapped his finger and whipped out his cell phone. "Hold that thought," he said, brandishing his index finger. "I keep thinking about that man in the dumpster over in DuPont Circle. His genitals were cut off and stuffed in his mouth. If I'm correct, he worked at N.I.H."

Tony Woo hesitated and then gave him a slow, skeptical nod. "Yes, you're referring to Stanley Hanes. He was the security guard for N.I.H. Why? We've profiled that case and the profile suggests there's no viable link. The DuPont slaying was a copycat."

The chief placed a hand over the receiver. "You're not a hundred percent sure, so how the hell do you know?" he fired back smartly. "Remember New York's Zodiac Killer? He had no set victims – black, white, man, woman. He slaughtered them all, and he killed for thirty years without getting caught. But there's a link between these killings; you just said so yourself. These killings aren't random, Inspector. These are controlled executions, and our perp isn't going to stop until we catch him!"

Tony Woo snatched off his glasses. "Where are you going with this line of talk, sir?" he questioned with a blustery sneer. "The Zodiac Killer? Come now, are you trying to jerk my chain?"

"What?" The chief snapped. "Have you forgotten your fucking position? Last I checked, I was still Head Nigga In Charge around these parts, so back off!" He punctuated his remark with a flick of his middle finger.

Tony Woo responded with a mocking chuckle. I've struck a nerve, he admitted quietly. How much longer will it be before this charade is up? He thought deep and hard with the most discerning spark in his eye.

Chief Holt cursed under his breath when Angel's voicemail picked up. "Fuck! Angel, where are you? I need to speak to you, it's very imperative that we speak. Something terrible has happened to Dee Dee, and I have a very bad feeling about your sister Renee. So please contact me as soon as possible." When Holt finally looked up, he was taken aback by the peculiar way Tony Woo was eyeing him.

"Inspector, is everything okay? Do you have something on your chest that you need to get off?"

Woo shook his head and mumbled something under his breath before walking off. His cold and divisive nature struck Holt as very odd and troublesome. The way Woo was carrying on was totally out of character. As the Chief of Police, he rationalized, It has to be this serial case.

It's wearing on everyone's nerves. So he gave his top inspector the benefit of the doubt. He also made a mental note. Holt didn't take lightly to crass, unprofessional behavior that could jeopardize or thwart their covert operation. He quickly made up his mind. First thing in the morning, Woo and I will have a private one-on-one in my office. But right now, he felt a serious urge to locate Angel. His gut feeling was so intense; the thought was starting to make him feel nauseous.

"Agent Steel!" Holt shouted and waved him over to the doorway. "Here, take my card," he said, scribbling his personal contact number on the back. "The moment you receive confirmation on the identity for both victims, I want you to call me at this number, ASAP. Understand?" He gave the agent a steely look.

"Yes sir," answered Steel, standing straight and tall, ready to salute his superior. "The moment I have confirmation, I'll be dialing your number." He looked the Chief in the eye for a brief second, and then dropped his gaze to the floor.

"Alright, Steel." Holt's tone was more cordial now. He handed over the card. "I'll be waiting for your call, so don't let me down." His expression was calm and amused as he watched the balding man turn the business card over and gaze upon the scribbled number, as if the card was the winning lottery ticket. "As you were, Steel," Chief Holt said and turned on his heel. He marched off down the hallway, his strong, overbearing presence following in his wake like a shadow.

The entire length of Michigan Avenue from 12th Street to Eastern Avenue, (about 10-blocks), was clogged in gridlock, from DC into Prince Georges County Maryland. At the intersection of Michigan and South Dakota, a glossy cherry red Aston Martin slowed to a crawl when the expensive coupe came upon the gridlock.

A few feet away, Bad Ass watched his older brother stroll across Michigan and make a bold stand against the sea of rolling metal, as if he was untouchable. Bad Ass grinned and tapped the accelerator. The sleek coupe lurched forward and surprised Shane. He came to an abrupt standstill and shot the Aston Martin a killer look, like he was about to dive through the windshield. Shane stood his ground for a full five seconds before he finally stepped aside.

The Aston Martin pulled up beside him and stopped. Shane peered at the dark passenger window and watched it slide open. His younger brother pulled his cherry Tootsie Pop out of his mouth.

"You got problems, Slim?" Bad Ass asked, flashing a dark grin.

Shane loosened the grip on his pistol the second he laid eyes on his brother. He glanced up and down Michigan, and then took a step forward and placed his hand on the roof of the car. He looked his brother in the eye. "You shouldn't play around like that, li'l brother," he told him seriously. "Because when I whip, I spit. Feel me?"

Bad Ass laughed at his remark. "Listen to the G-man trying to sound gangsta. You do know that G stands for government, not gangsta, right Cuz?"

Shane glanced over the roof of the car and instantly became agitated by the sight of Tony Woo looking his way.

"Check this out," Shane said, tugging at his collar. "This isn't the time or the place. You've got my number, so hit me up!"

Bad Ass cut him off. "Man, fuck that!" he retorted. "We need to talk right now. So where can we go?"

Shane smacked the roof of the car and gave his brother an aggravated look. "Alright, you got it. Follow me," Shane directed while keeping a close eye on Tony Woo. He stood up straight, whirled on his heels, and twenty seconds later the chief was standing in front of his Escalade.

Tony Woo observed the casual exchange and wondered what that was all about. His interest piqued when the Escalade rolled out with the Aston Martin following close behind. Before the two vehicles were out of sight, Tony Woo was on his cell phone.

###

Meantime, back over on Kendale Street, the special robbery task force was in full throttle mode with their investigation. Lieutenant Louis was lead detective in charge of operations, and at the moment, Louis was extremely pissed off. Maruchan and Nubie had totally disregarded departmental protocol when they decided against calling for back-up and instead engaged in a reckless shoot out with members of the Leonardi Crime Family and members of an unknown underworld DC gang.

"It's quite obvious to me the blatant dereliction of duty you both partook," Louis openly reprimanded Maruchan and Nubie while pacing the floor just inside the loading bay, his booming voice vibrated loud and clear. "In your failed attempt to apprehend some very big and dangerous fish, I presume." Louis cut Maruchan off with a wave of his hand when he tried to speak. "Please, Detective, I'm on a roll. Don't interrupt me."

Lieutenant Barnhart walked through the door with an arrogant smile stuck on his face. "Give me my props, Louis! I was right on the money! The improvised explosive device has the exact same detonator component and fragment make-up as the device we recovered from that nasty explosion on Columbia Road, the house on East Capitol, and the jewelry store bombing in Georgetown!" Barnhart paused for a minute, fixated on a piece of food that was stuck between his teeth. He was busy with his toothpick, trying to dislodge the food particle. "Well, Louis?" Barnhart waited, his brow crinkled slightly.

Louis moved to the middle of the floor and grimaced. "Barnhart, now is not the time. I'm dealing with these two wannabe super-cops!"

"Excuse us, fellas," a pale, geeky-looking coroner wearing bright yellow bifocal Gazel lens interrupted. "But we've got some more corpses on the move. They're extremely irritable and can't stand to be around the living," he told them as he flashed his yellow stained teeth in a creepy smile. The coroner's weird play at a joke went right over every one's head.

Louis eyed the strange-looking coroner and the black body bag he wheeled out on a gurney. Without saying a word, Louis stepped in the gurney's path. "Who do we have here, my friend?" Louis didn't wait for a reply. He leaned over and unzipped the body bag.

The face of Danny Boy stared up at Louis, his chest full of holes, head full of copper, as he lay inside with his brains in a shit bag and a toe tag on him.

"Well looky here," Louis snorted, "Caesar Leo's right hand man. What in the hell went on in here?" Louis's head whipped around. "Who in the hell did you two idiots let get away? There's a goddamn gang running around DC knocking off the mob! You get a golden opportunity to seal off this entire area. But no...instead of calling for back up, you gung-ho fucks rush in and fuck everything up!"

"Excuse me, sir." The coroner sneered with an obvious look of sarcasm. He zipped the bag shut. "We have a stack of bodies that need to be processed, tagged, and bagged. Let us do our work while you do your job. I'd appreciate it."

Maruchan and Nubie glanced at one another and snickered. Louis obliged the coroner and stepped aside. He cut his eye on the two detectives. "You know, sometimes your greatest triumph can be your albatross," he said while twisting his handlebar mustache. "So you two ass-wipes keep that in mind."

Maruchan and Nubie were tempted to make a smart reply, and then decided against it, especially in the midst of such a sobering and somber procession of the dead.

An eerie quiet settled over the men and the docking area as a line of coroners began wheeling out the gurneys, one by one, with their deceased baggage riding on top. The sound of wheels squeaking echoed in the dock area as the parade of the dead wound its way outside. The scene had an extremely grave and dismal effect that was profoundly felt, and that feeling would have a lasting impression on the men who witnessed the parade of the dead.

Outside at the corner of Kendale and Okie, news crews swarmed the vicinity. The beautiful and impeccably dressed Cynne Jennings was reporting on the recent bloodbath.

"Once again, murder and mayhem has captivated our Nation's Capital. I'm standing outside of a vacant warehouse on Kendale Street where last night a violent shootout occurred. An unknown number of casualties is being carted off by this motorcade of medical examiner vehicles you see lined up just behind me." The attractive reporter stepped aside and allowed the camera man to get a wide angle view of the vehicles parked in a straight line, just beyond the smoldering burnt wreckage that was once a Cadillac.

Approximately thirty minutes later, the Aston Martin and Escalade were both parked at the curb in front of the Florida Avenue Grill. Inside one of DC's most renowned eateries, Bad Ass and his brother Shane were seated at a corner table, the pair going at each other in a verbal sparring match.

Bad Ass leaned across the table with a fierce look etched in his brow. "Why the fuck you lay that bogus bullshit on me about Caesar? Huh, muthafucka!" he snarled with a scathing twinkle in his eye. "Those dago muthafuckas are the reason you where you are today! So why would you put me out there like that? Me, of all people! I'm your fuckin' brother!" A fleeting look of confusion and hurt flashed on Bad Ass's face for a split second and disappeared.

Shane's disposition was unaffected. He leaned back in his seat, his face emotionless, his demeanor nonchalant, his deep set gaze dark and chilly. Shane knew his brother well. He had him down to a science, knowing which buttons to push, which screws to turn, and just how far he could push the envelope before his brother snapped on him. At the moment, Shane sensed he was teetering right around the borderline. He listened to Chevar vent, but his words didn't faze him one bit. Shane was in his tunnel-vision mode and there was nothing Chevar could say or do at the moment that would deter his motivation except put a bullet in his head. The entire time Chevar was venting, Shane's fingers were busy tap dancing on the table's edge, drumming an incessant beat he was quietly grooving in rhythm to.

"Check this out, young killa." Shane's tone was slick and composed. "Those dago muthafuckas don't mean anybody any good. Whatever moves they make, whenever they give assistance, believe you me, there's always an ulterior motive with them dagos. Especially when there's a black man involved. They try to stick it to him every which way they can!"

Bad Ass gave his brother a suspicious look. "Hold the fuck up!" he said sourly. "You're trying to tell me that Caesar Leo put you at the top of the police department, while at the same time he's trying to bring you a move? C'mon, champ, what sense would that make? That would be like biting off your nose to spite your face." The smirk on Bad Ass's face screamed that he was totally unconvinced.

Shane hesitated and glanced around the restaurant before responding. "Look, young killa," he began more forcefully. "I deals directly with these dago muthafuckas! You don't know nothing about Caesar Leo, so how in the hell you going to go against my word?"

Bad Ass leaned back in his seat, his gaze deep and penetrating as he silently stroked his chin and pondered, What would my brother gain by eliminating Caesar? He mulled the thought over for a minute, and then flipped the question. What did Caesar's father gain by ruining our father's business? What would Caesar gain by helping out the son of the man his father supposedly wanted to destroy?

Not only that, the Leonardi's helped Shane reach one of the most pivotal positions held in DC government. There is only one position higher than the Chief of Police, and that is the Mayor!

Bad Ass sat across from his brother, a cool contemplative gleam shimmering in his eye as he weighed the pros and cons. Something just didn't sit right with him. He could feel it in his bones. There was something deeper at play here, but he couldn't quite put his finger on it—not at the moment. Bad Ass prided himself on being a savvy and shrewd street hustler, and he knew if he played his cards right, whatever was in the dark would eventually come to the light. It never failed...Universal Law!

Chapter Twenty-Two

Law 33: Discover Each Man's Thumbscrew
"Everyone has a weakness, a gap in the castle wall. That weakness is usually insecurity, an uncontrollable emotion or need; it can also be a small secret pleasure. Either way, once found, it is a thumbscrew you can turn to your advantage."

48 Laws of Power

One of Loso's prized chicken heads put a bug in his ear. "You know that bamma Demon you asked me about? Well guess what? He got a thing for my Puerto Rican homegirl, Bonita. Every night at 10 o'clock, Demon and a couple of his boys are at the club getting the VIP treatment. So if you're interested in taking care of business with him, I suggest you come down to the club after 10 o'clock."

It was around 10:15 p.m. that evening when a crew of Ducati motorcycles six deep came tearing down Georgia Avenue like they owned the street. At the intersection of Georgia and New Hampshire Avenues, the traffic signal flashed from yellow to red. The sound of bike engines roared a split second before the gang of Ducati's blitzed through the intersection in a streaking blur, as if the red light meant "Go"

Ten seconds later, the Ducati crew pulled up to the curb outside one of DC's legendary strip joints called the House. Six bikers hopped off their bikes wearing all-black biker suits and matching helmets. They made a beeline for the entrance.

The doorman was a big beefy sumo wrestler-looking dude name Rock. The moment he spotted the bikers rolling his way, Rock was immediately on guard. His massive frame blocked the entrance way like a stone wall. He stood erect, arms folded strong over his chest.

"Hold up, fellas," Rock told the men in a deep, robust voice. "The helmets have got to go. You know the rules."

Leading the charge was Bad Ass. When the doorman spoke up, he paused briefly, and then without saying a word, he calmly removed his helmet and stared the doorman right in the eye. His dark penetrating gaze beneath the ski mask was potent.

A dry smirk caught the corner of Rock's mouth.

"Hey, Slim, what's up with the skimask?" he scoffed, looking him up and down. "That's gotta come off also."

An irritated huff escaped Bad Ass's lips. "Is this the bamma Rock?" he sneered drily as he turned to Loso.

When Rock heard his name mentioned, a deep frown jumped across his meaty forehead.

"Yeah, that's the bamma," Loso confirmed with a sarcastic snort.

Bad Ass looked Rock straight in his bloodshot eyes and said with a sharp tongue, "Damn. Slim, it's like that? I thought you knew what time it was. But evidently not." Without warning, Bad Ass gripped his helmet and swung it like a baseball bat. He smashed Rock in the face and shattered his hooked nose on contact. The mountain-sized man stumbled backward, and before he could react, another violent blow to his temple made him shudder.

Loso rushed the door and slung it open. "C'mon! Get his bamma ass in here!" he ordered, sounding impatient.

Bad Ass cracked Rock upside the head again just before Midnight, Nightmare, Cut Throat, and Threat charged in and forced the doorman through the doorway and tackled him inside the vestibule.

Loso was the last man inside. He glanced up and down the Avenue, and then pulled the door shut and locked it.

"You the Boss, hey! You the Boss... You the Boss, hey! Rosay a born stunner, I can blow money, fifty when I'm shopping, that ain't no money!
I got my jeans saggin', money stuffed in 'em! I got forty whips, way too much in 'em!
I need me a queen...I need me a dime! Livin' this fast life, show me a sign!"

The voice of Rick Ross and Nicki Minaj echoed the hit "I'm the Boss" over the sound system. The heavy beat penetrated the wooden door leading into the men's room.

Inside, lewd grunts and moans echoed off the grimy beige tile. The source was the A-Team captain Demon and his Puerto Rican vixen, Bonita. Seated in a cramped bathroom stall, the half-naked dancer was crouched on bended knees between Demon's legs, her curly blonde head bobbing up and down in his lap.

"Aaaahhhh! Yeah, baby girl, deep throat that for daddy!" Demon licked his lips and flashed a greedy grin. His right hand cupped the back of Bonita's head. "Oh yeah, that's it!" he groaned, gently coaxing her to take his organ deeper into her throat. "Take all that, baby girl. Swallow that for daddy!"

"Mmph...mmph...mmph!" Bonita moaned and slurped and slobbered and sucked him off in a heated frenzy, like she couldn't get enough of him.

"Aaaah yeah!" Demon breathed, sounding rejuvenated. "Baby girl, I want you to do me a favor." A devious smirk appeared on his face.

Bonita paused mid-stroke and removed the saliva-coated meat from her mouth. "Yeah, papi!" She wiped the sticky fluid from her lips with the palm of her hand. "I'll do whatever you want, but I don't swallow," the slinky butter pecan vixen looked him in the eye and said flatly.

Bam! Nightmare kicked in the bathroom door and interrupted the freak session. Half a second later, Bad Ass and Loso stormed in, waving chrome-plated Desert Eagles in the air.

The sudden burst through the door jarred Demon. His head snapped upright, eyes popped out. "What the fuck?" he grunted, sounding rattled. He watched as shadows swept across the tile floor beneath the door stall. Demon held his breath and felt his entire body go rigid with fear.

Damn...bammas caught me slippin'! the little voice in Demon's head whispered.

Bonita felt the severity of the situation bearing down on her like a weighted force. Her body grew tense with fear as she silently cowered down between Demon's legs.

The sight of her disgusted him now. "Move, bitch!" Demon lashed out at Bonita, directing his sense of fear and defeat and dismay upon her. "Get the fuck off me!" He gave Bonita a violent stiff-arm to the head and jumped to his feet, and then took a couple deep breaths and tried to shake off the anxiety.

"C'mon, you bitch muthafuckas!" Demon snarled while rushing to fasten his belt. He figured it was over for him, so he might as well go dick-hard and face death head-on. His reputation was at stake. "Yeah, that's right! Let's do this! You bitch-ass - "

Bock! Bock! Bock! Bock! Bock! .40 caliber slugs exploded through the door stall. Three shots caught Demon in the chest, rocked him, and knocked him back into the wall. He was stuck for a second, and then he slid down the wall

and came to rest on the toilet seat. Bonita shrieked in horror and was trembling like a leaf.

The stall door slammed open and a ski-masked Loso
reached in and snatched the screaming, petrified, and half-
naked woman by her hair. "Shut the fuck up and bring your
ass here!"

Bad Ass watched in amusement before he casually
stepped into the stall. "Heard you were looking for Bad
Ass," he said with a victorious smirk pinched in the corner
of his mouth. "Well, here I am. Who's the bitch muthafucka now?" he mocked him. He put the chrome pistol to
Demon's head and continued. "Say your prayers, Slim. It's
time to meet your maker."

Coughing up blood, Demon struggled to raise his
hand and speak. "Wait a minute, Bad Ass." His voice was a
feeble whimper. "It's your folks..." Demon coughed up
more blood. "Your folks are setting you up."

"What? Setting me up?" Bad Ass muttered, looking
offended. "What the fuck are you talking about, Slim?"

A glob of blood spewed from Demon's mouth when
he tried to speak, but he willed himself to go on, and with
the last remnant of his life hanging by a thread, Demon
called upon everything within him. "Goldie and your brother and the cocaine...it was all a set-up." Demon coughed
and convulsed uncontrollably.

"Goldie and my brother?" Bad Ass sneered dangerously. "Muthafucka, you best tell me what the fuck you
talking about!" His head whipped around. "G, get that crying bitch out of here!" he ordered Loso. He waited for the
door to close, and then he turned around, ripped off his ski
mask, and yoked Demon by the throat. "Okay, what about
my brother? What about Goldie? Muthafucka, spit it out!"

Demon's head lifted slowly until both men were
eye to eye. "Bad Ass," he spoke in a voice just above a

whisper. "You're public enemy #1. When you fall. your brother is going to take credit for everything."

Bad Ass grumbled, "Muthafucka! You don't know me or my brother!" He pressed the barrel against Demon's temple, but hesitated just before he pulled the trigger. Bad Ass was struck by the knowing look in Demon's eye.

A weak grin parted Demon's lips. "Your brother...he's the Chief of Police right now," he said in a voice that was barely audible. "But when you go down...he's going to be the mayor of DC. Think about it."

Bad Ass face was unreadable, blank. The dire situation left him in an emotional abyss. He didn't respond to the accusation. Instead, Bad Ass stared Demon deep in his eye, as if he could see inside his soul. He paused and took a deep breath. "Okay, Slim, good looking," Bad Ass muttered and pulled the trigger.

Bock! Bock! He put two shots in Demon's head – dead bang.

Chapter Twenty-Three

"There goes my baby!" The charismatic vocals of Usher soared inside Shane's immaculate bachelor crib. The gentle medley wafted in the air as soft flames swayed in rhythm atop Ferragamo scented candles that were scattered around the room.

The master bedroom was alive and pulsing with the sounds of pleasure. Shane's Brazilian cherry wood canopy bed rocked back and forth with Mecca bent over in the center of the mattress, face down, ass up, gripping the black satin sheets, her face a deep crimson, mouth agape, eyes clenched tight, babbling incoherently. Shane showed her no mercy as he pounded her insides hard from the back.

Suddenly, their intimate frenzy was interrupted by the sound of Shane's iPhone. His pounding subsided and he slowed down and reached for the phone sitting on the edge of the nightstand.

Mecca's eyes popped open. "Fuck that phone!" she growled and slapped his hand away. The iPhone tumbled off the nightstand and bounced quietly on the carpet floor.

"Shane, you need to finish taking care of me before you do anything else!" she scolded with a catty smirk and then she cooed, "Take care of Ms. Punanny and Ms. Punanny will happily take care of you." Her hot, lusty eyes gazed up at Shane.

Shane liked the sound of that. "Oh yeah, baby? Be careful what you ask for, because what I'm packing will blow your mind," he boasted, oozing with self-confidence. Shane stiffened his back and commenced to pounding her from the back.

Thirty minutes and five pulsating orgasms later, Shane brought Mecca to an awesome, cranium-calming climax. He sent her into a virtual orgasmic conniption.

"You goddamn sonofabitch dog-ass pussy-beating muthafucka!" Mecca stuttered, her whole body shuddering from small volcanic eruptions of euphoria.

Shane paused. He wore a big haughty grin plastered on his face. "What I tell you, baby?" he said, hovering over her, his demeanor, strong and boastful. Another piece of pussy on smash! he gloated silently as he made a mental footnote. "I'm too much man for you to handle, baby!" Shane belted out a wild-sounding laugh, like a male lion's roar after a good kill.

Lying on the carpet floor, the iPhone sat face up, the phone line open through the entire freak-fest. A digital photograph of Angel with a gleeful smile floated on the screen. Her full name, Angel Rising, was inverted beneath her picture. It read, Rising Angel. A second after the intimate encounter ended, the phone line went dead. The words "Goodbye" slid quietly across the screen for five seconds, and then faded to black.

Approximately 1:18 a.m.

The fresh coat of metallic-sapphire blue sparkled under a moonlit sky as the Cadillac CTS blazed the road like a streak of lightning. Behind the wheel, a psychological battle between Angel and Natasha was heating up.

"I'm in love with a man that sleeps around! Why has God forsaken me?" Sadness and anger echoed in Angel's voice as if her heart had been ripped from her chest. Suddenly, Angel's face contorted and grimaced in pain. Her head whipped violently from side to side. "No!" Angel groaned through tight lips, attempting to keep the spirit of Natasha at bay.

Her upper lip curled in a sneer. "Has God really forsaken you? Or is it the fact of the matter that you're really that damn gullible?" Natasha snarled. Her piercing blue gaze eyed her reflection in the rearview mirror. When she spoke for the second time, she sounded totally disgusted.

"You were actually dumb enough to believe that lovey-dovey bullshit Shane was spitting, like you're some dumb-ass airhead! You really make me sick to my fucking stomach with that stupid-ass shit! By now you should know how those trash-ass men think! In their eyes, the only thing better than some good pussy is some new pussy!" Natasha's head snapped back abruptly in a violent whiplash.

"No...you fuckin' bitch!" she hissed, glaring up at the mirror, her face tense as she struggled to keep Angel at bay.

The Cadillac swerved suddenly, weaving left and right, cutting across the southbound lanes on the Baltimore/Washington Parkway. The dangerous maneuver prompted a flood of brake lights from the vehicles following behind.

"Fuck you, Natasha!" Angel spat, her expression wild, bordering on hysterical. "You don't know shit! Shane loves me! I know when a man is genuine and real! So stop hatin' on me, and get your own goddamn man!" Angel stopped short and stared at the rearview mirror, her eyes wide and nervous when she realized police lights were flashing in her rearview mirror. Instantly, she felt her mind spiral and her heart lurched in her chest, not due to the police, but because she was terrified by the wicked blue-eyed reflection looking back at her. A moment later, she felt herself being sucked under like quicksand.

"God! Please help me!" Angel screamed out a second before Natasha burst forth.

"Shut your gotdamn mouth!" Natasha admonished sharply. "Let a real bitch handle this business, because you're scared ass will fuck around and get us both hemmed-up and stuck in the can!"

The state trooper climbed out on the shoulder and adjusted his uniform. He looked fresh out of the academy, with his clean shaven face and boyish good looks. When he noticed there was a blonde redbone at the wheel, he quickly discarded the big clunky trademark state-boy brim. He leaned into the side mirror, finger brushed his thin mustache, stroked his chin, and gave himself a self-serving go-get-this-pussy wink.

If Mr. State Trooper/Wannabe-ladies-man would've been doing his job properly and run the license plates, he would've known that the tags on the Cadillac were stolen, which would've prompted a more thorough inquiry and revealed the vehicle's owner, the now-deceased Ms. Josephine Nubie – Jo Jo.

The trooper strode up next to the driver door.

"How are you tonight, Ms. Lady? Whoa! You're looking sweeter than a Georgia peach dipped in honey," he said, flashing his dazzling white teeth in a deep-dimpled smile. He leaned on the door to get a closer look at the pretty diva behind the wheel in the dark leopard print bodysuit. The trooper inhaled and caught a nice whiff of the feminine fragrance permeating the air inside of the cockpit.

"Mmmm, Ms. Lady, you smell almost as good as you look," he complimented while undressing her with his eyes. "So tell me, where are you going in such a hurry, gorgeous?"

The entire time the trooper was standing there talking and ogling over her, Natasha was contemplating his death. She held her eyes on the windshield and was finger tapping her favorite tune on the steering wheel – Beyonce's

"To the Left". Slowly, she rotated her head to the left and her icy blue gaze shimmered with hatred.

"To the left, to the left..." she uttered the lyrics in a weird-sounding chant.

The ominous tone gave the trooper the chills and he quickly covered his frown and replied, "Damn, baby, you have the prettiest blue..." His words died in his throat. The last thing the trooper saw was a flash of silver sweep across his eye.

Natasha slashed his jugular from left to right and snatched his service revolver from his holster in one swift motion. She looked down and grinned, satisfied, when the trooper collapsed to the ground with blood gushing from a deep neck wound, a look of utter shock splashed on his face as he choked on his own blood.

A minute later, the sapphire blue sedan was rolling south on the pitch black parkway, headed for DC. Natasha tossed the blue steel .357 on the passenger seat, wiped off the trooper's blood from the straight razor, and slipped the blade in the stash spot inside of her black La Perla bra.

"Alright, Mr. Dirty Dick Shane," she said with a dark, cynical grimace perched on her lips while she typed in the address on her iPad. "Let's see exactly where you are." A look of delight spread on her face when a digitally-enhanced image of DC and the city's roadways lit up the screen and a bright red flashing beacon marked the spot on the map. "There you are...you no good lying piece of shit for a man." Natasha licked her lips, grinned, and mashed the gas pedal to the floor.

Shane Holt's residence was a huge three story Victorian located in an upscale NW neighborhood called Mount Pleasant, which was a stone's throw from the National Zoo.

The chief's home was considered an architectural and historical wonder from the early 18th century, when the eloquent Victorian had served as one of Washington's most affluent lodging accommodations, catering exclusively to the city's rich and elite.

It was apparent the moment you entered Holt's swanky spread that the man spent some serious money on this back in the day high roller joint. His crib was straight flossed-out! Glazed black marble floors with inlaid golden trim greeted you at the front door. Once through the foyer, you came upon huge eggshell white cracked granite Roman pillars that soared from floor to ceiling. Also on display in the first floor lobby was a large polished black cracked marble fireplace with matching black leather Fernando Poo furnishings, which dominated the decor on the first floor, along with a collection of Rembrandt and Picasso replicas that canvassed the rouge silk walls. Shane's crib was on some next level platinum-coated shit, hands down.

Outside, under a cloudless starlit Washington sky, a cream-colored Audi A8 eased up on the rear bumper of Shane's black Escalade and a stunning Bahamian beauty, Mrs. Yolanda Holt, emerged from the automobile with a sassy cold sneer draped on her glazed pink lips. It was obvious; Mrs. Holt was pissed-off about something. She slung her long sandy tresses over her shoulder and strode across the small patch of grass and up the long concrete staircase.

Her long sandy hair whipped the air with an attitude. She brought to mind a prissy statuesque runway model dressed in a pretty pink Carolina Herrera pants suit, billowing with an air of class and arrogance as she moved up the steps.

A few blocks away at Connecticut Avenue and Columbia Road, Bad Ass's glistening new Aston Martin snaked through a thick logjam of traffic. Inside the exotic automobile, Bad Ass's eyes were glued to his Sony laptop monitor and the computer-generated GPS roadmap. A minute later, while he was in the midst of analyzing the screen, his body language went rigid with aggression. A look of pure disgust and anger flared in Bad Ass's facial expression when he recognized the address the white blip was now resting in front of.

"Oh yeah?" he hissed as he slammed his fist against the stern. "So that's why you said you couldn't hook up with me tonight, Yolanda! So you could get with my no-good-ass backstabbing brother!" Bad Ass paused and took a deep breath. "Fuck that! What the fuck you take me for? A sucka? Shit, we gonna get this shit straight tonight!" He gunned the engine out of frustration and then pounded the horn. "C'mon, muthafuckas! I got business to handle!"

A few blocks further up the road, at the busy 14th and U Street intersection, Nadia was cruising alone in her Dodge Charger, her eyes darting back and forth from the road up ahead to the glowing Apple Mac monitor on the passenger seat. She was locked on the small black blip floating across the digitally-enhanced city street and wondered where its next stop would take her.

An inquisitive gleam shone bright in Nadia's eye as she scrunched her nose and popped her lips. "I think I may be on to something," she said, thinking out loud, and then out of habit, she started pulling on her lower lip. "If I didn't know any better, Bad Ass, I'd swear you were following someone? I wonder... where's your partner in crime tonight, huh, bad boy? He's probably lying back in the cut somewhere just waiting for you to arrive so the both of you can indulge in a psychotic rendezvous. You want to make human chop-suey tonight, don't'cha bad boy? Well, not if I can help it...you sick fucker!" Nadia cursed at the screen, looking totally disgusted.

Approximately seven blocks west, at the corner of Georgia and Florida Avenues, Loso was driving a cranberry Escalade.

"Damn, this joint is wet!" Loso exclaimed with a tickled expression while focusing on the red blip gliding along the computerized image of 14th Street. "Bad Ass, I don't know how in the hell you pulled something like this off," he said to himself while glaring at the Sony laptop screen. "But you damn sure have to be connected to some pretty big bammas. If we can put five-O under surveillance, shit, who could stop us?" The possibilities were enormous, Loso figured as he slouched behind the wheel with a sly, seedy grin dancing on his lips as he watched Nadia's vehicle move silently on the computer screen.

Loso was so consumed with the computer monitor and the detective's movements that he was oblivious to the money-green Dodge Magnum driving up the opposite side of 14th Street. The driver inside the Magnum did a double take when he spotted Loso. The Magnum skidded to a halt and then hooked a hard U-turn in the middle of the street, totally disregarding the traffic moving in the opposite direction. The Magnum's low profile tires screamed as the car raced up 14th Street in pursuit of Loso's vehicle.

With all the dots on the various computer monitors slowly converging on the Mount Pleasant community and Shane Holt's residence, it was as if dark forces were aligning themselves with the stars. This gathering of toxic personalities meeting simultaneously at one place would be the equivalent of tossing a flaming match stick into a canister of gasoline. The aftermath would be something extremely catastrophic in nature...it would be inevitable!

Chapter Twenty-Four

Yolanda reached the last step and sighed when she stepped onto the porch, but something was amiss in the air and she felt a sudden chill shoot down her spine. She immediately stopped in her tracks, pivoted on her heels, and glanced around the dark empty porch. Nothing. She breathed a sigh of relief and proceeded to the front door.

She stood at the door for a moment, nervously fidgeting with her keys and silently hoping that Shane hadn't got around to changing the locks like he had threatened to do. She pushed the key into the lock – perfect fit. She held her breath and turned the key with ease. "Thank God..." she whispered before going inside.

Upstairs, on the 3rd floor, Shane and Mecca were relaxing on the bed, the both of them sweaty and sexually exhausted. Mecca was lying on her stomach.. Her plump derriere flexed and jiggled every time she moved. Suddenly she folded both her arms on the fluffy down pillow and propped her chin on top.

"Shane, you know you started something?" Mecca playfully insinuated as she flashed a soft pleasant smile. "Because with a woman such as myself - beautiful, passionate, career-minded, goal oriented, and a hot-ass freak in the bed with the bomb punanny - you know I'm not fling material, right?"

Shane didn't answer right away. He lingered, sucking on his teeth for a moment. He finally turned to Mecca and said, "Baby girl, you don't have to sell yourself to me. I'm not one of those young boy-toys just stepping off my momma's porch. I've been around the block a few times and I'm no fool. I know a woman's worth when it's presented to me, and you, baby, are without question one in a million, in a class all by yourself." He could tell by the spark in her eye he'd just scored some major fuck points with that line.

"Oh really?" Mecca replied, nibbling on her bottom lip. "One in a million....a class all by my lonesome, huh? I'd have to say that's a pretty admirable assessment of me." She moved her arm off the pillow and ran the tips of her fingers lightly along the side of Shane's thick chocolate thigh. A soft teasing purr fluttered from her mouth as she eased her hand into his lap and brushed against his flaccid organ.

"Oh my, look what I found!" Mecca licked her lips provocatively while fondling him. "I think he could use some extra tender, loving care. What do you think, big boy?" She flashed Shane a naughty look.

Shane looked her in the eye and chuckled. "Show me what you got, baby. I'm anxious to see how you mark your territory." Something moved outside in the hallway and startled Shane. "Shhhhh...." He pressed his index finger against Mecca's lips and then scooted to the edge of the bed and hopped up. Shane pulled a Glock .45 from his nightstand drawer, threw on his black Gucci robe, and headed for the door. He paused when he heard the sound of footsteps sprinting away down the hall.

A moment later, Shane crept quietly down to the second floor landing and peered over the brass railing. His face dropped. "Son of a bitch!" his voice cracked when he recognized his wife hanging out down in the lobby like she was waiting for him to come down and greet her. "Woman, have you bumped your goddamn head?" Shane said, charging down the stairs, ready for an argument. "What in the hell are you doing here? You don't live here anymore. You're trespassing!"

Yolanda stood there glaring, arms folded, foot tapping, her demeanor solid, ready for war. "Are you finished?" she grunted, giving him a fierce look like nigga, you better kill the bullshit!

Shane winced. "What?" He thought she had lost her mind or that wifey was on the juice, which she was prone to indulge on a whim. "Am I finished? You got shit twisted, don't you, baby? You're the one that's finished!" he retorted arrogantly.

It took Yolanda a half a second to close the four foot gap between them. Whack! She slapped the shit out of Shane and snatched a manila envelope from her matching Herrera purse. "What in the hell is this shit about?" she scolded as she pushed the envelope in his face. "We discussed a trial separation. These are divorce papers, Negro!" she hissed with a scathing look.

Shane had on his deaf and dumb face now. "Oh?" he mumbled under his breath. The divorce papers had totally slipped his mind.

Without warning, Yolanda's head whipped around.

"I hear your freak ass up there sneaking around, listening to me and my husband! You fucking hoe! Go crawl your funky ass back in bed and wait for this piece of shit! He'll be there when I'm finished with his dog ass!"

"Oh shit!" Mecca mouthed, looking surprised. She froze in place, whirled on her heels, and crept back up the steps with her tail between her legs.

"And you!" Yolanda snapped on Shane. "You think the sun rises and sets on your black ass? Well it doesn't! You pathetic, pitiful excuse for a man!"

Upstairs, Mecca quietly slipped back in the bedroom and closed the door. A few feet away in the corner, she failed to notice Natasha's dark silhouette slowly creeping up on her.

Meanwhile, downstairs in the lobby, Yolanda's tirade reached a fever pitch a moment before Bad Ass burst through the front door like a madman.

"Yolanda! What are you doing? This muthafucka treats you like a piece of shit! What the fuck are you doing back here? You want to throw away what we have for this no good muthafucka!" Bad Ass made it crystal clear that he and Yolanda were deeply involved. He didn't stop there. Bad Ass continued to ramble on and on.

The unexpected revelation by his brother rocked Shane to the core. He gasped, astounded. "What's going on, Yolanda? You mean to tell me that you're fucking my brother?" Shane looked away from his wife and glared at his brother. "And your bitch ass! You're fucking my wife?" His hand tightened on the handle of his pistol hidden in his robe pocket. Shane paused briefly and weighed his options. A second later, all the emotions drained from his face. He was frigid.

"You know what?" he grunted and gave them both a fervent stare. "Wifey trespassing and your bitch ass is breaking and entering! So guess what?"

Bad Ass was on point. The moment he walked into the room, he had immediately sized up his brother and peeped the pistol in his robe pocket. When Shane made his move, Bad Ass was ready. He leaped clear across the room in a single bound and pounced on him.

While the action in the lobby was just getting started, upstairs, Mecca was fighting for her life. She was on her A-game, utilizing all her martial arts skills and fighting techniques: fifth degree black belt in karate, red belt in jujitsu, and amateur woman boxer with a golden glove ranking.

"C'mon, you psycho bitch!" Mecca scowled, crouching down in a defensive stance grasshopper style, prepared to strike down her opponent. "You fucked with the wrong bitch tonight!"

A twisted grin rolled across Natasha's face. She paused, stuck out her tongue, and savored the taste of blood that was leaking from a fresh gash in her bottom lip.

"No, whore, I got the right bitch tonight," Natasha spoke in a low whisper, and then she charged Mecca like a raging bull.

Mecca vaulted in the air like a kangaroo. Crack! Crack! She landed a powerful double-kick to Natasha's head with lightning fast precision. Natasha took the full brunt of the blows, stumbled slightly as she brushed by Mecca, and managed to stay on her feet.

When Natasha turned around to face her opponent, Mecca noticed a silver blade in her right hand. Her eyes jumped wide with fright and she instantly dropped to her knees to inspect the damage. Her jaw fell open and she shuddered when she saw the deep gash and fresh blood oozing from the side of her torso. She stilled herself, took a deep breath, and concentrated.

"It's gonna take a lot more than that little razor you got, bitch, to keep me from whoopin' your ass!" she told her. She swiped at her nose with her right thumb, the way a boxer taunts his opponent in a fight.

Natasha looked on. The corner of her mouth turned down and she cast an evil eye. "Bitch, you ain't saying nothing," she scoffed and then reached for the small of her back. "Your ass belongs to me tonight!" She whipped out the .357 Magnum.

Mecca timed the move perfectly as she went airborne, simultaneously. It was like a move straight off a Bruce Lee flick. Mecca sailed through the air in a flying jump kick across the room. Her right foot crashed hard against Natasha's chest.

Bam! A single gunshot rang out.

In the first floor lobby, the brothers were getting it in, scrapping and tussling and trying to gain control of the gun.

"You tried to set me up, muthafucka!" Bad Ass growled and delivered a wicked bite to Shane's wrist.

"Arrrggh!" Shane moaned in pain. "You bitch-ass-muthafucka! You're fucking my goddamn wife! I ain't set you up, but I'm gonna burn your ass up now!"

"The Mafia, the cocaine...that shit you told me about our father!" Bad Ass spat. "You bitch muthafucka! All that shit was a lie! You set me up! Now you're a dead man, brother or no brother!"

"Stop it!" Yolanda screamed. "Both of you acting like fools! Act like a real man for once in your life, please!"

Boom! The gun went off unexpectedly. The powerful blast resonated in the lobby and rang like the inside of a giant bell. Both brothers instantly froze in motion when they saw Yolanda stagger backward and grab her chest.

"Yolanda!" Bad Ass shrieked. A shocked expression exploded on his face. He felt his heart drop in his chest when Yolanda's hand fell to her side and revealed a dark red splotch slowly spreading across her sheer pink chiffon blouse.

"Baby, no!" Bad Ass felt the air leave his body when Yolanda's gaze faded and she crumbled to her knees and fell flat on her face. Bad Ass forgot all about his brother and their heated fight and rushed to aid his fallen lover, although Yolanda was no longer there. He dropped to his knees and cradled her head in his lap.

"You killed her!" Bad Ass sobbed, sounding out of breath. "Everything you touch dies. You're like a curse!"

A savage smirk fell on Shane's lips as he watched and listened to his brother. "Call it what you want, young killer. I'll be your curse, your brother, and your killer...because your bitch ass is going straight to hell right along with her," he said matter-of-factly as he placed his finger on the trigger. His facial expression was smug and full of self-satisfaction as he looked on and gloated in the moment.

Back upstairs, Mecca's flying jump kick jarred the gun loose from Natasha's hand. Natasha watched the gun tumble to the floor as she stumbled backward but she was still able to keep her balance and stay on her feet.

Mecca's eyes went from Natasha to the gun on the floor. I need that gun! a small voice in her head yelled. She held her breath and lunged headfirst like a human torpedo.

Natasha had her sights set on the gun as well. She bared her canines, launched herself like a heat-seeking missile and collided head on with Mecca. Both women hit the floor hard and a muffled thump echoed in the room followed by the sound of painful grunts and moans.

Get up...now! the little voice shouted in Mecca's head. A jolt of adrenaline hit her and Mecca forgot about the pain. She hopped up and scanned the floor for the gun, but it was nowhere in sight. "You crazy bitch!" she hissed and bolted for the door. She didn't look back as she dashed out of the room.

Natasha was right on her heels. She sprinted full speed like a cheetah running down its prey. "I got your crazy bitch, bitch," she said to herself, racing out of the room.

Mecca felt her attacker bearing down on her and gave it everything she had, but that wasn't enough. Natasha ran up behind her, reached out, and grabbed a handful of Mecca's hair.

"Where do you think you're going?" Natasha muttered. "I'm not finished with you!" She clamped down on Mecca's hair like a weighted anchor and dropped to the floor, causing Mecca's head to snap back in a violent whiplash motion. Both her feet left the floor simultaneously and flew straight up in the air. She slammed hard on the floor. Her head and back absorbed the brunt of the fall.

Natasha rose to her feet, tongue wagging and salivating between her lips as she prepared to exterminate her most formidable adversary thus far.

"Alright, hoe, time to die," Natasha uttered. She reached down, wrapped a thick braid of Mecca's mane around her hand, yanked the discombobulated woman, to her feet and pushed her back against the railing.

"I'm sick of bitches like you! Don't know how to keep your legs closed and your nasty ass hands off other women's men! Bitches like you don't deserve life!" Natasha said with a tongue so sharp that she spit blades out of her mouth. Out of nowhere, the straight razor appeared in Natasha's hand.

Warning bells went off in Mecca's head and her eyes jumped wide, totally alert. She watched Natasha rear back with the razor shimmering in her hand, her evil blue gaze fixated on Mecca's jugular. A moment later, the razor sliced the air with deadly intent.

Mecca's instincts sharpened to a point. A split second before the razor found its target, Mecca's forearm shot up in the air, counter-blocking Natasha's blade-wielding arm in mid-swing. Natasha grunted and a look of surprise and hatred flared in her facial expression as she felt the sudden shift in momentum; Natasha's feet lifted off the floor. Her entire body propelled up and over the railing in one swift counter-move.

Natasha's survival impulses instantly kicked into gear and she latched onto Mecca's hair and arm. She used her weight, momentum, and the force of gravity. Natasha pulled Mecca up and over the railing right along with her.

In the lobby, a hairsbreadth before Shane pulled the trigger, he felt something wet drop on his hand. He paused and looked closely at the wet, dark red splotches on his hand and arm. Blood? Shane winced, looking startled, and alarms sounded in his head. His natural inclination screamed, Move! But Shane's intuitive nature got the best of him. He leaned back and looked toward the ceiling. Instantly he knew he had made a mistake.

Horror filled her screams as Mecca plummeted three floors. Her left foot slammed into Shane's right shoulder as he pulled the trigger and missed Bad Ass's head by a mere three centimeters. Shane thought he'd been shot when the right side of his body went completely numb and his right knee buckled under him. He grimaced in pain with a dumbfounded look plastered on his face. He fell to the floor and watched his gun go sliding across the black marble floor, and finally it came to rest two inches from his brother's foot.

Situated directly behind where Shane sat looking dumbfounded now, his black leather sofa helped break Mecca's fall and inevitably saved her life. But she was knocked out and in critical condition, busted and broken and bruised from the fall.

Shane glanced over his shoulder, hoping that the person lying behind him wasn't Mecca, but that was wishful thinking on his part. His face shattered in a thousand pieces when he realized it was Mecca lying on the sofa, busted up and dead – or so he thought upon looking at her.

"C'mon, muthafucka!" Bad Ass shouted, still cradling Yolanda's head in his lap. "I want you to go for it! I dare your bitch ass!"

Shane's head twisted around and he stared at his brother and the gun lying untouched by his brother's foot. It was tempting, but he quickly dismissed the idea of going for the gun. He knew if he made a play for the gun, his brother would whip-n-spit – dead-bang his ass.

The real dilemma facing Shane was the path to the front door. His brother was a human road block to his freedom. That's out of the question, he told himself and changed gears. I've got three other pistols upstairs, so fuck going out the front door! He caught his brother off guard when he popped up off the floor and made a mad dash for the stairs.

Gunfire exploded behind Shane as Bad Ass opened fire on him sprinting up the stairs. "Sonofabitch!" Bad Ass cursed himself for missing his target.

Upstairs, Shane burst into the master bedroom and caught Natasha by surprise. "Who in the hell?" he stammered. He quickly realized the woman standing in the room was Mecca's killer. "You murdering bitch!" Shane was livid, foaming at the mouth like a mad dog. His insides swelled into a ball of pure anger, anxiety, and uncontrollable rage.

He snapped out and pounced on Natasha without a second thought. He crushed her with vicious head and body blows that would make a grown man cringe.

The attack happened so fast; Natasha was blind-sided by him. The first blow to her head was so hard that Natasha thought he had cracked her with a bat. Shane rocked her with a wild haymaker and she stumbled, seeing stars for a moment, and almost blacked out.

To counter the punishment he inflicted on her, Natasha made the only move she could. She turned her back to him. Another blow like the first one and she knew it was lights out.

Shane was unmerciful in his attack and showed no signs of stopping. He continued to pummel her from behind, hell-bent on avenging Mecca's death. But a moment later, Shane made a critical mistake when he decided to strangle Natasha from behind.

Natasha figured he'd take the bait once she turned her back to him. She was absolutely correct. Dumb ass! she voiced silently when he grabbed her around her throat and squeezed. Natasha stomped Shane's foot with all her might, and when he doubled over in pain, she bottom-fisted him in the groin, snapped her head back, and smashed him in the face. Next, she twisted left and right, shooting elbows to his rib cage. She thrust her hips backward, getting separation. She spun around, .357 aimed at his head, her blonde wig on the floor between them.

"Natasha?" Bad Ass shouted from the doorway, sounding out of breath and waving the pistol in the air. "Is that you?" A puzzled dick-look hung on his face.

Shane was down on one knee groaning in pain, blood gushing from his busted nose like an open faucet. Slowly, he lifted his head and glared at the woman with the pistol pointed at his head. "It can't be?" he mumbled and felt his mind implode. "Angel?" Shane's mind opened up and he experienced a pivotal a-ha moment. He felt the sensation of his body lifting and his ears went into a tunnel as the face of each murder victim reeled through his mind.

"Fuck me." Shane's voice was flat. "You had access to them all." His tone sharpened abruptly. "Angel, you're the serial killer!" He didn't want to believe the words he'd spoken, but the reality of the situation was staring him in the face.

Natasha looked upon Shane with fire in her eyes.

"You stupid muthafucka!" she huffed. "No, I'm not Angel. I'm Natasha, bitch!"

At that moment, Shane felt panic perched on the rim of his gut. He realized his fate lay in the hands of a psychotic woman. With that reality in mind, Shane realized he had no other choice but to die trying.

"You sick bitch!" Shane growled and lurched forward, which amounted to a desperate attempt by a dead man. Gunfire exploded a split second later and a shower of lead riddled his torso as Natasha and Bad Ass pulled their triggers in rapid succession.

When the shooting stopped, Natasha looked over her shoulder. A twisted smudge cracked her lips. "I didn't need your fucking help," she said, sounding salty, and then she walked over to get a closer look at the damage they'd caused.

Natasha hovered over Shane. Her heart filled up like a balloon about to burst when she saw his mouth agape and Shane's dead, accusing eyes staring up at her.

"C'mon, Natasha, we got to get low!" Bad Ass said with a sense of urgency. "That gunplay gonna have five-O crashing this joint any minute!"

Natasha paused for a moment before her head twisted around like a cobra and her eyes twinkled like crystal blue ice. "And?" she snorted, glowering. "So what? Fuck the police!"

Loso rolled up outside and parked across the street. He opened the driver window halfway and quietly watched Nadia scale the concrete staircase, whip out her service weapon, and charge inside the house.

"Okay…what's going on now?" he asked himself, so focused on the actions of the detective that he was totally oblivious to the danger approaching him until it was too late.

By the time the Magnum rode up alongside of the Escalade, Loso's street senses didn't register danger until the vehicle had come to a complete stop. A sudden flash of recognition jumped in Loso's eye and his heart skipped a beat.

"Oh shit!"

His facial expression shattered when Tommy Gunz flashed a deadly grin and grunted, "Suck on this, bitch!"

Hellfire exploded from the barrel of his Mac-11 and the sound of automatic fire splitting the night resonated on the warm summer's breeze.

A few miles from the Mount Pleasant neighborhood, Bad Ass thundered through Rock Creek Park in his Aston Martin as if he had a death wish, careening and speeding along the park's dark, narrow, and winding roads.

Natasha was consumed with primping herself in the visor mirror, making sure that her blonde wig was styled perfectly.

Bad Ass watched her from the corner of his eye. He twisted his mouth and inquired, "What the fuck is up with you, Natasha? Who in the hell do you supposed to be? Wearing wigs and disguises like you a damn detective!

That's some whack shit! So what's up with that? And then my brother...he called you Angel?" He stopped short. "Hold up," he said with a tense and wary face.

"Didn't we meet at Club Lux?" Bad Ass snapped his fingers. "Yeah, that's it! You're Renee's sister, Angel?" He looked suddenly astonished.

Natasha blew him off and gave him a sideways look and snickered. "What? Pssst...child, please!" She sneered with her upper lip cocked. "You got me fucked up and I'm not into playing games. I'm about taking care of business."

She paused and stared him in the eye. "You got your business to handle, and I got mine. So don't go fucking up a good thing, alright? You said we were meant to be, so don't go getting all complicated on me. Let's enjoy one another while we're together. Agreed?"

Is this bitch for real? Bad Ass thought to himself. Crazy, unstable bitch! "Meant to be," he scoffed, thinking to himself, That was before I realized you don't know who the hell you are...let alone me! Hell no, I can't do the split personality thing! he admitted to himself.

Bad Ass went on to say, "At the time I may have said that, but that's when I thought you were the business. But you're not. Baby, we were never meant to be, we just happened!"

It was like a sucker punch to her gut. Natasha felt her heart constrict in her chest. Her breathing went shallow and her pupils dilated into narrow slits. It took a moment for Natasha to gather her senses. "Okay, so that's how you

feel? Well, in that case, fuck you too! You no good mutha-
fucker!" She gave Bad Ass a scathing look and whipped out
the .357.

A moment later, three quick bursts of gunfire ignit-
ed the dark cockpit. Seconds later, the exotic sedan ca-
reened out of control, left the road, hit an elevated
embankment, and went airborne for three seconds before
it crash landed in a pitch black ravine. Then the entire car
erupted into a ball of hot flames.

Chapter Twenty-Five

Later on, in the wee hours of the night....

Multiple law enforcement agencies kicked into high gear when the APB went out over the wire: DC's police chief had been found murdered inside his Mount Pleasant home!

A stout army of law enforcement personnel converged on the Mount Pleasant residence and military-style tents posing as police command posts were erected at both ends of the block and in the rear alley directly behind the chief's property.

Chief Inspector Tony Woo was automatically promoted to Interim Police Chief via the mayor. He immediately implemented a dragnet and lockdown for the entire Mount Pleasant and adjacent Adams Morgan neighborhoods; military curfew was in effect. The posh enclave where the commander's home resided, Summit Place, was transformed into a virtual militarized zone over night.

Clever, cunning, concise, and fearless were the four adjectives that summed up Tony Woo's disposition perfectly. His firm voice floated along the hallway and into the master bedroom.

"Mr. Mayor, I've designated individual CSI teams for every room on the premises," Woo advised the mayor via satellite phone, his voice strong and concise, like a man with a plan. He continued, saying, "Each team is under direct order to report any and all findings directly to me, and I will personally be assessing and overseeing each and every aspect of this investigation from start to completion. So you can rest assured, Mr. Mayor, the perpetrator or perpetrators responsible for this despicable deed will be swiftly brought to justice." He concluded his business with the mayor. "Here!" He thrust the phone into his assistant's hand and shooed him away.

Tony Woo folded his arms behind his back and stood strong. His low, portly frame filled the doorway leading in the master bedroom, and his sharp-slanted gaze was methodical and meticulous as he canvassed the crime scene with a vigilant stare.

Silently, Tony admitted to himself, I figured you was dirty, Holt...but your own colleagues? A gang leader assassinated out in front of your home and he has a department issued GPS tracking devise in his possession that's targeting Detective Dozier? It doesn't make sense to me. There's something missing here. Where's the common denominator? That last crucial piece of the puzzle? He thought hard and deep, but still came up with a blank.

"Chief Woo, sir!" A shapely Sergeant Dunn came strutting down the hall towards him. Her shapely hips swaying side to side, uniform hugging every curve on her cinnamon physique. Sergeant Dunn stopped less than a foot away and looked the chief in the eye. "Your presence is needed outside in the garage. We've unearthed a sizable amount of money and cocaine. I'm talking multiple kilograms, Chief."

The calm expression Tony Woo wore was a mask for the shock he really felt inside. Outside, just beyond the rear of the house and right along the property's edge, stood a dilapidated and aged red brick structure that served as the chief's two-car garage. It was the last original remnant still standing from the 18th century.

Chief Woo hovered at the entrance. He shrugged arrogantly and waited for a group of suits to move their asses out of his way. A moment later, without saying a word, the Chief strode the length of the shabby and cluttered structure. When he could go no further, he made an about-face and clicked his heels. He cast a curious gaze along the walls, which were adorned with an assortment of new Black & Decker power tools that looked totally out of place in the drab and dusty garage.

The chief's gaze drifted from the wall ornaments to the crowd of police brass congregating at the edge of a freshly-excavated ditch. Tony approached the ditch and took notice of the long wooden planks that had been recently removed from a section of the garage floor which stood apart from the rest. It looked to him like a carefully designed and hidden storage space. The chief paused and glanced around at the collage of faces watching him and hanging on his every move. He then walked directly to the edge of the storage space and stared in its belly.

Rubber-banded bundles of $20's, $50's, and $100's were stacked two feet deep in the hole, right beside a big pile of bricked-up uncut Columbian cocaine. The view jarred Tony's senses, and he felt suddenly lightheaded gazing down upon the large mound of drugs and cash. It was as if he were staring in the belly of the beast – literally.

A portrait of Chief Holt was starting to take form. My God...the chief was living a double life! Tony conceded to himself. A moment later he exhaled, rolled his shoulders, and found Detective Louis in the crowd.

"Detective Louis!" he spoke up, firm, while doing his damndest not to show his colleagues how hurt he truly felt. "I want you and three of your men to personally catalog every dollar and every gram of cocaine in this hole. Are we perfectly clear on this?"

Tony Woo turned from the hole, took three steps, and leaned on the hood of what he thought was one of the antique automobiles Holt was always bragging about. He looked a bit hesitant when he began to scrutinize the old cracked brown car cover. A concerned frown tugged at the corner of his mouth when he noticed a shiny chrome rim peeking out from under the car cover. He kneeled to get a closer look.

"What's this?" The chief ripped off the cover. A low grumble of curious whispers swept the area when the chief revealed a glossy sapphire-blue Cadillac CTS. "Well looky here," he snorted, wearing a shrewd smug. "I've got the best collection of DC's finest standing around with their thumbs stuck up their ass!"

Someone gasped and chuckled in the crowd.

"Oh, you think this shit is funny!" Chief Woo spat.

"Well, this ain't reality TV, asshole, so stop laughing!"

"Excuse me, Chief," Detective Nubie spoke up, "But isn't that decomp I smell?"

The moment Chief Woo stepped foot in the garage, he detected a slight odor of decomp in the air. And now, Chief Woo was grinding his teeth with such force, his jaw started to ache. He took a couple of steps and stood in front of the trunk. "Somebody remove the thumb from their ass and get something to open this fucking trunk!" Detective Maruchan was more than happy to oblige. He quickly located a rusty crowbar and proceeded to pry open the Cadillac hatch.

"This should do it," Maruchan grunted, flexing his 22-inch biceps. A second later, the latch gave-way and the hatch lifted open. "What kind of sick shit is this?" he blurted out. He covered his mouth as the stench of human decomposition filled the air.

Chief Woo shook his head and peered at the human wreckage. "We are living witnesses to the worst of humanity's work." He spoke as if in a trance. "This here is the darkest depths of depravity..."

Inside of the Cadillac's trunk they discovered a grisly human smorgasbord of bloody guts, gouged out eyeballs, torn, shredded, sliced limbs and ligaments, and a pair of decapitated heads. Judging by the ghoulish arrangement of human remains, it was apparent to the trained eye that some deranged psychopath had taken particular interest in packaging, preparing, and preserving this arrangement, as if this display of savagery was well thought out and planned long in advance.

Chapter Twenty-Six

The Double Set-Up

In the aftermath of Damon's murder inside of The House strip joint on Georgia Avenue, Bad Ass immediately led his CIX team south on Georgia Avenue, past Howard University Hospital on the left. At the intersection of Georgia and Florida Avenues, the squad of Ducati's made a hard left on Florida and raced at top speed. Within minutes, Bad Ass and his CIX assassins had stashed their bikes in a back alley garage off Florida Avenue in a NE hood called Trinidad.

Bad Ass walked outside the garage, pulled off his helmet and ski mask, and looked around at his men with a wild, crazy look pulsating in his eyes.

"What up, Cuz?" Loso asked, sounding concerned.

"I know that loo. You ready to go medieval on a bamma's ass!"

Bad Ass snickered and looked Loso in the eye. "That loot and that cocaine we supposed to deliver to my folks..." When he spoke, you could feel absolute hate radiating in his tone. "Well, I wanna give 'em a little somethin', somethin' extra on the side."

"Something extra?" Loso quipped with a question mark look. "Like what, Cuz?" He was prepared for the worst.

A sly, diabolical grin parted Bad Ass lips. "Let's give him Caesar Leo's body," he said, cold and blunt. "That secret stash spot on my folk's property, that joint will make for the perfect burial for that Mafia bamma. Besides, I owe my folks something. They played me fifty."

A strange look crossed Loso's face and he quickly wiped it off. "If you say so, Cuz. It's your call." Sounds to me like Cuz about to throw his folks to the dogs. Money, coke and a dead Mafia Don...somebody's ass is going down! Loso told himself.

While Bad Ass was plotting to bring down his backstabbing brother, thirty-five miles away, inside the basement laundry room of Angel's Clarksville home, Natasha was preparing for revenge in the most deranged and inconceivable manner possible.

She had already disconnected the washer and dryer, pulled both machines off the wall, and left them in the middle of the laundry room floor. She moved back to the empty wall space kneeled down, and carefully began to dislodge a disguised false wooden wall covering. A moment later, she eased the wooden covering aside, leaned it against the wall, and exhaled a breath of satisfaction when she laid eyes on a small 3x3 foot dark green cast iron door – her little dark secret that only she knew existed. Natasha removed a single skeleton key from her black La Perla bra, slid the key in the door lock and turned.

Click! She pulled the heavy cast iron door open, made herself small, and slithered inside of the dark open space.

Inside, the room was completely still and silent and dark – the air stale, no ventilation, the temperature a stuffy 90 degrees. Natasha knew her way around in the dark. She rose to her feet, moved her hand along the wall, until...

Click!

The low-sounding buzz emanated in the dark for about two seconds, and then a single elongated overhead lamp, hanging from the center rafters, illuminated the 10x10 foot enclosure in bright white light.

Natasha beamed, a look of sheer euphoria swimming in her ocean blue eyes as she gazed upon the multilevel wooden shelves tethered to the left and right wall. The walls' shelf space was occupied by large clear glass beakers, the kind used in medical labs. The contents in the beakers were hideous. A collection of female remains floated in a state of suspended animation, each encased in a glass prison: a pair of disfigured heads, organs and limbs including eyes, a heart, liver, uterus, and labia with the clitoris attached. It resembled a scene from a Dr. Frankenstein laboratory, heinous and totally beyond the boundaries of the normal human comprehension.

The center wall was blank, empty, except for a wall mounted body-length mirror positioned perfectly in the center of the wall.

Natasha walked toward the mirror, wriggling her palms jittery-like and glancing around the room, as if she was expecting a visitor to arrive any minute. She stopped and stared at herself in the mirror, a twisted, seedy grin sliding on her lips, as she combed her fingers through her honey-blonde wig.

"Didn't you hear the phone call, Angel?" Natasha spoke with a strange hypnotic spark in her eye. "Don't worry, girlfriend, I'm the business. I'm gonna show Mr. Dirty-Dick Shane the business!" She admired her reflection in the mirror for a moment before she cracked up laughing – a crazed cackle of a laugh that resonated off the walls in the small room and gave off a demon-like vibe.

Chapter Twenty-Seven

Two Days Later - George Washington University Hospital.

Angel's eyes popped wide open. Bright white light flooded her sight and she instantly winced. "Oh my God!" she stammered, grief-stricken, when she tried to move. A flood of pain seized her body, and a second later she felt a comforting hand massage her shoulder and a familiar friendly voice spoke to her.

"Everything okay, Angel?" Ronnie said in her usual soft spoken way. "Just lay back and relax, girl. The doctor says you need plenty of rest, because girl, you're one lucky bitch, you know that?"

Angel struggled as she turned her head toward Ronnie's voice. Her vision was blurry at first, but it gradually came into focus. Finally! She sighed when she could see Ronnie's smiling face looking down at her from the bedside. Worry creased her forehead when Angel realized her situation. "Doctor?" she voiced weakly. "I'm in the hospital? But why, Ronnie? What happened to me? How did I get here?"

Her voice was just above a whisper. "Ronnie...please, what's going on?" The more Angel spoke, the more worried she became.

Ronnie was hesitant for a moment. She dropped her eyes, took Angel by the hand, and held on. "You don't remember anything, Angel?" She looked her in the eye. Angel's silence was heartfelt, so Ronnie took a breath and continued. "You were involved in a very bad car accident, Angel. You were almost killed, but luckily you were thrown from the car before it exploded! On the news, they were saying no one could've survived that terrible explosion." Straining to speak, Angel replied, "I was riding alone?"

Ronnie shook her head. "I wasn't able to find out a whole lot, but I think you were the passenger. Matter of fact, I'm pretty sure you were. The car that blew up was one of those Aston Martins."

Angel gasped. "Aston Martin! So whose car was that?"

Ronnie dropped her eyes and shook her head again.

"Girl, I couldn't tell you. They didn't find anyone else. There was so much going on that night in the city. All the shit on the news, all over the radio! Girl, first they were talking about your car accident in Rock Creek Park...the car explosion and all that shit! And then a big-ass news flash about the chief of police! On my gosh, Angel! Somebody murdered his ass! I'm glad you left his ass! They found a lady detective half dead in his house and some gangbanger outside in the car with his head blown off!"

Angel was no good after the news about the police chief. Her heart went flat and she didn't hear anything after that. Her mind went tumbling down into that dark mental abyss and she began to reflect on the crazy dream. The laundry room...the secret door behind the wall...the room with the human remains in the jars...the woman in the mirror with the wicked blue eyes saying, "Don't worry, girlfriend, I'm the business! I'm gonna show Mr. Dirty-Dick Shane the business!"

A look of complete shock and horror shattered Angel's face. Her gaze was terror-stricken.

"Angel. Girl, are you alright? You look like you just saw a ghost," Ronnie said, her soft brow etched with concern.

"Oh my goodness...Ronnie, I'm scared," Angel whispered, sounding paranoid. Her eyes glazed over, tearful. "I need to ask you something, Ronnie. Please, just between you and me." Angel paused. Her eyes glanced toward the door, and when she realized it was closed, she exhaled. "Ronnie, do you think it's possible to kill people behind your own back?" She waited for an answer, a spooky look stretched on her face.

Ronnie giggled, tickled by her question. "Girl, stop the madness." She stood up and slapped the pillow. "I sure hope not, because girlfriend, it would be a rack of dead bitches in DC, I swear!" She stopped short and then started fluffing up the pillow for Angel. "Girl, don't go getting all upset and spazzing out over nonsense. You know you got more than just you to think about now," she told her before assisting Angel and propping her head on the pillow.

Angel frowned at the comment. "More than just me to worry about?" She repeated the words with emphasis and jerked her head toward Ronnie. "Ronnie...what are you saying?" Her tone was overly cautious.

Ronnie smacked her lips. "Oh, don't worry, the baby is just fine." She stopped mid-sentence when she recognized the anguish in Angel's eyes. "Girl, stop the madness," Ronnie said, covering her mouth. "What, you didn't know you were pregnant?"

Angel's gaze darkened. The whites in her eyes stressed with red veins now.

"Oh my God, Angel!" Ronnie sat down on the bed next to her and tried to comfort her. "Everything is going to be just fine; you just wait and see, Angel. If you want, I'll go with you to tell the father." She hesitated. "Who's the father anyway? You know I'm dying to know!"

Angel was at a loss for words. The thought of having a baby and the baby's father dead and gone crushed her insides. Angel broke down and let it all out - the emotions, the grieving heart, the uncertainty, the lingering sickness she felt gnawing at her core. Do you think you could kill people behind your own back? That haunting question galvanized her heart and she thought long and hard. Well...could I?

Chapter Twenty-Eight

Law 5: So Much Depends on Reputation – Guard it with your Life
"Reputation is the cornerstone of power. Through reputation alone you can intimidate and win; once you slip, however, you are vulnerable, and will be attacked on all sides. Make your reputation unassailable. Always be alert to potential attacks and thwart them before they happen. Meanwhile, learn to destroy your enemy by opening holes in their own reputation. Then stand aside and let public opinion hang them."
48 Laws of Power

Meanwhile, downtown at Police Headquarters, inside of Chief Woo's new office digs (previously Chief Holt's office), the new Chief of Police was accompanied by Detective Nadia Dozier and Internal Affairs Agent Dan Jarvis. The trio was just about to close out a private meeting when the local news report flashed across the 40-inch television monitor and caught their attention.

The always gorgeous and impeccably dressed news anchor, Cynne Simpson, was in the midst of critiquing the city's latest headline news events. The trio paused and gave their undivided attention to the news reporter.

Cynne's signature voice filled the office:

Chief of Police Shane Holt was found murdered in his upscale Mount Pleasant home along with colleagu, Detective Mecca Tomay, who's listed in critical but stable condition. At last check, Detective Tomay was still in a coma. Further investigation of Chief Holt's home has turned up evidence that has led the U.S. District Attorney's Office to open an in-depth inquiry into Chief Holt's professional as well as his private affairs. Consequently, a search of a separate garage on his property has turned up $1.5 million dollars, 50 kilos of cocaine...and buried along with the money and drugs, the body of Caesar Leonardi was discovered. Mr. Leonardi is the alleged Mafia Don for the Leonardi Crime Family.

This is unbelievable, but there's more. A secondary search of the garage uncovered a Cadillac sedan, which had been re-ported missing over a year ago. The owner of the Cadillac was a Ms. Josephine Nubie. Her skeletal remains were re-cently discovered buried in a shallow grave in Rock Creek Park. From my understanding, Chief Holt is also a suspect in Ms. Nubie's disappearance and murder as well. But it doesn't end there. Inside of the Cadillac's rear trunk, human remains were found, and the victim count is mounting.

And to make matters worse, less than fifty yards from the doorstep of Chief Holt's residence, a gangland execution was committed on the very same night the chief himself was murdered. The body of Dakwon "Loso" Blackwell was found riddled with bullets, his face virtually unrecognizable. The evidence in this case is so overwhelming, and the chief is now being investigated as the prime suspect in DC's infa-mous serial predator slayings, ties to Mafia dealings, and possible connections to unknown gang activities and mur-ders. There's a laundry list of incriminating..."

During the meeting, Nadia was busy trying to place Dan Jarvis's face, his boyish good looks overrun with freck-les and a head of bright orange curly of hair.

Nadia quietly pondered, and then it hit her. Dan Jarvis is the Mad magazine-looking character that was as-sisting Chief Holt at the condo where Sergeant Webb was murdered. He was the paramedic, Ted Andrews!

Damn...Internal Affairs had been investigating the Chief for a minute, she realized sadly.

"Well, I've heard enough." Chief Woo rose from his seat behind the wide mahogany desk, flipped the cover shut on a thick manila folder, and scooped it off the desk.

He marched around to the head of the desk. "Operation Black Hole." Chief Woo's tone was adamant when he spoke. "That was Chief Holt's misguided attempt to cover his blood trail of misdeeds," he concluded and handed over the heavy manila folder to Agent Jarvis. "Every single document associated with the covert operation is in this folder, Agent Jarvis. That should cover everything."

Agent Jarvis tucked the manila folder under his arm, looked Chief Woo in the eye, and extended his hand.

"Chief Woo, you've done quite a job, and on behalf of IAD, we appreciate all the good work you've put forth. You know these are some very serious allegations that will undoubtedly mar this department's credibility for some time. You are aware of that, Chief Woo?"

Chief Woo gave him a stoic face. "That's why I'm in this position, Agent Jarvis: to clean house and get this ship in shape."

Agent Jarvis nodded and smiled. "Tell me, Chief Woo, why do you think he did it? I mean, Chief Holt had it all, so why would he do the unthinkable?" he inquired with a mystified expression.

Chief Woo thought for a minute, looked Agent Jarvis in the eye, and said firmly, "Right this second, I really don't know why Chief Holt did what he did. What could make a man in his position go over the edge like that, go against every code, rule, and set of mores he pretended to obey, against better judgment, against every lesson of hindsight and every shard of wisdom that comes with our line of work?

Evidently, Chief Holt had no regrets in the moment. Agent Jarvis, we may never know, but in this line of work, always keep in mind that Satan comes in all forms..."

The End

RJ Champ

DC Bookdiva Publications
#245 4401-A Connecticut Avenue, NW
Washington DC 20008
dcbookdiva.com

Order Form

Name_____

Inmate ID_____

Address:_____

City/State_____

Quantity	Titles	Price	Total
	Dynasty 3, Dutch	15.00	
	A Killer'z Ambition 2, Nathan Welch	15.00	
	Smokin Mirrors, Mike O	15.00	
	Secrets Never Die, Eyone Williams	15.00	
	Up the Way, Ben	15.00	
	A Beautiful Satan 2, RJ Champ	15.00	
	Tina, Darrell Debrew	15.00	
	Trina, Darrell Debrew	15.00	
	The Diary of Aaliyah Anderson, Randall Barnes	15.00	
	Uppity, Jannelle Moore	15.00	
	Lorton Legends, Eyone Williams	15.00	

Sub-Total $_____

Shipping/Handling (Via US Media Mail) $3.95 1-2 Books, $7.95 1-3 Books,
4 or more titles-Free Shipping

Shipping $ _____
Total Enclosed $ _____

Certified or government issued checks and money orders, all mail in orders take
5-7 Business days to be delivered. Books can also be purchased on our website
at dcbookdiva.com. Incarcerated readers receive 25% discount. Please pay
$11.25 per book and apply the same shipping terms as stated above

www.ingramcontent.com/pod-product-compliance
Lightning Source LLC
Chambersburg PA
CBHW050518260626
47157CB00004B/1377